"*Deliverance* weaves a thrilling web of intrigue.
Eye-opening. A great read start to finish."
— Ali Miner, author and artist of *A Time to Awaken*

"A trip through the American West turns into a
life-or-death journey…a literary thriller…"
— Indie Reader

"Your words strike the heart…your ability to
articulate universal truths is extraordinary."
— Lily Hills, author of *The Body Love Manual*

"*Queen of the Sun* takes us on an amazing adventure. From
the first page on, this book is hard to put down."
— Louise Hay, author of *You Can Heal Your Life*

"*Alchemy of Sacred Living* is a gift to the planet."
— Peter Ragnar, author of *The Awesome Science of Luck*

"I absolutely loved *Queen of the Sun*! Your writing
is so inspiring and insightful!"
— Anna Enea, author of *Together Forever:
Using Adversity for Awakening*

"Emory Michael's words inspire every area
of our lives with wisdom."
— Nancy Mellon, author of *Body Eloquence*

"You write so brilliantly! I'm a fan. Bravo! Bravo!"
— Sally Faubion, author of *Numerology from A to Z*

DELIVERANCE

A ROAD TRIP TO DIE FOR

Other Titles by
EMORY J. MICHAEL

Queen of the Sun
Alchemy of Sacred Living
Jewels of Light
The Secret of Light

DELIVERANCE

A ROAD TRIP TO DIE FOR

EMORY J. MICHAEL

Mountain Rose Publishing

Sedona, Arizona

For information about this title or to order other books and/or electronic media, contact your local bookseller or the publisher:

Mountain Rose Publishing
PO Box 20191, Sedona, AZ 86341
www.emoryjohnmichael.com

Cover and interior design by The Book Cover Whisperer:
OpenBookDesign.biz

Library of Congress Control Number: 2024922829

978-0-9642147-3-6 Paperback
978-0-9642147-1-2 eBook

Printed in the United States of America

FIRST EDITION

*To those whose childhood has
been stolen from them.*

ACKNOWLEDGMENTS

With gratitude to my wife, Mia, for her steady encouragement, my daughter, Sera Maria, for her thoughtful advice, and to Jaren Anderson for his tips and pointers. Special thanks also to Kathleen King, Ali Miner, Trisha Alessandra, Marisol Jimenez, Ashlee Threlkeld, Edna Alvarado, Karla Hansen, Grandpa Ole, and Valorie Bauer for their kind support and keen suggestions. A special shout-out to Laurie Gibson for her meticulous editorial guidance.

PART ONE

"Be yourself. Everyone else is already taken."
— Oscar Wilde

CHAPTER 1

The Road Trip

It was as if demons danced in my head.

Scenes of an ancient battle surged in my brain. Valiant warriors wearing crested, bronze helmets struggled everywhere about me, locked in deadly combat. Gripping spears and shields, the fighters clashed on the idyllic beaches of a mythic, crystal sea.

Their shouts and curses were so vivid that I seemed transported to the center of the conflict. A warrior charged me with his spear aimed at my throat. I cried out and woke up with a start.

Sweating and agitated, I fell out of my hotel bed, my sleep shattered by the violent, recurring nightmare I'd endured since childhood. As I hastily dressed and placed my clothes in my luggage, my hands touched the book I'd been reading the past several evenings, which I suspected had triggered the lurid scenes. It was a volume of *The Iliad* by Homer, one of the foremost epics in world literature.

The Iliad and its companion volume *The Odyssey* had been my father's favorite books, and I'd cherished them as a child. I barely knew my father; he had vanished when I was four. His only gifts to me, the son he abandoned, were illustrated volumes of these ancient classics. I treasured them and had brought my childhood copies on my road trip from California.

So great was my father's love for these heroic stories of Greek and Trojan warriors that he'd christened me with the very name of the ancient, fabled city. *Iliad* derives from *Ilium*, the antique name for Troy. Troy is my middle name.

Jaden Troy Parker.

Pushing away the nightmare visions and my intuition that they signaled rough times ahead, I grabbed my water bottle and stepped into the sizzling heat of the Arizona morning.

With imposing Camelback Mountain as scenic background, I wheeled around the streets of Phoenix in my Jeep Cherokee, staring at businesses, feeling the vibe of the place. The desert metropolis was an enigma to me. Hellishly hot for five months each year, the giant, sprawling state capital kept magically expanding despite average daily temperatures in summer well over a hundred degrees Fahrenheit.

Hailing from Monterey's green, coastal paradise by the Pacific's edge, I failed to grasp the desert's appeal. Over time, I would succumb to the magical beauty of the Southwest, and grow, if not entirely to love it, at least to appreciate and embrace its subtle charms. Even Phoenix, with its ungainly sprawl, suffered less urban blight than that infecting most big American cities; the downtown was surprisingly clean, with broad streets, mostly graffiti-free, and it had an abundance of palm trees, to me symbolic of utopian easy living.

Seeking love, thrills, and adventure, I'd just set out on a holiday excursion through the American West. My first stop was in Phoenix to see a couple of former high school buddies, and it was here, in the Tempe Mission Palms Hotel, that my childhood nightmares returned.

Cruising the vast, hot city gave me time to reflect on my dream episode, and I wondered if there was a message in this latest nocturnal installment. The notion wasn't comforting due to the vision's extreme violence.

The haunting wail of a police siren behind me yanked me back to the present and I realized I was driving well over the speed limit. Pushing aside my reveries, I swung into the parking lot of a small business complex, sensing my life would soon change in shocking, unimaginable ways.

CHAPTER 2

Airhead

R elieved to see that the cop was after another driver, I stepped out of my Cherokee to get my bearings, grateful that I'd dodged a bullet. The tiny commercial area featured a coffee shop— the Coronado—and an Italian restaurant named Machiavelli's. Strolling into the Coronado, I ordered an espresso and headed to an empty table by the window.

Savoring the darkly pleasant atmosphere, I leaned back in my chair, energized by the strong coffee. I felt charged, vibrantly alive, on the edge of impending adventure, ready to grasp my destiny with both hands regardless of what the inscrutable Fates held in store.

The young, blond woman didn't seem to notice me as I sat at the table across from her, sipping my espresso. Instantly attracted, I forced myself not to stare, focusing on my cell phone, glancing at day-old texts. Her shining golden hair dropped below her neck and wrapped around her shoulders, and she projected a petite, elfin charm.

She peered into her laptop, clicking the keyboard occasionally, smiling softly. She was speaking to someone through her air pods, making references to planets and employing astrological jargon. I heard her say, "Neptune square Mercury," and "Venus in the seventh house." I knew enough astrological terminology to gather she was interpreting someone's planetary birth chart.

I scrolled through random TikTok videos, glancing up occasionally at the young woman. She laughed frequently as she conversed. A person's laugh is an indicator of their personality and character, and I knew I'd have to be fond of a woman's laugh to be attracted. Hers was warm, down-to-earth, and made me smile.

She finished her conversation with the words, "It's been an absolute pleasure, Nikki. Let's talk real soon. Love you! Bye!" Her voice had a songlike brightness and sincerity. She stood up and started to move away from the table.

"I'd be happy to keep an eye on your laptop," I blurted out, surprised at my boldness, concerned she might take it as an affront. "I mean…if you need to get something." Our eyes locked for an instant as she judged my trustworthiness.

"Oh, thanks, appreciate it…I'll just be a minute." *I passed her test.* She flashed a micro-second smile and moved swiftly across the room with a natural elegance, as if she'd been a ballerina. She was slender, about five feet four, and looked to be in her early twenties. Her white sandals revealed light pink toenails matching her nail polish. She returned from the restroom several minutes later. "Thanks for keeping an eye on my laptop."

"Of course," I said. "Only had to fight off two would-be felons and a lurking Neanderthal."

"Is that all? Neighborhood's looking up." Her eyes were bright and penetrating, the color of milk chocolate, with a depth that seemed to convey wisdom beyond her years, and not a small amount of hurt. She buried herself in her computer screen.

I didn't want to let the opportunity slip away. "Excuse me, but are you an astrologer?" Her mouth opened slightly, and her eyes flashed. I noticed a small whitish scar barely visible on her chin, with tiny tracers left from the stitches. It made her seem slightly vulnerable and imperfect, which I liked. *Perfect* is hard to relate to.

"How'd you know!?"

"Sorry, didn't mean to eavesdrop, but I overheard your conversation. It sounded like you were interpreting someone's horoscope. But honestly, you just have the air of one. An astrologer, I mean."

"You're right! I was doing an interpretation for a friend." After a pause she added, "It's funny you should say 'air of one' because I have five planets in air signs. Well, actually four planets, plus my ascendant." I knew enough astrological jargon to follow her.

"Gemini rising, Libra sun, with Mercury in Libra," she continued. "I'm all over the place. Guess I'm just an airhead, after all. But in a good way, I think."

"That's only three—you said five."

"Oh…didn't want to bore you with details, but I also have Neptune and Uranus in Aquarius. That makes five positions in air signs."

"So, you love communication, ideas, conversation, and learning," I said. "You must be an interesting person."

Her eyes brightened. "Oh, you know…just naturally mysterious and fascinating." She fluttered her eyebrows theatrically and gave an exaggerated, flashy, photo-op smile, revealing almost perfectly formed, pearl-white teeth. I say "almost" because one of her front teeth edged out slightly over the other one, creating a pixie-like impression.

"My name's Jaden," I said. "Jaden Troy Parker. Nice to meet you."

The blond astrologer stared at me, as if determining if I was worthy of being more than a mere superficial acquaintance. A playful fire danced in her chocolate brown eyes, a flame equal parts intelligence, curiosity, and goodwill.

"I'm Viviana. My friends call me Viva."

"I'll call you Viva, then, if that's all right." She smiled and nodded. I passed another micro test.

"Umm…could you do my horoscope?" I asked, surprised by my bluntness. I was aware that Carl Jung, arguably the greatest twentieth-century psychologist and an associate of Freud, had studied astrology, believed in its accuracy, and even successfully matched hundreds of married couples together using the position of the sun and moon in their respective birth charts.

Viva paused for a moment, as if considering the time commitment. "I'd be happy to. But it'll take me a couple of days to get to it. And I do have to charge, of course."

"Of course, I wouldn't expect you to work for free."

"My normal price is two hundred seventy-five, but if you don't need to know transits and progressions, I could do your basic natal chart interpretation for two hundred dollars."

"Okay, let's start with the basics."

I told the attractive blond astrologer the date and time of

my birth in Sunnyvale, California. Viva clicked the keys of her computer and glanced up at me briefly.

"Same year as me," she said. "But I showed up six months later." I learned later that Viviana's father hailed from Mexico City and her mother from Irvine, California.

"So, you owe me six months' respect."

Viva smiled. "Perhaps. I'll know after I look at your birth chart."

"I'm curious what you find," I offered. "You know what the Greek philosophers said: *know thyself.*" My effort to sound like a reasonably sophisticated truth seeker felt awkward, but Viva didn't seem to notice.

"Yes, the important thing is to discover who you really are," she said. "Not just the outer shell, but who you really are in your essence."

"Sounds challenging. How will I know *my essence?*"

Viva paused, taking my question seriously. "You'll know. Start simply. Become conscious of your inner life...the flow of your thoughts and feelings. Later, if you can still the thought waves of the mind, you'll touch the real self."

"I'll get right on it," I said. At that moment, I wasn't much interested in *stilling my mind waves*, if that were even possible, but I had always been acutely aware of the inner dance of my thoughts and feelings, so I suppose I was already on Viva's recommended path. Regardless, dazzled as I was by her presence, self-knowledge was far from my thoughts. My overriding impulse was to get closer to this lovely young woman and she must've picked up on it.

"You okay?" she asked, embarrassing me. *Chill, Jaden! This isn't the Orgy Room at Burning Man.*

"Super," I said. *Get a grip, man!*

We arranged to meet again at the Coronado in two days. I texted Viva so she'd have my contact, and she gave me her business card.

HIDDEN WISDOM OF THE STARS
Horoscope Analysis and More
by clairvoyant Viviana Vega.

"They have booths in the other room...people won't hear us," she said, turning off her laptop and folding it. "Pardon me, but I have to get to work." She stood, slid her laptop in its case, and grabbed her purse.

"Privacy's good," I said. "Best not to let the world know my deepest secrets, lest the paparazzi find out. Till Wednesday, then." I extended my hand as she was about to leave. She held out hers and I squeezed it gently and briefly. "Do you work nearby?" I persisted, not wanting to end the conversation.

"Actually, I'd like to do astrology full-time, but it doesn't pay the bills. So, I've got a side gig...it's around the corner. Kind of hard to explain, but I help the police solve crimes."

"Really? You *are* fascinating. Do you use astrology?" I recalled what it said on her business card, that she was clairvoyant.

She shook her head. "Like I said, it's hard to explain. I guess you could say I have a gift. Pictures come to me...that is, detailed images flash in my mind, and I've helped them crack some tough cases."

"None of my business, but may I ask what sort of cases?"

Viva paused and looked at me searchingly.

"Murder."

The word struck me as if someone had pushed me in the chest.

"Sounds grisly."

"It's tragic," she said. "I mean, that this sort of stuff actually happens."

"You mean murder? Tell me about it. It's a bizarre world."

Viva headed toward the door, and I followed her onto the super-hot pavement outside. I was about to say goodbye when I noticed her staring intently across the lot at Machiavelli's Italian Restaurant. There was nothing between the Coronado and the eatery except a wide swath of vacant parking spaces divided by a long hedge of gorgeous but highly poisonous oleander bushes. A gap in the foliage provided a clear view.

As we watched, a Honda Civic pulled up beside a parked, white Dodge van and a stocky man with a shock of black hair leaped out of the car and yanked a young girl from the back seat. It appeared she wore a medical mask.

The driver of the white van watched as the stocky fellow shoved the masked girl into his waiting vehicle and slammed the door. Moments later, both the van and the Civic pulled out of the lot.

"Weird!" Viva muttered. "Did you see that?"

"Looked damn suspicious to me," I said. "Like she was being kidnapped, or something."

"Trafficked, maybe." Viva's jaw tensed and her features hardened. "This stuff is going on right under our noses."

She waved goodbye and I watched her get into a sage Fiat 500. Reaching my jeep seconds later, I drove out and saw her pull into the parking lot of the police station a few blocks down the street. I slowly wheeled by and glimpsed her enter the precinct building. Curious, I drove twice around the block, gazing at her car each time, musing on the nature of her clairvoyant "gift," and wondering if she'd picked up anything notable about me on her paranormal radar.

Embarrassed that I was behaving like a stalker, I pulled into the left lane and sped up, singing softly as I wove through the labyrinth of streets to my hotel.

CHAPTER 3

The Day They H-Bombed Los Angeles

The Tempe Mission Palms featured a tranquil, oasis-like courtyard, but its main attraction for me was the rooftop pool, with exceptional views of the nearby desert hillsides. After a brief dip, I relaxed under a poolside umbrella, reflecting on my encounter with Viva, and the disturbing incident involving the young, masked girl.

The petite astrologer was attractive, bright, pleasant, and a magnet for my eyes, and her heart-warming laugh echoed in my mind. I could not picture her as a cop, so I figured she must have an arrangement allowing her to employ her clairvoyant gifts in crime investigation. Resolving to ask more about her work when we met again, I brushed aside my uncomfortable feelings about the possible kidnapping incident.

∼

MY HIGH SCHOOL FRIEND Seth Rosen was staying about a mile away. We were having a reunion with another hometown buddy, Maxie. After showering in my room, I set off on foot toward Seth's place.

Tempe, home to Arizona State University, is a city in its own right, yet its streets flow seamlessly into the greater downtown urban web of Phoenix. I took my time, exploring the area. The leisurely pace gave me the chance to reflect on the previous night's frightening dream episode of clashing warriors, and the unlikely events that had brought me to this moment.

Since my early teens, I'd noticed a bothersome pattern: the return of the violent nocturnal images always seemed to herald ordeals and pitfalls in my life. Their last appearance three years prior certainly fit the pattern. Coinciding with the nightmares, my mother had endured a stroke on top of a nervous breakdown and kicked me out of my childhood home. "I never want my eyeballs to land on you again!" she said, her once-impressive intellect wasted by her affliction. Her out-of-control alcoholism no doubt played a role in her, and my, fall from grace.

Booted by my mother from our Monterey dwelling, I'd escaped to southern California. Those were crazy days, living wild on the street, surviving hand to mouth, subsisting off oranges and avocados plucked from trees. It's a miracle I didn't end up like so many of the wasted, withered souls I met, roughing it in Palm Springs and California beach towns. Lost and confused, without a roadmap.

I could have easily ended up a felon, a drug addict, or a homeless zombie, but fate spared me. Miraculously, unlike the hardened ones I met, my heart didn't turn to flint, and I dodged the peril that consumed these citizens of the street. Through divine intervention or simple luck, my life turned around, and I was yanked from the edge of the abyss by the invisible hand of destiny.

It happened after a homeless, teenage buddy dared me to do something violent to land in jail; "something cool," he said, goading me. Out of cowardice more than good sense, I spurned his dare, though it happened the violence found me without my seeking it.

I had tried to avoid the fistfight that broke out in The Marine Room, a Laguna Beach rock and roll whiskey bar I'd wandered in to escape a springtime shower. Believing I was a "person of interest" in serious crimes, the cops pulled me in for questioning. The creep at the center of the fight was a wanted criminal, a Charles Manson type who'd murdered several people. My six-foot, athletic frame and tousled brown hair matched the description of one of the suspect's sidekicks, and in the confusion, the cops believed I was a member of his gang. Not only was it not cool, but my night in jail was the worst in my life.

The officer apologized in the morning, said it was a mistake, and let me go, but it was a frightening ordeal. Adversity teaches what nothing else can.

My salvation came the day after the cops released me, while playing basketball on the public court by the beach in Laguna. Exhilarated by the Pacific breeze, warm sunshine, and my release from confinement, on a whim I called my uncle from a borrowed cell phone to let him know I was alive. Not that he actually cared. Yet my timing was auspicious. "Damn!" he said. "I've been through all kinds of shit trying to find you. Your mom died two days ago!"

My estranged mother had suffered a heart attack, and I'd inherited her split-level and a smattering of stocks and bank accounts. A modest sum, it seemed a fortune to a twenty-something, homeless vagabond.

So, I hitched a ride back to Monterey, buried my poor mother, and went to work driving a truck for a local delivery company. Serendipitously, I plowed my earnings and inheritance into tech stocks and soon had a tidy lump of cash set aside to support my desire to travel. Quite a contrast from those desperate days stealing fruit from trees to stay alive.

Now, three years after my homeless days and my mother's death, I was ready to begin a new life. My holiday road trip symbolized a fresh start, a promising new cycle of possibilities and adventure, yet the return of my nightmares cast a shadow over my expectations.

Brushing aside the lingering dread caused by the dreams, I wandered into a lonely bookstore to escape the midday heat. I imagined in its heyday it might have been one of those fabulous, atmospheric places one could find in university towns before the Internet and Amazon killed many of the old legacy bookstores. A confirmed bibliophile, I loved perusing aged volumes and would compulsively invade bookshops when I found one. Sadly, despite its probable noteworthy history, this one appeared to be on life support, shadowy inside, dimly lit by grayish fluorescent lighting, with two customers moving slowly among the antique stacks.

I rummaged through the dusty fiction shelves, but nothing spoke to me, so I stepped over to the counter where an attractive, young brunette woman about twenty, with a long ponytail, roundish glasses, and wearing a black leather jacket, glanced up from the sci-fi magazine she was reading and smiled.

"Helpless?" she asked with a giggle, surprising me with her odd greeting.

"Umm, not exactly. Just looking for a good read. Any suggestions?" I wasn't really looking for anything but felt like chatting with her.

"How about this one?" She held up a thin, musty, yellowed paperback that looked fifty years old. "It's called, *The Day They H-Bombed Los Angeles.*"

"Sounds like fun."

"It's so satisfying! It's about humans turning into zombies after L.A. is hit with a nuclear strike. The zombies go through fascinating character development...they'll remind you of people you see on the street."

"And friends, probably. Sounds delightful."

She smiled and nodded. "My ex-boyfriend, definitely!" Her smile was slightly crooked, with the right side of her mouth a touch higher than the left, and there was a tiny trace of red lipstick on her front teeth. She paused, then added, "The first chapter is the best." I was amused at her sales pitch. *Downhill the rest of the way?*

"Sounds like a hidden literary gem," I said, "though probably not *Lord of the Rings*, exactly."

"No orcs, just zombies," she beamed. "And it's just two dollars. Worth every centavo."

"Can't say no to a deal like that. Looking forward to the best part."

"Chapter one! It's so exciting!"

I held my credit card to the machine, wondering how the

store could stay open selling grimy, ancient paperbacks for two dollars. She deftly placed the book in a thin paper bag, smiling cheerfully.

"By the way, what's the name here?" I asked.

"Lyla...Lyla French. French is an English name." She giggled cheerfully, her dark brown hair framing her pretty smile.

"Oh. Hi, Lyla. Your name is ancient...means 'night' in Hebrew and Arabic."

"It's also Sanskrit," she said. "It means 'play.' I spell it with a *y*."

"My name's Jaden. Jaden Parker. Nice to meet you. But what I meant was...I didn't notice your sign...for the bookstore. What's the name of this place?"

"Oh, of course. Tattered Pages. Clever name, don't you think?"

"Umm...it's memorable. Thanks, Lyla."

"Enjoy!" she said. "And watch out for orcs and zombies. Lots of 'em around here." She smiled and waved as I turned to go.

CHAPTER 4

The Reunion

My friend Seth lived full-time in Las Vegas but was staying at his parents' place, a condo in the heart of Tempe, while they enjoyed an extended Hawaiian holiday. Seth and his wife, Karina, had the place to themselves as he focused on a big story he claimed would make waves.

Seth, Maxie, and I had drifted apart since our high school days, which I suppose is to be expected. Then again, as high school buddies, we weren't really interested in sharing ideas and "issues." Our goals were scoring beer and looking cool enough to attract girls. High school for us was not the place for camaraderie based on intellectually similar views. And in those days, "ideology" was a word we didn't even know the meaning of. Now, six years on from graduation, I believed we still had enough in common to remain friends and looked forward to seeing them.

Oddly, Maxie also lived in Vegas, where he worked at a hotel casino, the Golden Nugget. We had arranged to meet here, as the Vegas scene was too crazy and distracting. The timing was perfect, coinciding neatly with the kickoff of my road trip.

"Nice place your parents have here, Seth," I said, flopping on a cushiony chair in his living room after my friends greeted me. Maxie sat comfortably on the couch, his shoes off, feet on the glass coffee table. Seth was tall and serious and wore wire-framed glasses that gave him a distinguished, professorial air, reinforced by a few premature gray hairs mixed with the black.

"Great place to practice safe sex, no doubt," Maxie chimed in.

"What do you mean?" Seth asked, staring at our mutual friend.

"Well, it's a *condom*-inium, right?"

Seth shook his head. "The lousy jokes never stop coming with you guys."

Maxie was wearing a wrinkled T-shirt emblazoned with a Grateful Dead, electrified skull logo, and his long brown hair fell to his broad, linebacker shoulders. He took out a small brass pipe, stuffed it with sticky marijuana leaves, and offered it to me, but I declined. Maxie was a survivor, more so even than me. After high school, he became addicted to heroin, which nearly killed him. He smoked hashish for a year to help stay off heroin, and marijuana after that to drop the hash. Now he was mostly drug-free but smoked pot occasionally. Drinking beer was a mission in his life.

I'd been through my own personal drug wars but had reached the point of near-total abstinence, avoiding even beer. My drug of choice was coffee. The three of us smoked weed together a few times in high school but didn't hang around with the druggies. My athleticism and love of sports probably saved me. Playing baseball and smoking dope don't synch well.

"I'll pass," Seth said, after Maxie lit the pipe, sucked on it deeply, and offered it to him. "It's fun for an hour, then it makes my brain feel like it's got cotton glued on it. Besides, my wife can't stand the smell. You're gonna make my parents' castle stink like an opium den." He stood and moved toward his office. "I'm getting some incense."

"Hey man," I whispered to Maxie when Seth was out of earshot, "you should ask permission before you light up in his house."

"Sorry, I wasn't thinking." Maxie took another hit from his pipe and placed it on the coffee table. He stood up abruptly, smoothed his grungy jeans at the knees, then ambled into the kitchen and swung open the refrigerator door. He pulled out a bottle of Heineken, then invaded the pantry and ransacked the shelves till he found some cookies, to which he helped himself. *Still the scrounging leech.*

Seth reappeared moments later. "Where's Maxie?" he asked.

"Bonding with your kitchen," I said, nudging my head in that direction. "Hasn't changed since high school." As a teenager, Maxie was famous for unabashedly making himself at home in other people's kitchens, and he'd obviously not outgrown that boorish adolescent streak.

Maxie strolled in from the kitchen clutching his bottle of Heineken, set three peanut butter cookies on the glass table, and reclined in the plush chair, his feet once more propped, shoeless, on the table. If Seth was put off by Maxie's brazen behavior, he didn't show it.

"How's your girlfriend these days?" Seth asked him.

Maxie crunched on a peanut butter cookie, gazing fondly toward the kitchen. "Sheila? She's okay, I guess...it's just that... she never stops talking, ya know what I mean?" Seth and I nodded sympathetically. "But deep down inside…" Maxie paused and stared into space, a faraway look on his face, "…deep down inside…she just never stops talking." Maxie took another bite of cookie, wiped the crumbs from his chin, and examined his pipe as if it were an ancient artifact.

"Actually, I don't smoke weed much these days either," he added. "Thought I'd share some fine herb with my ole best buds… fer *auld lang syne*. This stuff is from the hills of Mendocino, grown by a friend of mine. He's in prison now. There's no finer weed this side of Acapulco."

Seth took a deep breath and shook his head, as if he were wrestling with an inner dragon. "You know," he said, "I think I *will* have some. It's been a while, and I could use something to help me chill. I'll tell Karina we burned a rare blend of exotic Persian incense laced with traces of Indonesian frankincense and Sri Lankan sandalwood." He laughed, and I knew he wasn't serious about the incense story. I hadn't met Seth's wife yet, but he had texted me pictures of their wedding. She was a stunningly beautiful blond, born in Poland of Swiss parents.

"My life's too frickin' frenetic these days," Seth went on. He paused to place the brass pipe to his lips, inhaling, then breathing out a stream of thick, pungent smoke.

"Aren't you on a break from your Vegas reality?" I volunteered.

"Yeah, but it's a work vacation…got to finish this article. Everything is *work*. Even on holiday. *Work* on your relationship. *Work* on your tan. *Work* out at the gym. Work, work, work." He took another toke from the pipe and handed it to Maxie.

"Besides," Seth continued, "the world is going absolutely

to hell, and I've uncovered some super-weird stuff. Vegas is a wonderland, and a dangerous one." After a pause he looked at me and forced a smile. "Anyway, how do you like Phoenix, Jaden?"

"It's okay, I guess, as far as cities go. Way too hot, a little boring; I miss the ocean."

Maxie nodded enthusiastically, crunching a cookie. "Yeah, who doesn't? Phoenix is as hot as Vegas, without the pole dancers and gambling addicts. But hey, your wife used to be into ballet, right, Seth? You told me that. That means you're married to a *Pole dancer.*"

Seth rolled his eyes. "Haha. But I agree with you about the ocean—I miss it too. Truth is, Phoenix sucks. But what city doesn't? It's better than most big metro scenes. Less insane, less dirty, but the bottom line is it's screwed, like pretty much everywhere. The country's going down the tubes if you ask me. If things don't turn around, we'll end up a dictatorship with jackboots on our necks. The politicians in charge are crooks. It's a sick syndicate of corporate and political gangsters."

"Didn't know you majored in conspiracy theory," Maxie said, not expecting a response. He bit into another peanut butter cookie, then tipped the bottle of Heineken to his mouth.

Seth ignored Maxie's comment and looked at me seriously. "Just wait till I tell you some of the dirt I've uncovered," he said. After a pause, he switched tracks. "What brings you here, Jaden? Other than to see us. Pilgrimage to Mecca?"

"Well, yeah…obviously I wanted to see you guys—it's been a few years. California's not what it used to be, far as I can tell. Cities are hell holes, homeless everywhere, mile-long tent encampments...some places are starting to look Third World. Not Monterey, fortunately. Still dead boring, though. Anyway, I just needed to get away—go on a road trip. Explore."

"Find ultimate truth and gain limitless power," Maxie added.

"How'd you know? So, I'm headed to Sedona, the Grand Canyon, New Mexico. I aim to see Santa Fe and Taos. Wherever the spirit leads. Anyway, California's still home unless I find someplace that grabs me."

"The pilgrim continues his journey to self-discovery and enlightenment," Maxie said. "I'd wager it's more like till you find a hot chick who grabs you." He pointed to his crotch. "But I'm warning you, Hawaiian shirts aren't cool, man. Makes you look like a boomer." *And faded Grateful Dead T-shirts and grungy jeans are high fashion, I suppose.* I didn't reply to Maxie's complaint.

The Hawaiian shirts were a legacy from my father. Despite the fact he'd abandoned us when I was a kid, for some odd reason, my mother never removed all his clothes from the closet. He was known for his Hawaiian shirts, and I'd brought three of them along on my road trip. Generally, I wore T-shirts in hot weather but today I wore one of my father's Hawaiians to our reunion. Despite Maxie's take, the gaudy shirts made me feel relaxed and on holiday.

Maxie's sarcastic banter was edgy, and he definitely had an obnoxious streak, but he didn't *intend* to be mean. Usually. It was just part of his nearly continuous effort to be funny, a personality trait I shared with him. Truth is, he amused without trying. Always had. Once, in high school, in all seriousness and to the scorn and derision of the class, he defended himself to the English teacher who challenged his sources: "I didn't plagiarize! I copied straight from the book!"

"You always were a strange combo, Jaden," he continued. "A medieval bookworm in the body of a proverbial jock." Maxie was right. When I wasn't playing sports growing up, I spent most of my spare time devouring books.

"Always the seeker, Jaden," Seth added, a quick smile lit his features before his stern look returned. "That's good...the quest is what matters, wherever it takes you. And remember the saying: *Truth will make you free, but first it will make you angry.* And believe me, it will."

"You really sound pissed about something," Maxie said.

Seth *did* wear a somewhat worried expression. And to be honest, though it was almost six years since I'd last seen him, he looked as if he'd aged at least twice that.

"Actually, I am. The truth has turned out to be disgusting. Makes me wish I'd never become an investigative journalist." I knew Seth had nearly lost his job after writing a series of provocative exposés of criminal activity involving key figures in the Vegas political establishment. Despite the editor's misgivings, the articles had been published and he was working on a follow-up, but he had poked a hornet's nest. When Seth gave his editor a draft of his latest findings, his boss threatened to let him go. Top levels of management were forcing his hand, Seth believed.

"Nearly got canned from my position at the *Vegas Sun* after I wrote that article about drugs and child trafficking."

"Trafficking?" Maxie said, his hands folded on his chest. "I'm not going down that rabbit hole. I don't read papers. Sorry, Seth.

I know you write good. In fact, you're the smartest guy I know after my techie friend in Vegas, Dante Ferraro. And of course, Jaden here." He threw me an amiable glance. "Anyway, I get my news from TV or Twitter. You can trust it if you see it on TV." *Is Maxie really that naive?*

Seth ignored Maxie's skeptical remarks. "Yeah, trafficking. You know, sort of like kidnapping. Despicable stuff. Kids are taken from foster homes, from illegal immigration, brought across the border, you name it, and they end up being trafficked. Sexually exploited, and worse. It's really demonic, and it's a lot more widespread than you think."

Maxie seemed unimpressed. "Sounds like conspiracy theory, but I suppose it's true," he said. "Thing is, even if it *is* happening like you say, there's nothing us peons can do about it."

Seth shook his head. "It's not theory, and I intend to do something about it. This stuff is going on right under our noses and there's complicity at the highest levels."

Stunned, I recalled that Viva used the exact same words that very morning. "This stuff is going on right under our noses." I decided not to mention the bizarre incident at the Coronado.

"The fact that I nearly got sacked for investigating this crap," Seth continued, "is tantamount to proof that I'm on the right track. And what makes you think we're peons?"

Maxie took a sip of his Heineken and didn't answer. "C'mon, Maxie," I said, "Give Seth some credit. It takes a lot of courage to write about this sort of stuff." I looked at Seth. "Can I read the article?"

"Sure. I'll send it to you. The one I'm working on now is even more explosive, but it's not finished." He leaned over his laptop and clicked a few keys. I looked at my phone and saw his message hit my inbox.

Seth laughed nervously. "You know, this might sound crazy, but I'm actually a bit paranoid. I'm afraid if I publish everything I know, they might try and kill me. These psychos are evil. And for them, killing someone is child's play."

"Are you serious?" I said, stunned at his words. "I mean, that's crazy. Who *are* these scum?"

"Yeah. Who's *they*?" Maxie added.

"You'll get an idea when you read my article. At least, the new one I'm working on. But if something happens to me...for the record, I don't have a suicidal bone in my body." After a pause, he added, "Care to have a copy, Maxie? Of my article?"

Our friend was leaning back, his eyes half closed, hands folded on his belt buckle, cookie crumbs on his Dead T-shirt. I was shocked by Seth's revelation, but Maxie seemed almost blasé. "Umm...no, sorry. I feel for you, man. This stuff sounds freaking insane. But I'm not ready to swallow the Kool-Aid. I've got an open mind, but I'm no tinfoil-hat weirdo. Weirdo, yes. Just no tinfoil hat. Anyway, you might be deluding yourself. Reality is what you think it is." *Maxie, waxing philosophical.*

Seth glared at our Monterey bud. "Your mind's so open, Maxie, there's nothing in it. Feel free to remain in your adolescent stupor." It was unlike Seth to be cantankerous, and it was clear he was anxious and troubled. Maxie, on the other hand, loved to play the devil's advocate and be disagreeable for argument's sake. And the combination of THC from the marijuana, mixed with the beer, created a cocktail in his brain certain to contribute to intellectual obstinacy. So, despite his words lacking what I felt to be appropriate sympathy for Seth's dilemma, I let it slide.

"Look, Seth, I'm on your team," Maxie offered. "I know you're an awesome journalist, but can't you just, like, change lanes? You know, investigate something more chill. How about sports gambling? I hear they pay refs to rig games."

Seth shook his head and frowned. "This is what I've discovered. I've got to tell the world what's going on. Dangerous or not."

"You're a hell of a lot braver than me," Maxie said. "Or maybe just stupider."

"C'mon, guys," I interjected. "This was supposed to be a happy reunion. Seth's obviously onto something." I glanced at Maxie, whose arms were now folded across his chest. "'There are more things in heaven and earth than are dreamt of in your philosophy, Horatio,'" I added, quoting a line from *Hamlet* and poking Maxie on his knee.

"Ah, yes," said Maxie, "wisdom from the immortal English bard. Jaden, you're stuck in a proverbial time warp." "Proverbial" was one of Maxie's favorite words and he used it way too often.

"Maybe so. The foundation for our current world is built on the past. You can't really grasp the present without a sense of what's come before. Antiquity is underrated, in my humble opinion."

"Whatever you say, Mister Retro," Maxie replied. "At least we have technology nowadays. Smartphones for dumb people."

Seth's cell phone rang. He answered it and spoke softly. I

could make out a chorus of "Yes, sweetheart," and "Of course, sweetheart," and figured he was speaking to Karina.

"Sorry, guys," he sighed as he finished the call. "My wife's on her way home and I forgot she wants to make me a special dinner. It's my birthday in a couple of days."

"Happy Birthday, man!" Maxie and I said together. We jumped to our feet and began straightening pillows and cleaning up the coffee table.

"Birthdays are good," Maxie mumbled. "The more birthdays you have, the longer you live."

Despite the heat, Seth opened the windows and raced around, attempting to reassemble his parents' home the way it was before we two barbarians entered the sacred temple. Pushing aside the troubling edge in our conversation, we exchanged bear hugs, and Maxie and I strolled out into the blistering desert air.

CHAPTER 5

Lyla French

Next morning, I spent an hour at the rooftop pool enjoying the intense desert sun, relieved that my nightmares of clashing Greek and Trojan warriors hadn't returned. Blown away by what Seth had confided to us about his investigative writing and the peril he believed it conjured for him, I was determined to read his article before our next meeting. Despite my respect for Seth's intelligence and my concern for his safety, I believed his fears were exaggerated. Nonetheless, I was shaken by my friend's revelations on the heels of what Viva and I had witnessed leaving the coffee shop.

Maxie and I'd agreed to meet at a local restaurant-bar that catered largely to Arizona State University students in Tempe. On my way there, on a whim, I drove to a convenience store not far from Tattered Pages. I parked a block away and was ambling back to my car with a bag of plastic razors and shaving cream when I passed in front of the bookstore. The instant I reached the storefront entrance, the door swung open, and Lyla French stepped onto the sidewalk, gripping a small brown grocery bag, and started moving in the same direction as me. *Talk about good timing.* As if choreographed, we strolled shoulder to shoulder, though she apparently didn't notice who I was. The odd synchronicity at this chance encounter struck me as worthy of philosophical reflection.

"Hi, Lyla," I said, smiling, hoping not to cause alarm, not sure she would even recall me. She glanced over and peered through sunglasses, her brown ponytail bobbing in rhythm to our steps. "You probably don't remember me, but I met you in the bookstore yesterday."

"Oh right! You bought a book!"

"About zombies. *The Day They H-Bombed Los Angeles.*"

"I remember! Hi again!" It could have been an awkward moment, but we both took it in stride, literally. *Is there a message here? Some mysterious fate at work in this unlikely encounter?*

"What'd ya think of it?" she asked, as we stepped in tandem.

"So far, so good. Haven't finished yet, but the first chapter is definitely the best." I actually *had* read the first three chapters. The bomb had dropped, destroying most of L.A., and the survivors were starting to lose their humanity, becoming vicious zombies.

"I'm glad you like it." She paused, then laughed and said, "Maybe not the greatest book, but it's a sci-fi classic, ahead of its time. Anyway, lots of zombies around these parts, for sure." She made a sweeping gesture at the surrounding environs.

"I know. Got to stay sharp and watch for trouble. Dangerous business these days, going out your door." An odd picture flashed in my mind of Maxie and Lyla hitting it off and I surprised myself by doing what normally I found painfully difficult to do: randomly picking up on girls.

"Hey, I'm on my way to meet a friend at Zipp's here in Tempe. Care to join us for an hour or two? I could give you a ride back or pay for an Uber to wherever you want to go."

Lyla paused for an instant and I thought I might have been too sudden in my approach, but her response put me at ease. "That sounds like fun!" she enthused. "How about an Uber ride to New York City? All expenses paid. Or better yet, Miami!... kidding!" I liked her slightly dippy sense of humor. We arrived at my Jeep, and I opened the door for her. She slid in the front seat, and I sauntered to the driver's side, slightly wonderstruck at the unexpected and magnificently orchestrated encounter. *Do invisible powers really intervene in our affairs? If so, well done!*

"Hey Maxie, this is my friend, Lyla," I said a few minutes later as we strolled up to the table at Zipp's Sports Grill where Maxie was waiting. Zipp's was a darkish, noisy, atmospheric sports bar serving mostly as a watering hole for ASU students. He still wore the same seedy jeans and T-shirt featuring the electric skull, and he'd added a Los Angeles Dodgers baseball cap to his outfit. "Lyla, this is Maxwell Cooper, a.k.a. Maxie. The two of us go way back."

A feeling of immature pride arose in me as I introduced the bookstore clerk to my old friend. In high school, Maxie and I majored in attempting to meet girls; we would compare notes and strategies, suggest various approaches and pick-up lines, and study how to appear cool enough to attract the ones who stirred our teenage passions. Oddly, I felt a moment of post-adolescent enjoyment as Maxie stood up and extended his hand toward Lyla. *Maybe they'll click.*

"My pleasure," Maxie said, sizing up my bookstore

acquaintance, gazing at her attractive figure a bit too long. "Perfect timing. I've only been here a few minutes and I'm expecting my libation to arrive any moment." He studied Lyla as she took a seat on a stool between him and me at the high table. "Can I get you something to drink?" His question beat me to the punch.

"Rosé sounds good, but I'm only twenty, so I'll have to wait two months."

"That's a long time to wait, even in this palatial environment," I said. "Red Bull for me," I added, looking at the waitress as she appeared with Maxie's Heineken.

"I'll have a Red Bull too," Lyla said, flashing her charming, crooked smile at me. A soft breeze touched my heart, and I wondered if I might be seriously liking her.

The waitress brought our Red Bulls, a couple of glasses with ice, and a plate of nachos Maxie'd ordered. Our server was tall and slender, her black hair cut short, and her expression and demeanor seemed oddly serious in that environment. Her name tag read, Tiny.

"A toast to friendship and good times," Maxie said, holding up his glass. We touched glasses and echoed Maxie's words.

"How do you like Zipp's?" I asked him.

"Not bad," my long-haired friend replied. "But it's so dark I can't hear anything. It's a good place to chill, though. I need to slow down…pulled a muscle in my back a few months ago and it keeps acting up."

"Oh, no," I said. "Have you seen a chiropractor?"

"I saw one in a movie once. But no, I haven't gone to get my spine cracked. Don't need to…my doctor gave me some pain medication. Works great. It's called 'sukkfuxxium.'"

I glanced at Lyla, who was on the edge of her seat. "Are you *sure* you're pronouncing that right?" I asked.

"Absolutely. It's right on the label. Begins with an S, ends with an M. Also increases male hormone production, so I'm a regular testosterone monkey." Maxie gulped his Heineken as Lyla and I sipped our Red Bulls.

"By the way," my friend added after a pause to glance at his cell phone, "what's in the bag?" Maxie pointed with his chin at the brown bag Lyla had placed on the table, then swigged his beer.

"Oh, just some groceries," Lyla said, "I'm experimenting with a mostly fruit diet, all organic and non-GMO—papaya and grape-fruit. Gotta love those big naturals." Maxie's eyes bugged and he unintentionally shot a spurt of Heineken across the table at me.

"Absolutely…gotta love 'em," he affirmed, gulping hard. "Truth is," he continued, collecting himself, "I eat tons of fruit. In fact, I'm vegan. I also eat lots of meat."

Lyla and I glanced at each other and smiled while Maxie plowed on. "Ya know, I really can't tell if our waitress is a man or woman."

"Probably gender fluid," Lyla said.

"Genner what?" Maxie said, raising his eyebrows. "Sounds like motor oil."

"You know, non-binary," Lyla explained. "They don't iden-tify with being boy or girl. They kinda slide back and forth. Gender fluid."

"But they're still one or the other," Maxie insisted. "They've either got a penis or a vagina. That's standard equipment on all models."

"I bet he's a girl," I said. "'Tiny' sounds like a girl's name. Even though she's not tiny."

"I think she's a boy," Lyla said, holding the base of her glass of Red Bull. "Maybe it's a *he* and he's got a micro-penis," she suggested. "So, he chooses to be gender fluid and non-binary. It's a free-will choice."

"It's got to be one or another," Maxie insisted. "It's a biological reality, male or female. No third options. Sorry."

"How's everything so far?" Tiny said softly, checking in at our table and bringing Maxie another Heineken.

"Big yum," Lyla asserted, biting on a crunchy tortilla chip smeared with guacamole.

"*Big yum?*" Maxie said, his eyes squinting at Lyla.

"Yeah, tasty…as in, real yummy. *Big yum.*"

That apparently satisfied Maxie, who turned to Tiny and said, "By the way, don't mean to be nosy, but is Tiny a boy's name or a girl's name?"

"Can be either," Tiny said, black eyes shining.

"And for you personally…is it a boy name or a girl name?" *Maxie, not pulling punches.*

"Personally, I'm fluid," Tiny said. I looked at Lyla and her face said, *See, I told you so.*

"Sorta depends on the day, huh?" said Maxie, gripping his glass of Heineken for support. "If I may be so bold, what's your last name?"

"Brighter. Tiny Brighter. It's my stage name. I'm a dancer."

"And your birth name? Probably Hank," Maxie declared, trolling poor Tiny.

Our waitress frowned. "Don't be rude or I'll report you to management."

"Hey, I just thought you were possibly gorgeous, and I might want to ask you out," Maxie said. "But only if you're a woman of the female persuasion." Tiny swiveled and hurried away.

"C'mon, Maxie," I pleaded. "Leave him alone. Or *her*. Let Tiny be what he wants to be."

"This is some weird shit," Maxie said, draining his Heineken from the bottle. "The world is really going to hell. Look, I don't give a rat's ass if you're gay, or lesbian, or ambidextrous, or whatever ornamentation…I mean, orientation you might have, but you're either a guy or a girl, period."

"Guys and dolls it is, then," I said, hoping to steer the conversation another direction. "Did you grow up in Phoenix?" I said, looking into Lyla's Irish green eyes.

"Nah," she said. "I'm way too sophisticated for these parts. I was born in Chicago, moved to Texas, then Florida and California, but I came here to recover from a bad relationship. So, I'm staying at my dad's place till I can get back on my feet."

"Were you an army brat?" I asked.

"Brat yes, army no. My dad was a Marine. Special Forces. After that he was a pilot for Southwest. Then he worked for the FBI a few years. Now he's retired. Back injury."

"That's cool…I love to fly," I said, "but my arms get tired." Maxie winced and muttered something under his breath.

"You're a funny one," Lyla said, gently poking me in the shoulder. *Sometimes even bad jokes get the girls.*

"What do you think of Phoenix?" I asked her.

"Phoenix is not a place one *thinks* of," said Lyla. "It's a place one *endures*. But I suppose it's all right; humdrum, monotonous... but it has its virtues."

"Name one," said Maxie.

"Virtue? Well, of the four classical virtues, *fortitude* stands out as one required to endure this hellish heat. So yeah, fortitude is a Phoenix virtue, at least of the people who live here during summer. Also, regarding virtue, Phoenix is not, like, one of the world's leading vice capitals, though I hear it has a raunchy side."

"All big cities do," affirmed Maxie. "Have a raunchy side, that is. But this town's a nun's cloister compared to Vegas."

"I doubt you'd know much about nun's cloisters," I said.

"Not compared to the world's expert," he countered, pointing at me.

"Not sure if I follow you," I said.

"Well, c'mon, Jaden, you yourself told me one of your favorite spots to chill was that nun's church in Carmel, right?" Maxie was referring to the Carmelite Monastery, a charming seaside chapel that was also a home for cloistered nuns. Located just a few miles from me in Monterey, I enjoyed decompressing in the serene, historic chapel overlooking the Pacific.

"Guilty as charged," I said. "I like to meditate, and that's a great place to unwind."

"Cosmic rays, man. Dammit, Jaden. I really like you, but

you're weirder even than me…you meditate, hide out in nun's cloisters, and don't even drink beer. What went wrong?"

"I meditate," Lyla said, coming to my rescue. "And if you like churches," she added, glancing my way, "you should check out the one a few blocks from here…Old Saint Mary's Church. It's, like, real old…I mean historically ancient and charming, with great vibes. And it possesses a transcendent spiritual atmosphere."

Maxie stared wondrously at Lyla, as if she'd just admitted her diet consisted exclusively of earthworms. "Here I am," he said, "in a proverbial college sports bar with two saints, drinking beer and discussing meditation, nun's cloisters, and stratospheric churches. What's next? English literature and the meaning of fairy tales?"

"I think fairy tales are cool," Lyla said. "Straightforward good versus evil themes…with a happy ending."

Maxie eyed Lyla suspiciously. "Sounds like Drag Queen Story Hour. Goldilocks and the Seven Dwarves."

"Fairy tales have deep psychological meaning," I said. "Symbolizing aspects and layers of human consciousness."

Maxie frowned, tilted his second bottle of Heineken and rapidly drained it. "You guys are way over my head. Can we talk about something down to earth? Like, you know, sports. The Raiders suck. They should've stayed in Oakland… or even L.A."

"The L.A. scene is way too crazy for me," Lyla offered. "But I'll take Malibu any day." She plunged a chip into the salsa, then scooped guac from the nacho plate and devoured it.

"This is as close to L.A. as I want to get," Maxie said, touching his Dodgers cap.

"It looks good on you," Lyla said affably. "Fashionable, in a sporty kinda way."

Maxie seemed pleased by the compliment. "Thanks. But I don't pay attention to fashion," he said, stating the obvious. "Most guys don't, except gay guys…but I like clothes, which is why I wear them. I have a lot of cool T-shirts."

"Fashion's overrated," Lyla said, trying to be agreeable. "It's an elitist business run by a gang of billionaires. They, like…try and manipulate you. Know what I mean? To keep up with the new fads."

"It's definitely commercially driven," I pitched in. "Designers change styles seasonally so fashion enthusiasts, mostly women, provide a steady income stream. But at the same time, isn't it true lots of women…you know…really *like* to read *Cosmopolitan* and *Vogue*, and those type magazines?"

"I do myself," the bookstore clerk admitted. "Or used to, when they had print editions. I'm not exactly a Cosmo girl, if ya know what I mean. But I always liked those mags for the articles, which were pretty decent. I mean, you could learn a lot. And for the photography, which was mostly gorgeous. I'm not all that fashion trendy, though."

"The problem with clothes," Maxie said, "is you have to buy them. I mean, why waste time shopping when you can go to a bar?"

"It's an acquired taste," Lyla said, getting up and moving toward the restroom.

Tiny Brighter reappeared with our bill and Maxie picked it up. "I'll split it with you," I offered, reaching for my wallet.

"No, Jadie, it's an honor to dine in the company of two enlightened beings." My friend paid the bill with cash, and I noticed he included a hefty tip. Then he scribbled something on a napkin and left it beside the money.

"What's that all about?" I asked.

"I'm apologizing to Tiny. Just because I'm obnoxious doesn't mean I'm a jerk. Besides. Just in case there *is* a God, I need to polish my resumé." He winked at Tiny on the way out, and we gathered briefly on the sidewalk before Maxie sauntered to his car and Lyla and I headed toward mine.

"I have to admit, I'm starting to like Phoenix," I said to Lyla, opening the door of my Jeep. "It's clean. They take care of the roads. There's actually lots to do."

"True. Could be worse. By the way, nice car. Super fancy." Lyla gave me a thumbs-up as she slid into the passenger seat. *She's got the right attitude.*

"Thanks, it's fun to drive. The brakes are bad, but I compensate with a loud horn."

Lyla smiled and giggled. "You know," she said as we merged into the traffic. "I love the symbolism of the name—Phoenix, that is."

"Something about a creature that flies into the fire, right?"

"Right. The Phoenix is an ancient, mythical bird. Every five hundred years it flies into the flames and is reborn."

"I like that. A metaphor of transformation and new life."

"Yup. Only problem is...you have to die in the fire first." Lyla sighed gently and her voice had a melancholy tone I hadn't heard from her before. "Why's it always that way?" She looked at me quizzically, as if she were a soothsayer who'd lost her convictions.

"Good question. I never really thought about it."

"Maybe it's time you do," she said. Her piercing sideways glance surprised me. "In case you have to go through some fires."

I could only nod, struck by her strange suggestion. Moments later, we reached her apartment and parted ways with my less-than-certain guarantee I'd text her in a day or two. As we waved to each other, I made a screeching U-turn and drove way too fast back to Tempe Mission Palms.

CHAPTER 6

Saturn Transit

Perplexed by my possible connection with Lyla, I wondered if I should press it. The unlikely spontaneous way we'd met in front of Tattered Pages that morning seemed almost choreographed by an unseen hand.

My bookstore friend was cute, sexy, smart, funny, and she seemed to like me. Despite the positive prospects of cultivating her friendship, by the time I left the pool the following morning to take a short excursion around Phoenix, I'd made up my mind Viva was the one for me. Of course, it was mighty presumptuous on my part. After all, we'd met exactly once. She might think I'm an idiot, or she might have a boyfriend, or be otherwise unavailable. Regarding all these possibilities, I was clueless. So, hedging my bets in typical male-brained fashion, I decided if Viva showed no interest, I'd give Lyla a call.

Cruising around town, I spied a food truck parked at a corner with several people standing, eating off paper plates. I parked behind the Modern Tortilla Taco Truck and ordered a dish of incredibly tasty veggie tacos loaded with sweet potatoes, caramelized onions, roasted corn, and roasted red peppers, which I washed down with bottled water.

Refreshed after my repast and sparked by the thought of seeing Viva tomorrow, I wheeled around greater Phoenix, spent a couple of hours in the famous Scottsdale shopping areas, and sipped an espresso in Berdena's Café in the Old Town.

I made a wrong turn in the late afternoon and found myself in a dilapidated neighborhood when I again felt pangs of hunger. I spotted an old man pushing a cart along the sidewalk, similar to the ones I'd seen on a foray into Mexico a few years back. The hand-painted sign on the cart read, "Tamales Excepcionales. El Mejor del Mundo." Exceptional tamales. Best in the world. I hadn't eaten a tamale in years but felt compelled to pull over. Seconds later, I met the man at his cart.

"*Hola,*" I said, a bit taken aback by the grease on his clothes. He had a contented, smiling face, round as the moon, and yellow teeth that appeared to have seldom felt the scrape of a toothbrush.

"*Buenos tardes,*" he replied with an honest grin that seemed to say, "Trust me; you're in good hands." I inquired about his tamales.

"*Fresca?*" I imagined that might be the word for "fresh." My Spanish was feeble, but I could get by on a street level.

"*Si, pero tengo solo una más. El último del día.*" He was down to his last tamale. He pulled it out with some sticky wooden tongs, and I handed him five dollars. It was then I noticed the thick layers of dirt under his nails, and wondered if I should really eat *el mejor tamale del mundo.*

"*Es fantástico y muy sabroso,*" he said. He vowed it was tasty. Why should I doubt him?

My lunch at the taco truck earlier that day was one of the best ever, so I decided to risk a street meal from this questionable source. I unwrapped the corn leaves; the tamale smelled fine. So, I bit in and wolfed it down in three bites. The gristly sensation of the carne as I swallowed gave me a queasy feeling, but I thanked the man and slipped back into my car.

A dark, cumulus storm cloud characteristic of the monsoon season in Arizona had built up forebodingly and blocked the sun with dramatic darkness. Gazing at the awesome, brooding storm, a sinister intuition washed over me—just as the blackish cloud obscured the sun, so was my life about to be obliterated by the best tamale in the world.

The corn flour morsel quickly did its violent work. Thank God I'd eaten only one! I barely made it back to my hotel on the other side of town, and once parked in the lot, my sprint to the bathroom beside the lobby was scarcely in time. I spent the next ten minutes with severe diarrhea, my head clouded by a toxic sensation. I finally made it up to my room on the fourth floor and spent the next eight hours moaning, shivering, clutching my stomach, certain I was going to die, my solitary suffering on the bed frequently punctuated by nauseated dashes to the bathroom.

I'd read about the ravages of cholera, which literally means "diarrhea," and fantasized my desperate runs were similar to those caused by the terrible, legendary disease. Knowing untreated cholera was usually fatal added mental misery to my wretchedness.

Mercifully, I vomited early in the morning and rid my system of the last sickly remnants of the offending tamale before it could do further damage to my stomach, intestines, and my life. I didn't fall asleep till nearly dawn and slept for less than two hours before waking up with a jolt, remembering my meeting with Viva. By the time the first rays of morning sun glowed the Tempe skyline, my food-poisoning ordeal was over.

I sipped gingerly from my bottled water and took stock of my condition. My nausea had passed, and I sensed I'd be fine, but I'd lost tons of sleep and felt physically and emotionally drained. I texted Viva and warned her I might be a few minutes late but was on my way.

Moments after pulling into the Coronado parking lot, I entered the darkly lit café exactly on time. As is the case with so many establishments in hot locales, the air conditioning was too cold, and I needed a sweater indoors despite the temperature being in the high nineties outside. By three that afternoon it would reach 112 degrees Fahrenheit.

"Hi Jaden!" Viva's voice was bright and welcoming. "Right on time. I figured you would be. You're an Aries after all." She was seated in a booth in the small, secondary dining area of the café, sipping a latte, a saucer with a mostly eaten croissant beside her laptop. She wore geeky, metallic-framed reading glasses, which gave her a studious look.

I smiled and slid onto the seat across from her in the shoddily upholstered booth, trying not to gape at her beauty. Gazing at her almost furtively as she opened her laptop, I convinced myself she was one of the most captivating women I'd ever seen.

"Do you want some coffee and something to eat before we launch in?" she asked.

"Nah, I'm good. No appetite at the moment."

"Are you okay? You look like you ran a marathon, or something."

"I'm fine. Just lost some sleep…you know…the heat can get to you. Especially when you're a weather wimp from the foggy Central Coast. Besides, how could I sleep knowing that today my deepest hidden secrets would be exposed to the world?"

Viva laughed and combed her fingers through her hair, which fell in waves to her shoulders. "Not to worry. I won't tell a soul. Unless of course, the price is right." She flashed a mischievous smile.

"Do you realize you could've played an elf in *Lord of the Rings*?" Viva beamed at my words.

"Missed the audition," she said. "My bad luck."

"Nah. You were meant for bigger things. What secrets did you discover about me?" I didn't anticipate great accuracy from the reading, and I didn't care. I'd only asked for the interpretation in order to see her again and, if fortune smiled on me, get closer to her.

Nonetheless, I was curious. I tried to remain open-minded about things metaphysical, mixed with a healthy dose of skepticism. In my freewheeling study of psychology, I'd dabbled in what some call the paranormal or para-psychological and found it intriguing. An investment broker told me that to be a good trader you had to understand psychology. I learned that some successful investors even employed planetary cycles to gauge market timing.

I found Carl Jung's work in astrology remarkable. It prompted me to read an introductory book on the subject, and I soon realized the popular tabloid astrology was a pathetic caricature of the true ancient art, a science that had endured for thousands of years and often revealed deep insights.

"First, the important things," I continued. "Will I become rich and famous?"

"Actually, it's possible," Viva said seriously. She stared at her laptop screen, and I noticed she had a small, delicate tattoo of a red rose on her right forearm, just above her hand. "You have Sun conjunct Jupiter in Aries in the first house," she began. "You are impulsive and headstrong, and you might gain considerable affluence, and possibly even notoriety. Yet your Pisces ascendant keeps you modest."

"Thanks. I'm proud of my humility."

Viva smiled and continued. "You'll go out of your way to help people and you desire to make a positive difference."

"Just a few of the many services I offer."

Viva kept going. "And you're naturally philosophical. History and psychology would both be good fields for you, probably economics too." I was impressed that she immediately nailed three of my main interests.

"And remember, we're not looking so much at your future right now, but just what the basic horoscope reveals about your character and personality. So let me give some background, okay?"

"Shoot. I'm ready for the worst."

Assuming a serious expression, Viva launched into an explanation of basic astrological principles. "A horoscope is an abbreviated map of the sky at your birth," she began, "a picture of the planets in our solar system. Think of it as a snapshot or photograph taken by God or the universe and imprinted in each individual's soul structure or energy field. It operates throughout your life as a blueprint of character and life potentials. We carry it with us in our subconscious, a map of the heavens the moment we were born. It's a key in unlocking our deeper potential."

I smiled. "Couldn't have said it better myself."

Viva proceeded to talk for more than half an hour about what my horoscope revealed. I was astonished by her accuracy. She said that with my rising sign in Pisces, I was dreamy and imaginative, with a gentle disposition, which acted as a balance for my Aries brashness. And the position of natal moon in Sagittarius made me outspoken and adventurous, willing to take risks. She really had me pegged and I paid close attention, scribbling notes on a legal pad so I could refer to her words later.

"You're also innately positive and upbeat, with a resilient outlook," she said.

"Thanks for noticing. Glass-half-full kind of guy."

"And you're warm and affectionate..." *Not polyamorous, just amorous,* I almost interrupted.

"...but you can be stubborn and willful," she continued. "Once you know what you want, you're hard to deter. You're also a bit of a loner. At least, you're no stranger to solitude."

"I had a lonely childhood. Even my imaginary friends didn't like me."

Viva laughed her warm, endearing laugh. "You usually make your mind up quickly, but in relationships you're more hesitant." Her words brought to mind my feelings about Lyla. Yet in Viva's presence, hearing her voice and watching her mannerisms, there was no doubt that my heart's compass pointed toward this gifted, lovely, wise woman. "You can also be oversensitive," she added.

"Ouch. You hurt my feeling?"

"Feeling? You've only got one?"

"Just one. But I've got two more in the developmental stages."

"Probably more than most men." I smiled and nodded. "But seriously, once you've got your heart set on something, you're determined and steadfast. You're also loyal but can be rather possessive." I was scrawling fast to record her surprisingly accurate assessment of my character.

"Oh, and though this interpretation is not so much about your future. You do happen to have Uranus transiting in strong aspect to your natal sun and Mars. Your life is about to get dramatically eventful in unexpected and astonishing ways." She went on to elaborate that the current positions of the planets in relation to my birth chart signified sudden, startling changes.

"I don't know whether to be intimidated or excited."

"Both, maybe." I gazed deeply into Viva's inscrutable eyes, the light in them springing from a deep source in her visionary soul. *Are there things she sees in my chart she's keeping to herself?*

"I'll watch my step and keep the lights on at night," I said, wondering if she glimpsed something in our mutual planetary configurations that might attract her. I knew of a field in astrology called "synastry"—comparing horoscopes to assess compatibility. An astrologer friend once confided to me that all astrologers know their own birth chart better than the layout of their bedroom. Was there something she perceived between her and my chart that signaled attraction? Or the reverse: something to trigger warning lights?

After a pause, I impulsively added, "Will I fall in love?" *Did I really just say that? She probably knows I'm thinking of her.* The answer to my question was seated across the table, but I wanted to know, in her words, if the planets confirmed it.

"You just might do that." A smile flashed across Viva's face, and I thought I detected something flirtatious in it, as if she wanted to wink but held back. It was probably wishful thinking, yet I felt a swell of hope.

"You could also get into a lot of trouble with authorities," she added seriously. If there had been a hint of flirtatiousness, it was now gone.

"Why is that?"

"Saturn."

Is Saturn a bad thing? The way she said it made it sound as if the ringed planet was fraught with danger. "Saturn," she continued, "is making a powerful transit for you now. It represents authority...and karma, bringing tests and trials. You may have to walk through some fires." Her words jarred me, echoing Lyla's odd remark the day before.

"Trial by fire, huh?"

Viva nodded. "You're entering a crucial phase of challenge and transformation. Spiced with a real possibility of danger, so watch out."

Wrapping up the reading, she added, "And did I already say this? You're very generous. Thanks so much, Jaden, for letting me read your chart. You're amazing." She smiled and held out her hand, and I realized the reading was over. The skin on my arms tingled at her touch, and I took hope from the fact she didn't instantly let go.

"Okay if I Venmo you?" I said, as she gently withdrew her hand.

"Perfect."

I tapped my phone and sent her two hundred fifty dollars. "Thanks for the tip!" she said, glancing at her cell. "See! I knew you were generous!"

"It's nothing. I really enjoyed talking with you. And the interpretation was amazing. I'll stay indoors for a month." She tilted her chin slightly and laughed. I hesitated for an instant, then added, "Honestly, though, I'd love to get together again for coffee or maybe a walk. Chat about the stars, or, you know…asteroids and comets…meteors, black holes, galaxies, whatever."

"You're so cosmic." Viva smiled playfully. "Sure, why not?" She waved and stepped back, and it seemed she wasn't in a hurry to leave.

"Do you work your other job today?" I asked, thinking of her employment with the police.

"Nah. Today I'm off the hook." She brushed her hair back and I tried not to gape at her figure.

As we stepped outside, I saw her staring across the lot at Machiavelli's. The gap in the colorful oleander hedge still provided clear visibility. Unfolding before our eyes was a re-run of what we'd seen a couple of days earlier, and this time my attention was glued.

Beside a white Dodge van with the engine idling stood a man who could've been an older version of me, with longish brown hair and wearing a blue Hawaiian shirt. The van's sliding door was open wide, and he leaned casually against the driver's window.

As we watched, a Honda Civic pulled up beside the van and a stout, swarthy man in a yellow vest, like those worn by road maintenance crews, jumped out of the passenger side, yanked the door open, and roughly pulled a girl from the back of the car. She had long black hair, and wore an overly large, green face mask. I guessed she was about ten. It occurred to me the mask might have gagged her.

The Hawaiian-shirted man appeared to be expecting them and leisurely returned to his driver's seat as the swarthy guy shoved the girl inside the open, sliding van door. Slamming it shut, he stepped to his Honda as the Hawaiian-shirted man backed his van out and accelerated away. Seconds later, the Civic drove off. The two men hadn't spoken and barely glanced at each other during the weird exchange.

"Damn!" Viva said in a tight whisper. "Get a picture of their plates!" I already had my phone out, taking pics until they vanished from view.

A bizarre feeling welled in my gut, and Viva's prediction about sudden, startling changes echoed in my brain.

The hot, hard concrete of the sidewalk beneath my feet seemed to grow soft, as if volcanic. I suppressed the urge to lean against the wall for fear of sinking.

CHAPTER 7

Good Cop, Bad Cop

Viva swiveled toward me, shaking her head slightly. "Looked like the same white van and Honda Civic we saw the other day," she said. "Wish now I'd been more observant."

"Lightning strikes twice," I said, regaining my composure. "In broad daylight, no less." Then I paused. "This doesn't seem like that kind of neighborhood. Three blocks from the cop station."

"Machiavelli's is a shady operation as far as I can tell," Viva volunteered. "Mafia stuff, or something gang related, from what I hear. I ate there once—they're famous for their pasta and pizza. It's funny, because one of the owners is a cop."

She hesitated, frowning, then added, "Before it was a restaurant, it was a private home. Rumor is there was prostitution going on."

"You mean a whore house?"

She nodded. The words seemed coarse spoken in Viva's presence.

"Fun establishment," I muttered. "Should we make a police report? Just in case?"

"Just what I had in mind. My psychic gig with the cops is normally Fridays, but I'm definitely gonna go there now."

"Mind if I come along?" I asked, not wanting to be pushy.

"I was hoping you would," Viva responded.

We drove our own vehicles, and minutes later I followed her into the nearby precinct, amused that Machiavelli's, with its questionable reputation and trashy history, should be located just a few hundred yards from the police station. Even more curious if what Viva said was true about a cop being part owner. I recalled Seth's words. "This stuff is going on right under our noses and there's complicity at the highest levels."

Inside the station, everyone seemed to know Viva. Despite her ethereal persona, my elfin friend was firmly grounded in the realities of this dimension. She had to be in order to work with cops. She told the receptionist behind a glass-shielded counter she wanted to make a report about suspicious activity, and moments later a police officer appeared in the corridor.

"Hello, Viva!" the officer said, his voice and gaze effusive with affection. "What a nice surprise. I didn't expect to see you today. Bringing glad tidings?"

"Hi, Luca." She gestured toward me and continued. "Jaden, this is lieutenant McCloud. Luca, this is a friend of mine—Jaden." I shook hands with Officer McCloud and took notice of the lieutenant stripes on his uniform.

"I wish, but no good news," Viva continued. "*Au contraire*, we want to report some suspicious activity."

"Is that so?" the officer said. "Never a dull moment around here."

Luca McCloud was the picture of a perfect cop. He was about six feet tall, muscular, with a Marine haircut. I guessed him to be about thirty.

"I know, unfortunately. Anyway, we were just down the street at Coronado's. We were coming out into the parking area adjoining Machiavelli's lot...and this guy...he, like...he shuffles a young girl out of a car and throws her into a van. The whole thing looked suspicious."

"I see. Did you get the plates?" McCloud asked.

"Got them both," I said, holding up my cell phone.

"All right, then," the lieutenant said, "That sort of stuff does happen, though I've never come across it in Phoenix. Closer to the border, around Tucson, we've had reports and activity." He typed his badge number into the computer on his desk, which was angled so Viva and I could just see the screen. Then he typed the license plate numbers we gave him, and a database scrolled up. "Hmm...that's strange. Nothing comes up. I'll have to look a bit more. I'll make sure a report is filed and we can get on it."

Viva filled out some paperwork, while I emailed the photos to the police website, and as the two of us got up to go, another cop stepped into the office. He was a couple inches shorter than McCloud, and his balding scalp displayed a Gorbachev-type birthmark, a large reddish splotch just above his forehead and shaped oddly like the state of Texas. He had a massive torso and bodybuilder arms that could've belonged to a heavyweight boxer. The air of importance he projected was diminished by the odor of his cheap cologne. I noticed that his badge and stripes were of a higher rank than McCloud. The heavily built senior officer stared at Viva, his dark eyes shining with dull brightness.

"Well, if it's not the successor to Nostradamus herself, the seeress Viviana," the captain said.

Viva's smile was tight and lacked the open warmth she'd shown McCloud. "Hello Captain Darko," she said stiffly.

"Isn't Friday normally when you consult your crystal ball? What brings you here now?" His chin jutted forward, and the slightly sagging fold of his cheeks gave the impression of a pit bull. *Who is this guy? Darth Vader's understudy?*

"Yeah, normally Friday, but my friend Jaden and I...we're making a report...about some suspicious activity." She gestured toward me, and the big cop and I exchanged glances and nodded.

"Is that so?" Captain Darko said. "Nothing surprising about that, I suppose. Altogether too much weirdness these days."

Viva stepped away from him toward the door. "Always a pleasure bumping into you, Captain Darko," she said coolly, then smiled and waved at Officer McCloud and turned to go.

"Nice to meet you," I droned to the two cops, and followed Viva into the brilliant afternoon light.

"Whoa, that was interesting," I said. "Those two dudes are about as different as night and day. Good cop, bad cop."

Viva laughed. "You got it. I like working with Luca. He's a good guy. Captain Darko pulls a lot of weight in the cop bureaucracy, but he gives me the creeps."

"He's got the look of a grifter who guzzles six-packs and watches NASCAR in a trailer by the river."

"Luca tells me the cops call him 'the snake.' I suppose it's because he has a couple of pet rattlers, but the name matches his character. There's even a rumor he's got a rattlesnake tattoo on his butt."

"Weird dude."

Viva nodded. "Regardless, he's earned his stripes and has a lot of responsibility. He's actually the cop I mentioned who's part owner of Machiavelli's."

"Really! Captain of police. Who'd of thought? Bizarre world."

Viva nodded and leaned against her car. "He's head of this police district. I think he has even wider authority. Wouldn't want to be in his shoes, though. Tough job." She abruptly stood straight and extended her hand in a businesslike manner, her mood suddenly cool.

"So nice to meet you, Jaden, and to get to know you. And thanks again for the opportunity to do your chart. It was awesome." I clasped her hand briefly and had to thwart an impulse to hug her.

"My pleasure," I said. "Umm…can I call you? I mean, I'm curious about the result of the police report, and everything."

"Uh…sure," she said. Her hesitation hit me like a punch to my stomach. "I'm busy the next few days, though, but feel free to text me."

"No problem…maybe we can get together over an espresso. And let me know if McCloud or anybody gets back to you."

"Of course. I'll let you know if I hear anything solid. And I'll be back here next week sometime. So maybe we could touch base. At Coronado's maybe."

"Great. I'll text you to confirm." Our eyes locked for an instant before I turned and marched toward my Jeep, hit with conflicting emotions. Grateful to have strengthened my connection with Viva, I was also deflated by her sudden coolness. Nonetheless, I took solace from the fact we'd get together at least one more time, and was almost grateful, in a peculiar way, that the puzzling incident with the young girl in the white van had bonded us in a possible unfolding mystery.

I rambled slowly through town, touching the radio till I found a classic rock station. An old Beatles tune came on, one of their early hits off the *Help!* album. "You've Got to Hide Your Love Away."

Back at the Tempe Mission Palms, still unable to eat anything solid, I collapsed on the bed. Long after sunset, my thoughts revolved around the events of previous days, musing over Viva, Lyla, Seth and Maxie, and the girl in the van, wondering what lay in store on the road ahead. I fell asleep with Viva's warning vibrating in my brain: *Your life is about to get dramatically eventful in unexpected and astonishing ways.*

I could never have imagined how prophetic her words would be.

CHAPTER 8

Seth Rosen

N ext morning, I awoke in a sweat, besieged again by the distressing dreams of Greek and Trojan warriors battling along the coast of the ancient Aegean. The fact my recurring nightmares seemed always to presage trouble, coupled with Viva's warnings, was an unsettling start to the day.

Sipping coffee and nibbling a banana, the only food my stomach would tolerate, I flicked on my laptop and copied the file Seth had sent me. He'd since emailed me a second file, which I presumed might be the draft of the article he was currently writing.

Seth made a name for himself with his hard-hitting stories about crime and corruption in Las Vegas. He'd unearthed dirt about some political figures and had earned their enmity. This article went even further, and as he'd hinted, revealed even more sinister stuff he'd discovered in his investigations. Mind blowing info that clearly unnerved him. It was this new material that formed the subject of the piece which he was focusing on while staying at his parents.

Fortified by my second cup of java, I delved into his article about a human trafficking ring in the Vegas area that the cops had busted. My investigative reporter buddy suggested there was evidence the ring might have connections with some of the most violent Mexican drug cartels. There was much more, including involvement with top-level politicians and corporate leaders, but I skimmed the last half, so did not digest many details. Resolving to get back to the article soon, I called Seth and told him I was impressed with his writing, his courage, and his forceful journalistic style.

He was grateful for my words but wasn't encouraged by his editor's response when he'd sent him a draft of his new exposé. He had a long phone conversation with him yesterday. His editor said the material was too explosive and the *Vegas Sun* would not publish it. Seth countered that he would self-publish online when he'd finished, probably in a week or two. He insisted he'd get the material out, even if he had to set up his own website and broadcast via every possible social media channel. The editor advised him to watch his step—he was poking into a den of vipers. Seth wasn't sure if he was being threatened or merely warned.

We ended our conversation with him inviting me over to his place that afternoon for refreshments with Maxie and to meet Karina. "We've got a surprise to share with you," he said, an upbeat tone in his voice. I told him I'd be there by late-afternoon.

I turned off my laptop and stared out the window at the barren desert hill rising like a prehistoric burial mound in the heart of Tempe. Seth's article made me think about the strange encounter Viva and I witnessed as we left Coronado's the day before. Trafficking was a reality. According to some authorities, hundreds of thousands of children were trafficked each year in the United States alone. Most ended up sexually abused, others practically became slaves. In some cases, it was both. In Seth's view, even more sinister things were going on.

Filling time, I strolled around the Arizona State University campus area, coming across a striking small chapel. Realizing it was Old Saint Mary's Church, the one Lyla had mentioned, I stepped inside and sat in a pew toward the back.

The historic shrine was built with special red bricks formed from clay native to the area, and as Lyla described, possessed an uplifting vibe.

I'd recently developed an appreciation for small chapels, particularly those of cultural value due to their sacred art. Greek mythology and art history fascinated me—in school I'd written a paper on the Italian Renaissance that my teacher said was nearly publishable. I became obsessed with this remarkable period, one of history's most illustrious. A high point of my life was a two-week excursion to Europe the previous summer, focusing on Rome and Florence, viewing the works of the great masters: Leonardo, Michelangelo, Raphael, Botticelli, and my personal favorite, Fra Angelico.

Back in the States, I sought out some antique works on the West Coast, mostly from the Spanish colonial period. Though slightly repulsed by formal religious orthodoxy, I nonetheless gained an appreciation for the special charm and unique atmosphere of the California Mission chapels along the coast from San Francisco to San Diego, the famous Mission Trail. I'd visited them all, and from these sojourns, developed a sense for the

value of *pilgrimage*, which for me meant a quest for wisdom and
enlightenment.

I sat peacefully, savoring the solitude, gazing at the mural of
Our Lady of Guadalupe. Despite cultivating a casual outer persona, I was vividly interested in matters philosophical and spiritual. My struggles in early life found their apotheosis in an awakening that literally saved my life. For a time during high school,
my education had been a school-free drug zone. Fortunately, I
came through the tunnel quickly and quit the dope. The final
epiphany came after being tossed from my mother's split-level,
while homeless and roughing it, sleeping outside, eating fruit
off trees in Palm Springs and Palm Desert. Early one morning,
under a starless sky, I woke from a restless sleep, cold and hungry.
Stumbling a few steps, I stood motionless, absorbed in the desert
silence, when I heard—or imagined I heard—an ethereal voice,
clear as a tuning fork. *In the silence you hear the voice of God.* I
was stunned, moved to tears, and yearned to hear more from the
mysterious voice, but none came. That moment changed my life.

An instant benefit was that I gave up weed for good.
Hammered the final nail in the coffin of drug and alcohol use.
No AA meetings required, effortless full stop. I never told anyone about my experience but cherished it as a precious secret. I
looked forward to a day when I could share the memory with
someone I loved.

My burgeoning inner life had been reinforced by another
surprising discovery. When I returned home after my mother's
passing and went through her things, I discovered a small library
of inspirational books. It was a side to her personality I hadn't

known, never realizing she was secretly devout…a mystic of sorts. Sadly, the end of her marriage to my father exposed a vulnerable spot in her psyche and her inner life failed to prevent her eventual breakdown and descent into alcoholism.

Over subsequent months, I read several of her volumes. *Dark Night of the Soul* by Saint John of the Cross made an impact. In his descriptions of the soul's interior life, you first experience *the dark night of the senses*, which in some ways I'd gone through by giving up substance abuse. Would I now encounter some kind of dark night of the soul? A difficult letting go of worldly attachments? This I doubted, enthralled as I was by Viva's loveliness.

Leaving the chapel and feeling the first pangs of appetite after my bout with the toxic tamale, I wandered down Mill Street.

My cell phone rang; it was Maxie.

"Hey dude, what's up?"

"It's Seth…it's Seth, man." Maxie was breathing hard, and his voice sounded distant. "It's Seth, man. They did it."

"Did what? What's the matter? Get a hold of yourself, Maxie. Are you drunk?"

"No, dammit. Seth's dead!"

"What! What do you mean he's dead? I just spoke to him a few hours ago. I'm on my way over there."

"I'm at his fuckin' place, man. He's fuckin' dead! They…they… killed him, man. Like he said might happen. Karina's practically hysterical. The bastards pushed him off his balcony! They shot him in the head! Man, I don't believe it. They killed him!"

My world became a dark tunnel. "Hold on. I'll be right over."

I tapped my phone off and sprinted toward my car, my brain

frozen with shock. Ten minutes later I was at Seth's condo unit. Three police cars were parked out front. The area below the condo was cordoned off. I could see blood on the pavement. I learned later they'd already taken his body to the morgue in an ambulance.

A policeman stopped me, and I told him I was a family friend, and that Karina Rosen was expecting me. I showed him my driver's license and he looked me over, then nodded me through, so I bounded up the steps. The door to Seth's apartment was open.

Karina leaned back on a plush armchair, her head propped by a pillow. Her blond hair was short and straight, eyes light blue. Her black mascara had run down her cheeks and dried on her face, making her look like a pre-teen who applied makeup for the first time and botched the job. Her hysteria had vanished, and it appeared she'd sobbed out her grief for the moment and was stone cold sober.

Maxie was sitting on the couch, not far from Karina. His eyes were red. I'd never seen him cry before. He nodded to me. "This is Jaden," he said, looking briefly at Karina before dropping his glance, as if staring too long was disrespectful.

"I'm so sorry," was all I could say. Words were drugs to stop the feelings.

"Seth told me so much about you," Karina said, almost in a whisper, her features frozen. "He thought so much of you... both of you." She glanced at Maxie; his eyes filled with tears. He wore newer clothes today, probably because he knew he'd be meeting Seth's wife. He had on a clean yellow T-shirt and had washed his hair.

Karina answered my unspoken question. "They broke in when I was gone," she said, her voice cool and soft. "I left to get a few things at Seven Eleven. There was a van outside with two guys. They stared at me when I left the house. They must've been waiting. I'm sure it was them."

"Do you remember what kind of van?" I asked.

"A commercial van, mostly red. Something about home maintenance." She paused and let out a long, slow breath. "Seth must've let them in. There was a fight. They pushed him off the veranda. Then they went down and shot him...in the back of the head. I'm sure they shot him after they pushed him because there's no blood on the veranda. The only thing they took was his laptop." Karina confirmed that her husband's wallet, her purse, and all of their and Seth's parents' belongings were untouched. All they wanted was his computer containing the dirt he had on the powerful elites.

"They wanted his story," I said. Karina nodded.

"They killed him," she sniffed. "They murdered him...he was so beautiful...my life...everything." She broke down and sobbed into her hands, and I began crying, choking back tears. I snorted and got hold of my grief. I would have time for that later.

Maxie and I were silent; what could we say that didn't sound cheap? My heart went out to Karina. Finally, I spoke. "He's such a great man," I said, my voice subdued. "He'll always be my hero." The words seemed no match for the silence.

"Mine too," Maxie echoed, hanging his head. "If...if I'd come a bit earlier, I could've stopped the bastards. I'll aways regret it. I should've been here."

"It's not your fault," Karina said in a barely audible whisper.

"I'll…I'll do my best to find out who did it?" I said, surprised by my own words. They sounded almost stupid, but I wanted to say something. Anything. Maxie looked at me as if I was crazy. But my cold stare made him drop his glance.

"I don't expect you to do anything," Karina said softly, managing a grim smile. "I don't know what *I'll* do, except bury my husband." She sobbed again, and her grief was like an open wound, too much for me to bear.

I stood and looked at Maxie. "If I…if I can help you in any way, Karina, don't hesitate to reach out."

"Thank you," she said, also standing up. I noticed the rounded curve of her belly and realized she was pregnant, and it occurred to me this was the surprise Seth had wanted to share that afternoon: they were expecting a child.

"Can I call you in a day or two?" I asked, my emotions caught between anger and sorrow.

"Please, if you would," she said. "Thank you." I wanted to give her a compassionate hug, but we just shook hands stiffly.

"I'll call you soon," Maxie whispered to me as I was leaving. I figured he wanted to spend a few more minutes with Karina, since he was planning to leave in a couple of days and might not see her again.

A stout cop arrived at the door as I departed, and we blocked each other's path. He looked familiar and I recognized Captain Darko from the police department. The timing seemed supernatural. *Surprise* does not convey my astonishment at confronting him there.

"Hello…Captain Darko," I said, slightly repulsed by the scent of his cheap cologne. "I met you a couple of days ago with Viva… at the station."

"Oh yeah, I remember. What brings you here to the scene of the crime? Or suicide, rather, as it appears to be." His words jolted me. *It's obviously a murder. Seth was pushed off the balcony and shot.*

"I'm a friend of Seth's. We went to school together."

"So sorry. Terrible to have to deal with these matters. Just terrible."

"Pardon me, ma'am," he said to Karina from the doorway. "May I have a few words?" The police captain glared into the room with the dogged look of one who expected to have his way.

"Please come in," she sniffled.

Glancing back at the cop's hulking frame, I nodded to Maxie and stepped out of the condo, down the steps, out onto the oven-hot streets of Tempe.

CHAPTER 9

To Everything There is a Season

Somewhere, in the heart of the world, a silver liquid light is flowing, filling the hearts it touches with joy and laughter. Somewhere, in the heart of the world, there is an eternal streaming fountain of song and living water, soothing souls and quenching thirsts.

Somewhere.

My mind and my senses were traumatized. Leaving Seth's, I wandered aimlessly, barely conscious of my surroundings, before finally wending my way back to Tempe Mission Palms. I slept fitfully that night. Shock and grief vied for ascendancy in my overworked brain as I strained to process the stunning events.

In the early morning, I sat up with a start. It occurred to me that Seth might have sent me a draft of the copy he was working on. The draft of the article that had probably got him killed, and which the perps wanted to squelch before he could distribute it widely. What could it have contained that so frightened the murderers that they'd kill to prevent the info from leaking?

Apprehensively, I turned on my laptop and downloaded Seth's final email and skimmed the article. It was indeed the draft his editor had rejected with a stern warning he was treading dangerous waters. Not only did Seth's article contain far more detailed information about the trafficking operation he'd unearthed, but it named names. Mostly corporations rather than individuals, but Seth considered that management of the listed organizations was complicit. My journalist friend had discovered a pedophile ring in top levels of corporate and government circles and his article exposed several leading personalities, with evidence to back his claims. Powerful people in high places. Some household names.

Damn! That's why they wanted him dead. And I might be the only person in the world with a copy, besides the killers who'd stolen his laptop.

Later that morning, my phone buzzed, and I was surprised and delighted to see that it was my clairvoyant astrologer friend. "Hi, Viva!" My voice sounded foreign to me, as if it belonged to someone else. "So nice to hear from you. What's going on?"

"Hi, Jaden. All's well, thanks. But I did hear from McCloud about the report we made."

"Great. What'd he say?"

"Honestly, it's strange. They ran searches with the Motor Vehicle Department database, and they, like, couldn't find that license plate number, the one for the Dodge van. Which is really odd. The car...the Civic...well, it had Mexico tags, and they did find conflicting data on that one. He said he couldn't say too much about it, but there were several names in the US. connected to it, all with different addresses. It's weird. He said Captain Darko took an interest in the case, which is unusual, I gather. Anyway, Darko handed over the investigation, if you can call it that, to one of his subordinates. This cop…Darko's man, is in another department… across town. McCloud doesn't know the guy. So, we might not hear much any time soon, if at all. It's odd, if you ask me."

"Definitely weird," I whispered. "Should've reported the whole thing to the local sheriff."

"Are you okay, Jaden? You sound different." Her words made me think again about her "gift"—the clairvoyant thing. She sensed my feelings.

"Actually, I feel pretty bad at the moment. It's…it's hard to talk about, but a good friend was just murdered."

"What? You're kidding! I'm so sorry! How? Why?"

"It's a long story…I…I can't really explain. Not over the phone, but…his name is Seth, an old high school buddy from Monterey. Happened right here in Tempe yesterday. I'm in absolute shock."

"Oh, no! I think I just heard about it on the news. *Seth Rudman*, I think his name was."

"Seth Rosen…that's him!"

"So sad. He committed suicide, they said."

"Suicide!" I could barely contain my anger. "Who said that? He was murdered!"

"I…I believe you. The police, I guess it was…they said it was an apparent suicide." I recalled Captain Darko's words as I passed him leaving the crime scene at Seth's condo. That the murder of my friend *appeared to be a suicide.*

Viva's clairvoyant gift flashed in my mind, and her work with the cops in solving murder cases. Adrenaline from my anger at the lies kickstarted my brain and drove out the lethargy. "Listen,

Viva…something really strange is going on. Seth was murdered. I'm certain. A hundred percent."

"I don't doubt it, Jaden. I'm just telling you what the news said."

"I understand. Listen. Viva…maybe you can help us solve this case…get some leads…you know…using your gift."

"I'm open to trying. We can get together about that."

"That would be great. I'm stunned by everything. Got to sort things out. Can I call in a day or two?"

"Sure. That'll be fine. I'm…I'm so sorry about your friend."

"Thanks, Viva. He was such a great guy. And his wife…she's… it's just so devastating."

"I'm so sorry. Take care. We'll talk soon."

Though dazed by Viva's words, I was at the same time pleased that she had called. I googled *Seth Rosen* and pulled up the local news. Viva was right. *Suspected suicide*, police said, though officially they were waiting for the coroner's report. *Yeah, a suicide. Pushed off a balcony and shot execution style in the back of the head!*

I texted Maxie. He'd heard the same lies on local TV and was depressed and angry. Karina had told him the funeral was planned for Tuesday at a local cemetery. He was staying for the service and flying back to Vegas the following day. We agreed to connect again tomorrow.

I left the hotel on foot and ambled through downtown Tempe. I thought of going past Karina's place but decided against it. I couldn't fathom that Seth's parents' condo was now a crime scene. It was unbearable to contemplate their devastation at the news, the horror they'd be going through, cutting short their

Hawaiian holiday to fly back for their son's funeral. *God, what a screwed-up world!*

I found myself on the same street as Tattered Pages and drifted that way, figuring I'd say hello to Lyla if she was working. Turned out she was.

"Hi," I said softly. She was sitting behind the counter near the cash register, leafing through a magazine.

"Hi, Jaden! Nice to see you!"

"Nice to see you, too. I was in the hood, looking for zombies, and just thought I'd say hello." My effort at silly humor surprised me, given my emotional funk. Seeing Lyla's slightly twisty smile was a boost, as if rays of sunshine streamed from her eyes.

"A few just left the store," she said. "Just missed 'em."

"Bad timing."

"Next time. Are you okay, Jaden? You look different."

"Honestly, I feel awful. A friend of mine was just killed."

"No way! That's dreadful. I'm so sorry! You must feel terrible! Then I won't ask you what I was going to ask you."

"What? Tell me."

"Well, please just say no. It's nothing...I mean it's kinda silly really, but my dad wants to take a piece of furniture across town. The secondhand store's truck is in the shop till next week. And Pop's got a bad back, so I thought, like, you might be willing to drive his van. But forget about it now."

"I'm glad you asked. No problem. But it'll have to wait till Wednesday. The funeral's Tuesday."

"Oh! I'm so sorry! Please, Jaden...forget I asked. I don't want to be a pain."

"It's no problem. Really. It'll be good for me to get my mind off things." A customer stepped up to the counter with a stack of paperbacks. "You're busy, so I'll text you in a day to two."

"Sounds good!" Lyla's voice and manner lifted my mood, and I was flattered she thought of me to help her. I managed a faint smile and waved as I left the store.

~

TUESDAY MORNING ARRIVED, AND I wore the least shabby clothes I'd brought along: black shoes and trousers with a white shirt I picked up on Mill Street the day before. Maxie and I met at his hotel before driving to Karina's. He had on dark trousers and a cream-colored shirt.

Seth's parents had arrived the day before. It was so heartbreaking to see the three of them. Karina wore a black dress. Seth's dad, Sam Rosen, looked like a weathered version of his son, with snow-white hair. His mother, Angela, was a dignified woman, nearly as tall as her husband. She had on a small black hat covering her dark hair. They looked so grievously serious, yet so calm.

The mass was short, and the priest seemed to go through the motions mechanically. My head was a blur, and I still can't recall much. The casket was closed in accordance with Karina's wishes. The damage done by the gunshot to the back of Seth's head wasn't pretty.

From the church, Maxie drove everyone in his rental car, and we assembled at Holy Redeemer Catholic Cemetery, waiting for the hearse. There were only a few guests, close friends and family.

I was disgusted to see a photographer from the local media. Maxie wanted to punch him, but I held his arm.

My last surviving close bud from Monterey school days and I were pallbearers, along with two of Seth's colleagues at the *Vegas Sun* who'd flown in. Seth's brother from San Diego was another, and our deceased journalist's father rounded out the grim detail. I was barely able to keep it together.

The priest spoke the Last Rites, commending my heroic friend's soul to heaven, and they lowered his casket into the ground. I was bawling like a baby. Maxie too. Karina was surprisingly calm. She wore a diminutive black veil sewn to the front of her black cap. Her shoulders heaved slightly as she touched her eyes with a tissue, but her tears and sobs were silent. Seth's mother was shaking, and Sam Rosen's head was bowed so completely I couldn't see his face. It was the most dismal thing I've ever seen.

The priest softly intoned the words of Ecclesiastes: "To everything there is a season, and a time for every purpose under the sun…

A time to be born and a time to die;
a time to plant and a time to pluck up that which is planted;
a time to weep and a time to laugh;
a time to mourn and a time to dance.
a time to embrace and a time to refrain from embracing.
a time to lose and a time to seek.
a time to rend and a time to sow;
a time to keep silent and a time to speak;
a time to love and a time to hate;
a time for war and a time for peace."

As per Karina's wishes, the line, "a time to kill and a time to heal…" was stricken from the rites.

It was only then, as the casket dropped below the surface, that I realized they'd murdered Seth on his birthday. *Monsters!*

This was no time to celebrate, so we didn't gather after the funeral. Maxie was a wreck. I had never seen him so devastated. His flight was mid-afternoon tomorrow and we agreed we'd touch base before his plane took off.

My cell phone pinged at nine the next day and I lifted my head from the pillow. It was Maxie.

"What's up?"

"Man, the bastards are at it again. You won't believe it!"

"What now?"

"You know, I don't read papers much, but they put one under your door at the hotel here. There's an article about Seth. The police said it was a suicide!"

"But that's ridiculous! They shot him in the back of the head, for God's sake!"

"I know! It burns me up, man. Phoenix police passed the buck. They let some dude with elite connections do the autopsy. Freakin' flew him in from out of state!"

"Crazy! What's wrong with the local coroners? Not good enough?"

"Yeah. You won't believe it. I made some calls. The coroner's a guy named Victor Ahmed. From Las Vegas! He's the perps' coroner. It's all a frame-up."

"I thought you weren't into conspiracy theories."

"I am now! But dammit, Jaden…I still don't get it. I mean,

why would they kill him? Was the stuff he was writing about really that dangerous?"

I thought of the draft Seth had sent me, his latest article, the one the editor of the *Vegas Sun* refused to print and which I was sure got him killed so he wouldn't spread the info online. "Listen, Maxie, this is only for your ears, got it? This is what I think… based on some hints from Seth. It wasn't the published articles. It was what *he knew*…what he was gonna reveal. He…I think he uncovered a pedophile ring involving top-level people. Our bro was planning to name names. And he had evidence. A digital paper trail. I think that's what pushed them over the edge." Afraid I'd already said too much, I determined not to tell my friend that I had the article on my computer. At least not yet.

"Ya think that's it?" He paused, mulling it over. "Yeah…you're probably right…something like that. Makes sense to me." Maxie paused a second and it sounded like he was choking back his emotion. "Dammit! He…he didn't deserve this. He was such an awesome dude. Those goddam fuckers! Why did Seth have to investigate that crap? He could've stayed in his lane and left that stuff alone."

"It's water under the bridge, my friend. Listen…stay in touch. Let me know what you dig up in Vegas. And be careful what you say. Understand?"

"Yeah…I get it. I'll see what I can dig up, but I'll watch my ass. And my mouth. You take care, bro, and let me know your plans. By the way…I think that Lyla chick really digs you. If you want my opinion. Damn! She's hot. Even if she is a bit of an airhead. You lucky bastard."

I managed a laugh. "Maybe so. But I've got my eye on another beauty at the moment. Anyway...thanks for watching out for me."

We ended our call, and I headed back to Tempe Mission Palms where I spent the day poolside, trying to make sense of the bizarre unfolding mess overtaking my life.

CHAPTER 10

Machiavelli's

The ancient Greeks declared that out of *chaos* emerges *cosmos,* or divine order. Though I believed them, the cosmos part wasn't happening for me, and my personal drama kept descending into madness. According to Viva, the transits of Saturn and Uranus were triggering a bizarre series of events that spelled trouble for me. If she was right, this was just the start of things—with more to come.

Next day, I searched online for the most recent news about Seth in the local press and read the same lies about my friend's death being a probable suicide. The articles didn't even mention the break-in.

Other than the horrible fact of Seth's murder itself, I was most disturbed by the official lies coming from police and media. The deceit was getting to me, and it brought to mind Mark Twain's words, "A lie can travel halfway around the world while the truth is putting on its shoes." Lies arrive with trumpets blasting and sirens wailing; truth comes on cat's feet, softly and gently. Truth has its own fresh scent and needs no cheap perfume or gaudy spotlights. But our world enthrones falsehood.

I was in a funk all morning. Looking in the mirror, I was shocked at the redness in my eyes and the gloom in my face. *Man, you need to get away.*

Wait...I am away.

Mostly, I stayed in my hotel room, only going out for a brief stretch and some time at the pool. By early afternoon I felt slightly better and actually looked forward to seeing Lyla. Doing something novel might be good for my attitude.

"Hi! Nice to see you! Nice shirt, too." Lyla greeted me at the door of her apartment with a warm smile. I had on my floral-print, blue Hawaiian shirt.

"This is my dad, Hunter," she continued. "I told him all about you." She gestured to her father, Hunter French, seated in a big white lounge chair, a TV remote in his hand. Lyla's father had the muscular build of an athlete, and other than a slight paunch, he seemed lean compared to many men in their early sixties. He stared at me with penetrating, dark brown eyes, waved, and nodded slightly.

"Nice to meet you, Hunter," I said, grinning like Alfred E. Neuman, the dude on the cover of *Mad Magazine*. As I stepped over to shake his hand, I noticed a tiny flask of liquor protruding from his shirt pocket. "Your daughter is the smartest young woman this side of the Colorado River."

"Damn pretty, too, I reckon," Hunter said. He glanced to his left with a slight, almost imperceptible nod, where I saw a rifle resting against the wall. I wasn't sure if his gesture was a subtle warning to watch my step with his daughter, or just a normal glance around his apartment. I grinned at him again. *What, me worry?* Lyla laughed, as if she could read my thoughts.

"My dad wouldn't hurt a flea," she said. "But he used to hunt wild pigs and javelina." *Appropriate name, then.*

As Lyla had said, her father was ex-military. Special Forces. He walked with a slight limp from an accident. Not a combat injury, he was sorry to admit, but the result of landing awkwardly in a parachute drop. He *had* been wounded, though. Took shrapnel in his back on a secret mission in Southeast Asia. A covert operation that didn't make the papers. The surgeons didn't get all the metal out, and the pain flared every few weeks. I later learned from Lyla that when discomfort did arise, he resorted to frequent sips of his ever-present miniature flask of Jack Daniels. *A clever ploy to indulge in the booze,* the skeptic in me thought.

Hunter doted on his daughter. Lyla was his life, his source of meaning. He admired her brains and adored her loving smile. The doting father made sure his daughter received a good education, and he'd sent her to a private school for four years. His own formal education was sparse, but he became a voracious reader after his military duty, stint as a pilot, and several years in the FBI. Retired now, his hobby was reading, and it absorbed much of his time. Mostly history, but also novels in the style of Tom Clancy and John Grisham. Hunter had a passion for unearthing secrets buried beneath corporate and government propaganda. Politicians he loathed, but he loved the country he had pledged to defend.

"My Apache grandfather taught me to hunt as a kid," he

explained. "That's ancient history now. Haven't hunted in years. My back's not what it used to be." He pointed to a desk in the corner of his living room, and I gathered it was the one he wanted us to transport.

With Hunter discharging unnecessary advice, Lyla and I loaded the desk onto a piano dolly and managed to get it out the door, down the steps, and into the back of his white Dodge van.

We didn't say much on the drive across town to Twice Loved, the second-hand furniture store. I sensed Lyla was being respectful of my mood, in light of my friend's death. I acknowledged to her that the funeral had been a somber affair.

At Twice Loved, two young assistants removed the desk from the back of the van, and we shook hands and drove off. Lyla was delighted to have helped her dad, and I was pleased she was pleased. The errand gave me a chance to get my mind off the week's stunning developments and I was beginning to feel halfway normal again. We headed back through Phoenix's maze of streets and passed less than a mile from Coronado's and Machiavelli's.

"How about a slice of pizza?" I said, recalling my experiences with Viva the week before. "If it doesn't conflict with your mostly fruit diet."

"Nah. Fruit…pizza, it's all good."

"Sounds like me. I'm mostly vegetarian but I do eat animal crackers."

When I told Hunter's daughter where I had in mind, she raised her eyebrows. "Oh, you must mean Machiavelli's. If it's the place I'm thinking of, it has quite a reputation."

"Lousy food?"

"Nope. The pizza's supposed to be great, but there's lots of rumors and urban legends, so I hear. Even my dad mentioned it when we drove by once. He said the food's good but it's, like, mafia-owned, or something. He thinks mafiosi types hang out there and make deals."

"Drug deals?"

"Whatever deals mafia types are into. Could just be rumors, but my dad thinks the place is shady and has police protection."

"Corruption's rampant everywhere these days. Nothing would surprise me," I said, recalling Viva's words about Captain Darko being part owner. I made no mention to Lyla of the suspicious incident with the white van my clairvoyant friend and I had witnessed just days before.

"That's a fab coffee shop," Lyla said as we passed the Coronado before pulling into Machiavelli's parking lot. "Definitely laid back and funky in a good way."

"I know what you mean…been there a couple of times. That's how I learned about this place."

I rolled Hunter's white Dodge van into the lot and pulled up beside the Italian eatery, bemused that I parked in nearly the exact spot where the other suspicious white Dodge van was stationed the week before, the day of my reading with Viva. I thought it odd the restaurant had no windows on the parking lot side, just a brick wall.

As we waited for the hostess to take us to our table, I pointed to a *USA Today* resting on the bench beside us, with the headline:

**Congress Approves Thirty Billion
for Military Budget.**

"War mongers in D.C are at it again," I muttered.

"Yuck. Not interested," Lyla said. "My brain's a demilitarized zone."

The hostess led us to a table against the wall. "Except for the fact it's dark as a cave, the place looks normal to me," I said as we settled in the heavy wooden chairs. "Doesn't look like a mafia hang."

"I'm clueless what a mafia hang looks like," Lyla said as the waitress brought her iced coffee and iced tea for me.

"Oh, you know…pictures of the Sopranos on the wall, Sinatra playing over the speakers. A pool hall in the back with a kiosk to bet on the races. A guy named Guido waiting on you, who says, 'you no lika my pizza I breaka you face.' The usual stereotypes."

"Just as I pictured. My mom was Italian, and she disliked stereotypes, but admitted they had a kernel of truth. She was smart and beautiful."

"She took after you, then," I said, tearing a pack of raw sugar and pouring it in my glass. Lyla smiled and thanked me. Referring to her mom in the past tense made me pause, reluctant to inquire further in case it was a sensitive topic. She answered my unspoken question.

"She died when I was sixteen. Cancer. I miss her so much."

"I'm so sorry," was all I could manage to say.

Following an awkward silence, I asked, "So, what's on your mind these days?"

Lyla mused a moment, smiling her engaging, lopsided smile. She wasn't one to remain moody for long. "Well…I was just reading an article about cancel culture. You know, people who don't like it if you say something they disagree with…so they, like, try to censor you. And now some of the big internet outfits are censoring people. How can you have a free society if people aren't allowed to express themselves?"

Her statement, a sensible one, caught me off guard and I sipped my tea while gathering my thoughts.

"Maybe they want to ban intelligence, so the idiots aren't offended."

Lyla burst into a laugh and nearly spit out her coffee. "You're funny, Jaden, but didn't Dostoyevsky say that?"

"Wow, you're good. He *did* say something like that. Can't put anything past you."

"Just a random quote my high school English teacher made us learn, but it's true…big tech and big media have gotten way too powerful. With their algorithms they can practically bury the truth. News becomes propaganda."

"I *know*. And since when are somebody's bruised feelings more important than truth? Far as I can tell…the ones who push censorship are the ones with something to hide." I noticed I was drumming my fingers on the tabletop and stopped, thinking it might be annoying. "Information needs to flow freely," I added, "if we don't want to end up mind-controlled zombies."

Lyla took a sip from her cup and touched her napkin to her lips. "Yuck. Zombies everywhere. No H-bomb required."

I paused and drank more tea. "Anything else on your mind?"

"Well…I'm thinking of going to nursing school."

"I didn't realize you were studying to be a nurse."

Lyla nodded. "I've taken a few courses…decided to take

a break for a year. Just not sure if it's really what I want to do with my life."

"I know what you mean. But you could do it for a while, and if you get tired of it, switch tracks. Most people change careers at least once in their life."

"True, just look at my dad. A professional career-changer. What about you? Any plans?"

"As a matter of fact, yes. I plan to share this pizza with you." The waitress conveniently arrived that instant with our order. I hesitated divulging to Lyla my planned road trip. Perhaps because I sensed she'd volunteer to come along, which I'd be open to, but I had my heart set on asking Viva first.

Lyla held up her coffee. "I'll drink to that."

We savored the gooey, hot mozzarella liberally topping the mushroom and olive daily special. Extra parmigiana added.

Lyla's wavy dark hair fell in a cascade past her shoulders. Her light red lipstick was slick and sensuous. Her skin, white as the Queen of the Night despite the harsh Phoenix sun, was smooth and clear. Her deep greenish eyes were wells of mystery and intelligence. I began to realize how exceptional she was.

"Well…what's the verdict?" I asked, sliding the last of the uneaten pizza into a to-go container. Though Lyla exuded sensuousness, my attraction to her was not initially sexual. Yet I knew the most powerful romantic relationships often begin with simple friendship. I couldn't suppress the thought that her nymph-like manner would no doubt translate into bedroom entertainment.

"It's so pleasurable!" she said with fervor.

"Beg your pardon?" I said, jarred by her exclamation.

"The pizza. It's delicious…big yum! But this place definitely has a strange vibe." At her words, I saw Captain Darko and another cop enter and move to a booth in the back of the restaurant. Lyla noticed the surprised look on my face, and the fact I flinched slightly.

"What? Bigfoot come in?"

"Nah…just imagined I saw someone I knew. LSD flashbacks are a nuisance."

"I wouldn't know. I only have coffee flashbacks."

We got up from the table and strolled out to Hunter's white Dodge van. Relieved not to have encountered Darko, and savoring the sunshine on my face, I put on my Ray-Bans and felt a wave of contentment. *Almost back to abnormal.*

I opened the door on the passenger side for Lyla and she slid in. I couldn't help but admire the way her blue jeans molded to her legs, as if designed for her, and was relieved she hadn't caught me staring. I ambled around to the driver's side and swung open the sliding door, checking to see if my backpack was in order.

A Honda Civic with Mexican plates swung in and parked too close to us. I stopped myself from grumbling aloud that the lot was practically empty, and they didn't have to crowd us. But I held back. *Best not to make a scene.* The back door of the Honda opened wide and a swarthy, stocky, black-haired man jumped out.

"*Hola,*" I said, but he didn't seem to notice.

Ignoring me, he reached into the car. I watched, transfixed, as he pulled a young girl out by her arm, about twelve, dressed in a light blue dress and a thick red sweater. *Inappropriate for the Phoenix heat.* The dark-eyed girl was double masked, a light medical-type covering over a second heavier one, designed possibly as a gag. Her hands were tied together in front of her. Moving quickly and calmly, the man shoved her into the back of our van. Shocked, I neither spoke nor moved.

"*Ella es Marisol,*" he said in a low voice, speaking to me without looking directly at me.

"*Su hermana llegó ayer. Las dos están aquí por un hombre muy importante. Buena suerte.*" I gathered he was saying the girl's sister arrived yesterday. The two of them were intended for someone important.

Never looking directly at me, the swarthy man jumped back in the Honda and the driver reversed the car out. I held my tongue, staring at the frightened young girl in the back seat as Lyla eyed me, open-mouthed.

"What the hell…" she started. My finger to my mouth stopped her in mid-sentence. *Not a time for words.*

I slid in the front seat, heart pounding, knowing my life was about to explode in unimaginable ways. Starting the engine, I backed away, hands gripping the wheel as if it was a life preserver. As I veered toward the exit, a white Dodge van swerved into the lot, and as it pulled beside us, I stared at the driver—a man who could've passed as an older version of myself. His brown hair fell a little over his ears, like mine, and he wore a floral-print blue Hawaiian shirt similar to mine. His sunglasses hid his eyes completely, and I realized he was the same driver Viva and I had seen the week before, the driver of the white van whose license plate I photographed.

"Damn!" I snapped. "Let's get the hell out of here." I squealed out of Machiavelli's lot and gunned the engine.

Realizing I was driving conspicuously fast, I slowed to thirty-five and headed toward central Phoenix and out onto a freeway bypassing the slow-moving street traffic. *Was I trapped in a dream?* Glancing nervously every few seconds at my review mirror, I caught the gaze of the dark-haired girl in the back seat of the van, her eyes wide with the fright of a cornered animal. *What the hell mess had the Fates just gotten me into?*

Damn! Oh God! Jesus! I'm not cut out for this. You chose the wrong guy for the job!

Lyla was clutching her phone, her knuckles white. I imagined if I could hear her thoughts, they'd be screaming perplexity and alarm.

My mind was screaming, too, and I was grumbling under my breath, but my whispers were inaudible even to my friend seated beside me. I accelerated on the freeway, certain the young girl in the back seat was far more terrified and confused than either Lyla or me. But at that moment, my concern was for my own well-being and safety.

I'm not sure what the universe has in mind, but I'm giving notice!

CHAPTER 11

Trafficked

"The future's not what it used to be," said Yogi Berra. His words were frighteningly true in my case.

Already shattered by Seth's murder and the info I had from him on my laptop, my summer road trip plans veered hellishly toward oblivion. Now, for the second time in a week, my life pivoted in an instant. I'd fallen into a spider web so intricate that my head spun dangerously close to madness. Despite the dread gnawing my brain, a hot adrenaline rush gave exhilarating wings to my thinking. Only problem was, *I couldn't think clearly.*

What now?

Do I call the cops? Hide in my room? Drink hemlock?

I decided to drive with the girl to Lyla's and call Viva. Maybe the two women currently in my life would, like ancient Greek goddesses, protect and inspire me on my odyssey into peril.

And what about the little girl I had accidentally just abducted?

Then it hit. *Of course! The girl holds the key to everything!*
Everything!

"What the hell's going on!" Lyla asked, her voice almost a shout. "This is insane. Who is this girl and why is she in my van?"

"Lyla…I…I'm…it's a plot so thick it's beyond belief. Listen… the girl's being trafficked, I'm certain. The van we saw pull in as we were leaving…that's the one they were *supposed* to put her in, but they thought we were the van!"

"That's crazy!"

"Psychotic."

"So, what now? Call the sheriff?"

"No. Let me drop the van off at your place. You give the girl something to eat. And I'll take her to a safe place tonight or tomorrow, okay?" Despite my confident words, I was confused and uncertain.

"Sure. I guess."

I pulled off the freeway not far from Hunter's place and parked to let Lyla remove the girl's masks and untie her hands. One of the masks was a tight gag. My bookstore friend knew some Spanish and told the girl we'd take her to safety. We were going to get her home. Lyla's smile and reassuring voice comforted her, and the girl seemed to realize it was in her best interest not to scream or fight.

I reached Viva, and though confused by my fevered story, she grasped the gravity of the moment and agreed to meet us at Lyla's within the hour.

Reaching Lyla's, my companion took the girl by the hand and led her upstairs to her dad's apartment. Hunter opened the door.

"What the hell…!" he began.

Lyla put her hand to her lips. "Hold on, Dad. I'll explain." She escorted the dark-haired abductee into her apartment, and I followed.

While Hunter gave the young girl a plate of spaghetti and meatballs and a glass of cold milk, Lyla and I told her father about the bizarre events in Machiavelli's parking lot. When Viva arrived an hour later, our unexpected guest was sitting beside Lyla on Hunter's big brown couch.

"Viva, this is Lyla and Hunter...uh...friends of mine." My astrologer friend was casually dressed in a turquoise cotton top and navy-blue shorts. The top of her right ear stuck out a bit from her hair, befitting her elfin aura.

The two goddesses shook hands awkwardly. Viva's expression was sober, but when she saw the refugee girl, some instinct kicked in and she relaxed and smiled. She sat beside her, took her hand, and spoke gently in Spanish.

The trafficked girl's name was Marisol. She said she and her twin sister had been kidnapped and hauled across the Mexican border in a truck. Her sister had gotten separated the day before. Her words confirmed what the swarthy driver said in the restaurant parking lot.

It pained me to think of the terrifying ordeal the child must've been through, and I was relieved to see that Viva's and Lyla's presence calmed her. Not surprisingly, their warm smiles and gentle manner eased her fears. She was mostly worried about her twin sister, Marisa.

"We'll find her," I said, adopting a stupidly confident air. *This'll look good on my resumé.*

"*La encontraremos,*" Viva translated.

Leaving them, I drove to my hotel, grabbed my toothbrush, razor, shaving cream, deodorant, cologne, the clothes lying around my room, and threw them all into my carry-on bag. With my luggage and laptop, I rushed down to the lobby and paid for my room. *Something tells me I might never see the Tempe Mission Palms again.*

As I stuck the hotel receipt in a zipper pouch of my luggage, I vaguely noticed two men in dark suits stride purposefully to the counter. One of them spoke words that caused me to quiver violently.

"We understand a man by the name of Jaden Parker is staying here."

I crammed my cell into my pocket, hurried out the front doors, and rushed to my Jeep. Gunning the engine, I drove with fevered madness toward Lyla's.

Insanely, the lyrics of the song "Bad Boys" kept jackhammering my brain. "Bad boys, bad boys. What cha gonna do? What cha gonna do when they come for you?"

But why me?

The answer struck with the force of falling granite.

The killers had Seth's laptop! They could see he'd emailed me his article! How could you be so stupid not to think of this before! Dumb as a rock!

Obviously, the perps who'd murdered Seth had hacked his computer and searched his mailbox. And with digital hotel registrations, it wasn't hard to track me to the Tempe Mission Palms. Some sort of crazed good fortune had prodded me to leave the hotel. Literally not an instant too soon.

Talk about luck!

Back at Hunter's, Viva and Lyla still sat on either side of

Marisol, holding her hands. The girl's innocent features had lost their earlier tension, and her large brown eyes glistened in the room's subdued lighting.

I hid my newly hatched terror, and the fact my life was in immediate jeopardy. To my surprise and relief, Hunter insisted Marisol stay the night at his place. The girl seemed comfortable with Lyla and her dad, so I agreed it was the best way to go.

"I'll be back for her in the morning," I said, glancing at our little refugee, hiding my nervousness. Truth was, I had no idea where I'd even be tomorrow.

I smiled weakly and waved at Marisol, then, with Viva watching curiously, I hugged Lyla. After a fist bump with Hunter, I stumbled down the stairs to my jeep with Viva steps behind. She said we could meet back at her place, and I followed her as she drove to her apartment.

The drive gave me time to think.

Obviously, it took Seth's murderers several days to break into and search my friend's device to discover he'd sent me the latest, unpublished, taboo article he was writing. Whoever they were, they were after me and I needed to figure out what to do. Fast!

Now that I was on their target list, they might track my vehicle, so I'd have to abandon it. Tomorrow if not sooner.

So much for my road trip!

I had to tell Viva. Not to do so would be dangerously irresponsible. I was a renegade, and I'd have to figure things out on my own. With nowhere to go that night, I wondered how much of my predicament I should share with her.

Keeping my eyes on her Fiat ahead of me, I mused at the

bizarre unfolding pattern of events—as if the shocking transfer of the girl to me and Lyla at Machiavelli's had been orchestrated by arcane ethereal powers. On top of that, the almost scripted, theatrical timing of my departure from the Tempe Mission Palms, just as the thugs arrived to apprehend me.

Were we just playthings in the whimsical games of omnipotent universal overlords? Characters moved about on the earthly game-board by agents of cosmic central casting? Pawns for the amusements of the gods? In any event, the cloud of peril engulfing me held an ironic silver lining. Despite it being under terrifying duress, I was on my way to Viva's, soon to be alone with the object of my amorous longings. *Why let disaster interfere with a little romance?*

"What now?" I said, as much to myself as to Viva as we arrived at her place.

My friend's apartment was small and cozy, a blend of Zen asceticism and snug Bohemian comfort—with a few pieces of comfortable, showy furniture, including a large, puffy saucer-like Papasan chair, a plump, cushiony couch, and an antique armchair, all of them cream-colored. Other than a bookcase and a few plants, there was little else. I noticed a black, faux-leather guitar case against the wall.

"I think we should let Luca know about Marisol," Viva said, resting her purse on a small wooden table. "He's a good guy. He can advise us."

"Bad idea. I don't trust the cops."

"Me neither. But I think it's the best plan."

I shook my head. "I don't think so." Then after a pause, added,

"We've got to find the girl's sister. I promised Marisol." I wasn't really serious. Just wanted to put off telling her the whole truth.

"Jaden, be realistic. We can only do what we can do."

"Agreed. So, let's do what we can do."

Viva spent a few minutes in her bedroom while I lounged on her couch. I could hear her muffled voice speaking on the phone. She soon returned and busied herself in the kitchen making sandwiches, as if anticipating we'd need them. My astrologer friend had changed clothes and wore blue jeans and a beige sweatshirt, seemingly out of season for the Phoenix summer. *Anticipating a sudden move?*

As the sun set, I lay on the couch in Viva's living room and closed my eyes, figuring if I dozed off for a few minutes I'd be able to think more clearly. Despite my fatigue, the anxiety gnawing at my brain prevented sleep. We had to do something, but what? I couldn't just call the sheriff; I had no idea whose side anyone was on. And then there was Marisol. My brain clouded over as I contemplated her and my predicament.

"I'm ready to place my order," I said after an interlude of glum silence, thinking maybe ideas would flow if we talked. "Anything exciting on the menu?"

"Specials tonight are corn flakes and Wheat Thins."

"Nah. I'm on a diet to gain weight. I'd like red curry soup, seafood paella, and quiche Lorraine. Doctor's orders."

"Sorry, sold out…what about Cheez Whiz on crackers and Gatorade? And I'll need your credit card." I wondered why she didn't offer me the sandwiches.

Not exactly Chez Viva. "I'll stick with corn flakes. I should have the money tomorrow." My clairvoyant friend was smiling. After a pause, I continued, "Don't mean to shift gears on the French chef, but any ideas where we can go? With the girl, that is?" It was a leading question. I wasn't at all sure Viva wanted to get further involved in the messy situation. And I hadn't the faintest idea what to do about the trafficked kid we'd so outrageously "acquired."

"Actually, yes...Sedona."

So, that's what the sandwiches are for. "Why Sedona?" I thought it curious she would mention the tourist enclave in Arizona's famed red rock country, which happened to be a destination on my road trip.

"I know someone...a good friend. We can stay at her place. I texted her and she said fine."

At least she didn't say "boyfriend." I was secretly thrilled Viva was still on my team. *Stick with me. The fun's just beginning.*

It occurred to me my personal astrologist didn't have to get herself embroiled in all this. She could've ducked out, declared ignorance, and simply said "see ya!" But she willingly engaged. I was impressed with her apparent sudden devotion to helping Marisol. And I nurtured a secret hope she was willing to stay involved because she enjoyed my company. My momentary buoyancy collapsed, knowing I'd have to tell her I also had an invisible target on my back.

"It's all your fault," I said teasingly after a quiet interlude. "It's your astrological forecast coming true. How'd you put it? 'You're entering a time of danger and might get into a lot of trouble with authorities.' Self-fulfilling prophecies...and your reading triggered it." I playfully shook my finger at her in mock accusation.

"I'm innocent," Viva said, sticking her hands in the air, as if under arrest. "Truth is…the fault is in your stars."

"That'll be my alibi: the stars made me do it. But isn't that passing the buck?"

"Not what I meant. It's just that some things are destined."

"Ah yes…the Fates. I'll have to take this up with the lords of karma."

The doorbell rang, and I abruptly sat up.

"Who's that?" My voice edgy and nervous.

"It's okay…someone I know." Viva reached the door in seconds, opened it, and ushered in a muscular young man wearing jeans and a denim jacket, sporting a bootcamp haircut. Stunned, I recognized Lieutenant Luca McCloud in street clothes.

Damn! She called the cops!

It must've been McCloud on the phone with her in the bedroom. I felt betrayed she hadn't cleared it with me first.

McCloud nodded to me, and I got to my feet and shook his hand. *Might as well play along.* Despite my anger at Viva acting against my wishes, I realized that with his connections it was vaguely possible the "good cop" could be an ally. It was a calculated risk.

"So, you've run into a little problem," McCloud began, gazing at me with a serious expression. "And you've found a girl you think is being trafficked." I was surprised by what Viva had already told him.

"Yes. A problem. A girl. That appears to be the case, officer," I acknowledged reluctantly.

"You can call me Luca."

I nodded and gave a half-hearted smile. At this point, I figured I might as well divulge the bizarre events of the day and hope for the best. But I still nursed my anger at Viva and avoided looking at her.

I launched in about the serendipitous way Lyla and I parked outside the restaurant that afternoon, in the same spot as the suspicious van the week prior. The Honda Civic with the Mexican license plates. The swarthy driver. The little girl he pushed inside our open van. The whole crazy thing. Viva added a few details, tying it all together.

The officer listened intently as we recapped our story. "Maybe we should tell the big guy," he suggested after hearing us out.

"The big guy?"

"Darko. Captain Darko. He's chief of police, after all. Shady character, sure, but he's got connections. He'll know what to do."

"Don't tell Darko," I cautioned, warning lights flashing in my mind. "Let's figure out what's going on. Maybe we can find out something about the whereabouts of her sister." The notion seemed far-fetched, but I wanted to see how he reacted.

McCloud frowned. "Don't count on it. Wishful thinking. Let me mull this over for a day. By tomorrow I'll have a plan."

"Promise?" Viva asked.

"Promise." McCloud left in a hurry and drove off in his Ford truck.

I was silent, still simmering with resentment at Viva.

"You're mad at me," she said. "Because I called Luca."

"I guess you could say that. How can you be sure to trust him? Just because you like him, he's still a cop."

"True," she said, examining her nail polish. "But he's also more than that."

"What do you mean, *more than that?*"

Viva stood and moved swiftly into the kitchen. She placed her hands on the counter and exhaled deeply.

"Luca is my brother."

CHAPTER 12

Fugitives

My thoughts raced back to the moment I first saw McCloud in the police station. His manner with Viva was warm and friendly, almost casual. But there was nothing in their exchange or in my conversation with her that suggested the two were family.

"I get it," I managed to say. "I see now why you trusted him."

Viva shrugged. "We've got to do something, and Luca's got connections. But I agree he shouldn't tell Darko. That guy's got a shadow on his heart."

I thought of Marisol, struck by the irony that the trafficked girl and I were now both refugees. I wondered if I should go back to Lyla's apartment in the morning as I said I would. To attempt running away with a trafficked child seemed beyond crazy. *Where could I even go with her?* The whole thing was insane.

"I need some air," I said, standing up and moving toward the door. "Catch ya in a few."

I strolled into the warm Phoenix night, making my way toward a cluster of small convenience stores. I ambled down the aisles of a Circle K, not really looking for anything in particular. The junk food and packaged snacks had no appeal, and I ended up buying a plastic bottle of purified water. Tucking it under my arm, I headed back to Viva's.

Inside, I sat in my power spot on her cream-colored sofa, sipping my water.

Viva stepped out of the kitchen and flopped beside me on the couch. She stared at her hands and the rose tattoo on her wrist. I savored the nearness of her presence.

"I'd like to help you if I can, Jaden," she said. "But I honestly don't know what we can do. The girl's better off if we can get her to some government agency. Luca will know. He'll call us tomorrow, I'm sure."

Her cell phone rang.

"Oh, that's him now," she said, glancing at her screen. She flicked her phone to speaker mode, and I heard every word.

"Listen! We're up shit creek! You need to leave town with the girl now!"

"Why?" she asked. "What's going on?"

McCloud was gasping, as if he'd been running.

"Darko tried to kill me!"

"Damn! Luca! What the...? What do you mean he tried to kill you?"

Between gulps for air, Viva's brother spilled his story. "You two were right. Should've kept my mouth shut. I told Darko about the girl—that you had her. Less than a half hour later, they tried to run me over...right in the parking lot! Not Darko himself... another cop. Darko gave the order, I'm certain."

"You're kidding! Why?" Viva asked. I already knew the answer.

"He's obviously involved in the whole operation," McCloud

continued, still breathing heavily. "He's in on the crime. Now his cover's blown, and his actions incriminate him. He knows you've got the girl, so he'll come after you. I know too much—and so do you."

"Unbelievable!" Viva's voice was almost a whisper. "But couldn't he have just played nice? Told us he'd take the girl under his wing?"

"Maybe, but he panicked. Too late now. His operation's been exposed. Besides, playing nice is not his nature. A snake will always be a snake."

"Listen," Luca continued, his voice subdued. "I barely got away. They shot at me. Thank God it was dark. I was lucky... ran like hell and caught a taxi. I can't go home. My only hope is to expose Darko and his crime network before they kill me. It's him or me."

"Damn! Luca!"

"Don't worry about me. I've got contacts. Take care of yourselves. You're in just as deep shit. They'll track you and try to kill you and get the girl. She and her twin sister are prizes in some vile trafficking ring. And Darko is complicit. You need to get the hell out!"

"What do we do?"

"They'll find you in no time if you stay in Phoenix. You need to leave with the girl. Now!"

I was standing up. My stomach felt as if I'd swallowed a lump of concrete. *Let's hit it! Like right now!*

"Got it," Viva told her brother. "We'll leave this instant."

"Good. Where will you go?"

"North. To a friend's place."

"Michaela?"

"I'll connect with her, too."

"Figures. Don't text me in case something happens and they take my cell. Law enforcement has technology that can unlock mobile phones, in case you didn't know."

"Luca! What are you gonna do!?"

"I'll figure it out. I'm in hiding. Who knows? Maybe I'll meet you somewhere. Bye for now."

Viva's phone fell silent.

"Sorry about your brother," I said. "Dammit! I knew that Darko creep was evil! We've got to split, but where?"

"Sedona." Viva's voice was surprisingly calm. "Like I said. We'll hide and protect her at my friend's place till we can get her to safety." Her expression was grim, but there was confidence in her voice.

"Then let's move!" I feared the cops were already on our trail.

We decided Viva would drive her car to a girlfriend's place and we'd take mine to Sedona. In the heat of the moment, I couldn't tell her about my own predicament, that I was already a target for possessing Seth's article. I'd have to ditch my Jeep at some point and figure things out on the fly.

She put the sandwiches she'd made in a small cooler, then grabbed some toiletries and clothes and tossed them into a travel bag. She hesitated a moment by the front door, then rushed back and grabbed her guitar.

"Going on tour?" I said, taking the guitar case from her hand.

"Nah. The gig's canceled."

"Good. Not a time to be in the spotlight."

She locked her door and raced to her Fiat. We both pulled away and I followed her. She dropped her car off in her friend's lot, piled her belongings into mine, and jumped in the seat beside me. I shot a text to Lyla saying we were on our way to pick up the girl and to have her ready. It was an emergency.

I drove maniacally to Lyla's, and we were there in half an hour.

"Say nothing about anything to anybody," I warned my bookstore friend as Viva took Marisol by the hand. "And for God's sake, hide your dad's van and don't under any circumstance drive it anywhere. Any white van that fits the description is a target for the cops. Heads will be rolling for sure. Pray it's none of our heads."

"Big storm's coming," Lyla said. "Monsoon tonight. Take this." She handed me a raincoat. One of Hunter's. "Come back soon, Jaden," she said, and planted a kiss on my cheek. Viva watched us intently by the front door, holding Marisol's hand. I hugged Lyla and waved to Hunter on my way out.

"We'll be in touch," I called back to him. "Might need your Special Forces magic down the road."

"I'll be ready," Hunter said. "I could use an adventure."

Marisol, Viva, and I plunged down the stairs to my Jeep. The girl we were trying to help seemed to grasp we were the good guys, and she mercifully kept her mouth shut. She'd been pampered, fed, and treated kindly by Lyla and Hunter. And no doubt she loved the clothes Lyla gave her, some of her childhood best she'd stored away. The trusting look Marisol threw me as I opened the car door for her touched my heart. *I just might do anything for this girl.*

It was ten that night when we merged onto Highway 17 north toward Sedona. As I drove, Viva sang a Mexican folk song, "De Colores," popularized by Joan Baez, and Marisol sang along. We were in the same boat and we'd either sink or swim or perish all together.

I was falling in love with Viva. Though we might never live together, the chances were promising we'd die together.

The monsoon rains cascaded deafeningly on the Cherokee's roof in the heaviest downpour I'd ever experienced. Torrents crashed like a river on the windshield. With thunder booming and lightning exploding in a symphonic light show around us, I drove toward the famed red rocks of Sedona, wondering if any of us would live to return.

PART TWO

———

"When exposing a crime is treated as committing
a crime, you are being ruled by criminals."
— EDWARD SNOWDEN

CHAPTER 13

The Curandera

The drive to red rock country, normally about two hours, seemed to take all night due to the crazy, violent storm. Lightning tore the sky and lit the landscape with sunlight brilliance. The windy downpour ripped down giant tree limbs, making the highway an obstacle course. Thunder roared so loudly that Marisol buried her head in a pile of clothing and blankets. I'd never seen such a display of nature's ferocity.

It was after midnight when we drove through the Village of Oak Creek and meandered into downtown Sedona, which resembled a ghost town. During the day it was a bustling tourist village, with red rock views second only to the Grand Canyon.

Viva directed me to a mountain road leading high above the tourist enclave. The drive wound upward several miles before we turned into a gravel driveway. The deluge had dwindled to a light shower as we stepped wearily from the Jeep and knocked on the door of a modest, beige stucco home. A young woman greeted us and led us to a guest room. Viva and Marisol took refuge in a double bunk bed. I collapsed on a couch in front of a dry fireplace.

In the morning, I woke to sounds in the kitchen and the rich smell of coffee. The storm had lifted, and the cloudless sky was bright, eggshell blue. Viva sat at a table with a young woman and introduced me to her friend Jenna, a thirty-something redhead of medium build, with a spray of freckles across her nose.

"Thanks for letting us stay at your place," I said. "Nice view." Her home was scenically perched on a boulder-strewn hillside overlooking the village of Sedona. The famous red rock country was stunning in its beauty and visual power.

In the late afternoon, people began arriving at the house. The living room was warm and inviting. Several candles burned, along with a stick of incense on an altar covered with white cloth and adorned with a bouquet of fresh red roses. On the altar was a framed picture of Our Lady of Guadalupe, the Hispanic Madonna that was the sacred national image of Mexico.

Eight people sat in a semi-circle on assorted pillows and chairs, and two more on a white couch. Marisol lounged on a pillow near the door of her guest room, gazing shyly at the group. Viva and Jenna waited in the kitchen for someone who I gathered was a special personage. Sure enough, a woman arrived who they warmly greeted. They talked quietly, allowing time for the guest to refresh herself from what was apparently a long drive.

The mystery woman entered with Jenna and moved to a seat arranged for her. *The evening's entertainment,* I thought. Viva took a seat beside me. The newcomer looked to be about sixty, had mostly whitish hair, shot through with streaks of original black. She was tanned and attractive, and I imagined she could've been a model in her youth. The white-haired guest wore a colorful traditional Indian shawl and exuded a gentle, thoughtful aura.

Her expression was serious, and wrinkles framed the outer edges of her deep brown eyes.

Viva whispered to me that this was indeed her mentor, Michaela, a North American who had lived half her life in Mexico, spoke fluent Spanish, and had trained in the native Southwest healing arts, earning the title of *curandera*—a learned elder and practitioner of the ancient, folkloric healing path of Mexico's Aztec and Maya.

Michaela greeted everyone in the circle, clasping hands with each. Jenna introduced me simply as Viva's friend Jaden. She nodded with a cheerful smile, her eyes probing me. The curandera then sat in a plain wicker chair upholstered with several colorful pillows embroidered in bright Mexican floral designs. She folded her hands in her lap and closed her eyes. I noticed I was the only one with eyes open. I was also the only male.

We observed five minutes of silence before a heavyset Indian woman recited a verse. We joined hands as the white-haired leader said a short prayer asking for grace, enlightenment, and protection for those assembled, as well as for loved ones everywhere. Then she addressed us in a soft, clear voice.

"My dear friends, behind the familiar scenes of nature bathed in the light of the sun, shines another world not discernible by our ordinary physical senses, yet more real and enduring than our everyday reality. A higher world, a spiritual realm, and our true home, from which we have come and to which our souls return after this period of physical embodiment. We are here to learn certain lessons that enable our souls to evolve through the school of experience we call earthly life."

"We are now in a time of great upheaval. Not the end of the world, but the end of an age or cycle. Nothing will remain untouched by what's to come."

I nudged Viva with my elbow and whispered, "Hang on tight." Michaela glanced at me, and a trace of a smile flashed across her features. Viva's mentor spoke for nearly an hour. Her message and vocabulary seemed to me a mixture of shamanism, Zen, and Christian mysticism infused with her personal brand of warmth and wisdom. She wove it all together in a verbal tapestry that blanketed the atmosphere with a magical presence of serenity, a delicate uplifting mood I had rarely experienced.

She said it was a time of personal and planetary *initiation*, as she called it, in which we would be pushed to develop new ways of action and thinking. Would we grasp the opportunity to overcome differences, to heal ourselves and the wounded planet, or would we descend into fear, violence, war, and chaos?

I was intrigued with her concept of "celestial law," which in her view governed all areas of life. She said nature is an interwoven fabric, a seamless web, and all things are bound together. She quoted physicist David Bohm, saying, "Everything interpenetrates everything else." Our actions rebound back on us, and no one can escape the consequences of their thoughts and deeds.

"Life is a garden," she said, "in which we are always planting seeds in the form of thoughts, feelings, intentions and actions." She explained that the "seeds" we plant bring forth "fruit" in time, in accordance with their nature. Because the universal fabric is a seamless tapestry, the subtle waves we trigger by our thoughts and actions extend outward in all directions, much as a pebble thrown into a pond creates a ripple effect. Our thoughts are forces that shape our lives, and our deeds have consequences far beyond those of which we are aware.

She finished with a shamanic ritual of sorts, lighting a stick of Palo Santo wood placed in an abalone seashell, then intoning a short prayer in a language unknown to me. After, she invoked the four directions using traditional Indian names. She then stood up and proceeded around the circle, her eyes half closed, holding the burning Palo Santo stick close to each of us as she said prayers of blessing and protection.

During this time, Marisol left her seat on the pillow and knelt beside Viva, observing curiously. Michaela stood a long time by the dark-haired twin and touched her forehead as she spoke. The trafficked girl seemed enchanted and comforted.

Following the gathering, Jenna served tea and freshly baked cinnamon cookies. Viva gestured to the elder wise woman who came up to me softly as a shadow and graciously held out her hand. "Jaden, I want to introduce you to Michaela…Michaela, this is my friend Jaden."

After exchanging pleasantries, I thanked her for allowing me to attend the ceremony. Michaela and Viva then discussed a seminar on traditional healing methods happening in two days at a nearby hotel. The curandera was scheduled to be a keynote speaker, and the event featured a kind of psychic fair in which Viva would also participate. Not only was my friend an astrologer, I learned, but also an adept in interpreting the cards. Tarot cards. *She had been planning to come to Sedona all along!*

"So, you're a regular gypsy," I said, deflated to realize she hadn't come on the journey just to be with me.

"Ha-ha. Not quite. But I am rather good at reading a card layout, if I do say so."

"How about doing that session we talked about, to see if you come up with any clues about the murder of Seth? You know... that clairvoyant thing of yours."

Viva laughed. "Of course. That was always part of the plan. We'll give it a try in the morning."

Viva took Michaela aside, and from their expressions, I gathered my friend shared some of what had transpired for us in Phoenix, and the drama in which we were enmeshed. The two approached me, and the curandera touched my arm and motioned for us to follow her. I glanced at my astrologer friend, who shrugged and trailed behind her teacher as she headed toward the door. Mystified, I followed.

Michaela led us behind the house, to a small clearing illumined only by star shine, moonlight, and several candles placed strategically on a stone wall. "The two of you have entered a difficult phase," she began, "and I want to give you something." She pulled from a woven pouch around her shoulder two leather cords with small leather pouches attached, apparently filled with sage and dried flower petals. On the leather were inscribed geometric glyphs, possibly some kind of Native American script or symbols. She placed the corded pouches over our heads.

"Wear these," she said. "They will connect you to me in a vibratory resonance and will help shield you in the days ahead. If the current danger passes, if you do not fail, pass them onto others who may need protection and blessing." She paused a moment and added, "God be with you. That is all." She blew out the candles, pivoted, and vanished in the darkness.

I looked at Viva. Her eyes were lit by the moonlight as she gazed in the direction her teacher had disappeared. Without a sound, she turned toward the house and I followed, wondering at Michaela's confusing words. *Oh great. More fun stuff ahead.*

And did she have to say *if* the danger passes?

As we reached the house, I glanced at the crescent moon. A dark cloud engulfed the silvery orb and devoured its light. I stepped into the warmth of the house, anxious about what the coming days held in store.

CHAPTER 14

Red Rock Fever

After breakfast next morning, when the last of the overnight guests were gone, Jenna took Marisol out for a stroll among the red rocks, while Michaela, Viva, and I gathered at the kitchen table. The curandera spoke a short prayer and Viva slipped into a deep meditation. After several minutes of silence, her eyes opened slightly, and she nodded as if ready to begin the session. I showed her a picture of Seth I carried in my wallet and Michaela began to ask questions. Could she tell us who killed Seth, and did she know the whereabouts of Marisol's twin, Marisa?

Viva seemed distant, as if she'd entered an altered state. She didn't appear to be aware of me or her environment as she began to speak in what seemed to be a semi-trance. I grabbed a pen and pocket notebook to make notes, and Jenna did the same with a legal pad.

"There is great sadness at the untimely death of this good man," she began, her voice soft and subdued. "The decision to kill him came from a high place in the business world. That is, a man of worldly prestige and power. A man…several men, but mostly a prominent individual…I'm not sure his name, but

I see a bitter cold morning. It's winter. No leaves on the trees. There is frost on the ground. Not snow, but a heavy frost. That's what I see." She paused; her eyes half closed. I realized she was describing, or attempting to describe, the man or men involved in Seth's murder. As Viva spoke in greater depth about the group, I gathered all of them were part of a circle of top-level corporate executives.

"There's more," she said after a pause. "Something to come. A big gathering, a convention. Large buildings…with lights on them. I see a pyramid and a Greek temple. Or maybe Roman. There is something like music or jangling electronic bells in all the buildings. Lots of people…people in the group that wanted Seth dead. They feared what he had to say. This is in the future, but soon. In a large, hot, sinful city. I see Marisol there…with a friend who looks just like her. The building is tall…an entertainment center, perhaps a hotel."

"The people who ordered Seth's murder are in this place. Most are innocent. It's the leadership. There is something vile about them. They're gathered for a celebration. The ones in charge have evil thoughts. They are dangerous and powerful."

"How do we find this place?" I asked, hoping for more detail.

"Follow the bow and arrow," Viva answered.

"And you see Marisa there?" Michaela asked.

"You'll not find her in this century, but in the last year of the last decade of the eighteenth century." *Great. Riddles. Can't you be less ambiguous?*

I furiously wrote down Viva's bizarrely cryptic words, while Michaela probed her a with few more questions about another matter. Then Viva slowly returned to her normal consciousness and sipped some green tea.

"Well...any clues?" she asked.

"Strange stuff," I said, glancing at my scribbled notes. "You're a regular Oracle of Delphi." The famed Delphic Oracle in ancient Greece was a world-renowned priestess in the temple of Apollo who often spoke in riddles that required interpretation. "Kinda vague. Lots of puzzling images. Definitely some clues, though not real detailed, but I guess it's something to start with." Viva's reading left me confused and frustrated, but I didn't want to say anything to hurt her feelings.

In the afternoon the five of us—Jenna, Michaela, Marisol, Viva, and me—hiked along the trails of Sedona's stunning red rocks. Marisol clasped Viva's hand as she walked, and they spoke together in Spanish. The pretty twelve-year-old called her Viviana and seemed radiantly happy to be coming on our hike. I was impressed with my intuitive friend's fluency, as I could make out at best half of what they said. Viva filled in the gaps later.

When she asked Marisol about her sister, Marisa, the girl's face lit up as she talked about their life growing up in a village not far from Guadalajara. Then she grew serious and described their abduction. They were strolling together into town when some men stopped them. Before they could react, they were bound, gagged, and thrown into a truck headed for the border. From the men's conversation, they gathered that twin girls their age were sought for some reason, and someone was paying a lot of money to abduct them.

Marisol was separated from her sister the day before we so bizarrely gained guardianship of her. It happened after the twins had reached the border for transfer into another truck. But Marisa got into the wrong one. Apparently, the missing twin arrived at Machiavelli's restaurant in a car the day before we encountered Marisol. I recalled the brief verbal exchange with the man at the restaurant when they pushed her into Hunter's van. Something about her sister getting separated and arriving at the targeted destination earlier.

Marisol and Michaela fell behind us as we hiked, giving us a chance to talk about Viva's session. From the reading in her trancelike state, we gathered that the people responsible for Seth's murder were attending a conference in a big, hot "sinful" city. And we presumed the "friend" she described who looked just like Marisol was her twin sister, Marisa.

"There are a lot of hot cities in the US this time of year," I said. "In fact, all the cities are hot; it's still summer. Not much to go on. You said it had a pyramid and a Greek temple."

"It's got to be Las Vegas," Jenna said. "There's that pyramid hotel casino. And Caesar's Palace has some architecture and columns like a Roman building. That might be the Greek or Roman temple Viva saw. But the clincher is she said it was a sinful city. They call Vegas 'Sin City.'"

"Of course," Viva and I said together.

"And the jangling bells are the sounds of the gambling machines," I concluded. "They have these electronic chiming sounds."

"It's got to be Vegas!" Viva said emphatically.

"Lots of companies have events and seminars there," I said. "There are dozens of casinos. The place is huge."

"Right. So which company and which casino?" Jenna asked, brushing her wind-blown red hair from her face.

"And what about that weird riddle about the bow and the arrow?" I persisted. "Downright mysterious."

Viva shook her head, and her face flushed slightly, as if embarrassed that her words were so vague. "That will take some sleuthing," she admitted.

We stepped cross a manzanita branch blocking our path. "You also talked about a winter scene with frost on the ground," Jenna said. "Not sure what that's all about." Viva shrugged and shook her head.

"And the most bizarre thing of all," I added, "was the brainteaser about finding Marisa in the last year of the last decade of the eighteenth century. Guess we'll need a time machine."

Viva pressed her lips together, seemingly flummoxed at her own words. "Sometimes I say weird stuff."

We came to a boulder-strewn area at the base of a large, impressive red stone cliffside, characteristic of the stunning rock formations of the area.

"Feel anything unusual?" Viva asked me, combing her fingers through her hair.

"Am I supposed to?"

"No, but there are vortexes around here. They're scattered in a few areas of Sedona. This one isn't on the tourist map, but I've felt it."

"Me too," Jenna confirmed.

We climbed the high desert hillside and Viva pointed to a large boulder rising like a massive ruby monolith. "Go lean against that rock, Jaden."

"As you command, oh wise one." *I've got a feeling we're not in Kansas anymore.* I strode over to the prodigious rock and leaned my back against it. I felt nothing unusual, but the blue sky, spectacular red rock views, and oxygen-rich air were enlivening. "Guess I'll have to remain a vortex skeptic," I said. "But it keeps the tourists coming." I leaped over a branch and felt a surge of energy flow up from my feet, almost like an invisible stream of air. "Whoa. That was strange! It's like this weird energy...*whoosh*... streaming up and rushing through me."

"You felt it!" Viva cheered. "Congratulations!"

I had in fact felt an unmistakable energetic flow through my body that triggered strong feelings, almost bringing me to tears for no reason.

"Now I'm one of the zombie-clan of true believers," I said. "Maybe at last people will accept me for who I really am."

Viva laughed as Michaela joined us, Marisol in tow. "So, you experienced the vortex, did you?" Viva's mentor said.

"I felt something powerful, for sure," I admitted. "Physically and emotionally. It's convincing. I'm a believer now. Where do I get my membership card?"

Michaela smiled. "Vortexes can prompt deep emotions," she explained. "They can even make people think they're going crazy."

"Too late. I've already crossed that threshold."

"Well, they're real, as you can see," the curandera continued. "I believe they're caused by the pressure of tectonic plates, as well as the iron in the rocks, which gives the area its reddish character. Some attribute them to intersecting ley lines of criss-crossing subtle energy. They can seem mystical and otherworldly, but I believe they're a geologically created phenomena."

Arriving back at Jenna's house, Michaela went to the guest room to rest while Marisol, Viva and Jenna took naps. I lounged on the couch exploring a magazine about Sedona hiking paths.

"How do you like my outfit?" Viva appeared several hours later from Jenna's room wearing a Moorish gypsy costume. "For the psychic fair on Saturday. It'll be fun to look the part."

I gave out a low whistle. She looked exotically stunning in the outfit. "Wow. Impressive. Now all you need is a crystal ball."

"I've got that, too."

"You look amazing. But black hair would be more fitting. Best to drop the blond look. Got to have a convincing disguise, right?"

"Good idea. But what about you? Shouldn't we both be camouflaged?"

I'd already come to that realization. "Of course. When you're a celebrity, people notice you. Misplaced my blanket of invisibility, so I'll go as a blond."

"Perfect!" Viva enthused. "Join the party. Go incognito—after all, you're a wanted man."

"Still getting used to the idea and I'm not comfortable with it. But life's a masquerade and we're all in costume anyway. I just hope it doesn't become our Day of the Dead."

"Don't be morbid."

We drove Jenna's Camry into town and stopped at Walgreen's. Ominous cumulus clouds darkened the sky, and a light drizzle began to fall. I put on a nerdy green beanie to keep my hair dry. Despite the gathering darkness, I wore my shades, now a permanent fixture of my hunted-man wardrobe.

We dashed into the store, and I followed Viva to the personal care aisle where she picked out a box of black hair coloring and plunked it in my hand. As she glanced at cosmetics, I found the men's brand for blond hair and tossed it into the shopping basket. *One easy application. Professional results.*

I purchased the boxes of hair dye and some shaving articles at the self-check register and swiveled to look for Viva. Through the front door strode a burly man in a brown leather jacket, moving with the resolution of an ox. He had a pronounced reddish birthmark on his balding forehead, and I recognized him instantly. Darko.

I hunched my shoulders and stared at my shoes, beyond grateful I was wearing my sunglasses and had on the silly beanie. I pivoted and stumbled into the heart of the store, found Viva with some toiletries in her hand and whispered that Darko was here. "Forget the stuff. Let's get the hell out!" As she ditched the merchandise, I glanced around the aisle and saw no sight of the cop. Signaling Viva, we rushed nervously into the drizzle, like teenagers shoplifting for the first time. We raced to Jenna's car and huddled inside. With raindrops pelting the windshield, I nervously keyed the engine, skidded out of the parking lot, and headed through town toward the turnoff to Jenna's.

We had dodged another bullet.

"How'd the jerk find us?" I grumbled.

"He knows about Michaela," Viva said nervously. "Must've

figured I'd seek her out. Probably learned she'd be in Sedona at the conference."

"To think we'd stumble into him in Walgreens! Like seeing a demon on an ayahuasca trip."

"Not many places in Sedona to get personal care stuff. It's a small town."

"Too small," I said. "That was scary." After a pause I added, "I bet he needed cosmetics. Darko's favorite spot's probably in front of a mirror."

Viva stared pensively. "The bastard's got a detective's mind," she said.

"And the police department's comprehensive database to track people," I added, surprised at her wording, as she generally avoided crude language.

After a pause, she added, "I'd say that's two cat's lives down for us, hopefully seven more to go."

"So, you think we're cats?"

"Well, we're not super-heroes."

"Speak for yourself. Fact is, Superman and I have never been spotted together. Just sayin'." Truth was, we could use some super-powers. *Faster than a speeding bullet. Leaps tall buildings in a single bound.*

Viva's cell buzzed. It was Jenna.

"You're kidding!" Viva said, alarmed. "Are they gone? Okay. We'll be careful. See you soon."

Viva was shaken. "What now?" I asked.

"Two cops showed up at Jenna's, looking for us and the girl. Thank God she was out with Michaela. Jenna played dumb."

"Crazy! How'd they know to check her place?"

"Who knows? I'm an independent contractor but they do have my employee file. Besides…lots of ways to get leads. Michaela's connections. Something on Instagram. Nothing's private anymore. Maybe I mentioned Jenna in a conversation at the cop station."

"Surreal," I muttered, wondering how much longer our luck would hold. Viva guided me on a longer route back to Jenna's to make sure the coast was clear.

Life is a kaleidoscopic theater. The issue was whether our unfolding drama would end as a divine comedy or a blood-stained tragedy.

We would soon find out.

CHAPTER 15

Enchantment

Friday, the first day of the conference, dawned with a cloudless, blue September sky. After breakfast Michaela performed an elaborate protection ritual, designed especially for Marisol and her missing sister. Viva stood behind the girl and placed hands gently on her shoulders. The curandera seemed a supernatural agent of spiritual mysteries and Viva, her apprentice.

Viva's mentor burned sage and Palo Santo wood and asked Marisol to hold a picture of Our Lady of Guadalupe, touching it to her heart. Michaela made it clear to the girl, who didn't seem to need convincing at this point, that she was safe with us, and we'd get her back to Mexico. But first we'd try to find Marisa. This pleased the dark-haired exile, who smiled radiantly.

We decided to bring our fugitive twin with us to the hotel, despite the risk. She would go with Michaela. Viva and I traveled into town in Jenna's Toyota, sporting our new hairstyles. Mine dirty blond and Viva's raven black.

Our destination was a secluded hotel in nearby Boynton Canyon, nestled beneath steep stone hillsides that featured ancient cliff dwellings—Enchantment Resort. Viva told me that powerful vortexes dotted the stunning hidden gorge.

The conference was a gathering of people from all over North America and Mexico. Some even from Europe. The theme was healing, with an emphasis on Indigenous traditions. Not only was she a keynote speaker, but Michaela would also teach a class in *curanderismo*, the shamanic healing art.

Normally the cost for a conference and lodging at the five-star luxury resort would be prohibitive for most. Because management knew Michaela and held her in esteem, room rates for the event were discounted. Attendance was limited to a hundred people, and it had sold out quickly. Michaela's keynote remarks that evening would kick off the event. Saturday morning after breakfast featured the psychic faire.

The curandera reserved a room for Viva and me in her name in order to shield our identity from Darko and the cops. Jenna also had a room, with Marisol under her wing.

Viva and I took refuge in our lodging, a small cabin-like adobe with a fireplace. We were watchful and cautious, convinced Darko would make an appearance at some point. The entire drama engulfing us produced a dissonant medley of contradictory feelings. On one hand I was fearful of what might befall us. At the same time, I experienced deep happiness having Viva as a near-constant companion since our escape from Phoenix. My moods swung from extremes of paranoia to the thrill of being in the presence of one who electrified me. I imagined I could withstand perennial insecurity in order to remain close to this exceptional companion, who so intensely sparked my romantic feelings.

I intended to confess these feelings to her, despite the risk of having it all blow up in my face and to endure her rejection. Though her birthday was two weeks away, I ordered flowers to be delivered at the hotel and planned to present them to her that evening.

The conference room and main restaurant boasted stunning views of ancient canyon cave dwellings. Knowing Darko might be at large, we hesitated to dine with the other guests. Jenna called Viva on her cell and said there were several cops at the hotel and one matched Darko's description. She saw them talk with the receptionist and wasn't sure if they'd left the grounds.

In late afternoon, we decided to hike on the local trails through the canyon before having dinner in our room. We headed out onto a path, eventually ascending high over the valley floor.

"Tell me about your family," I asked as we traipsed the dusty, red-hued paths. Viva smiled and seemed to enjoy the clean air and invigorating late summer hike. She wore peach-colored shorts and a beige halter top that exposed her trim, tanned waistline. She was slim and gorgeous, and it was a challenge not to constantly stare at her.

"Nothing much to say, really. My dad was a businessman from Mexico. He had a jewelry store in Mexico City, and also owned a wholesale jewelry company with some accounts in the US. That's how he met my mom. She was working in a jewelry store in Newport Beach while going to school. They got to know each other, and I guess the sparks started to fly. Anyway, they were married for ten years, but it didn't work out, obviously. Luca came a year after they married. I arrived a few months before they split up. I'll give my dad credit, though: he tried to spend as much time as he could with me growing up. At least till I was in my teens. By then he was mostly in Mexico."

"Was your mom's maiden name McCloud?" I asked, figuring that might account for her and Luca's different last names.

Viva nodded. "You must be psychic too!" Despite her sarcasm, her mischievous smile made my heart quiver. "When he was older, Luca took Mom's name...he and Pop didn't get along. I kept Dad's last name; it's on my birth certificate. He moved back to Mexico, and he's mostly retired now. Dabbles in international finance. Lives part of the year in Mexico City and has an apartment in Florida. I see him every two, three years or so. We're on good terms, just don't connect that often. My mom lives in Albuquerque. I see her a couple times a year. How about you?"

"Your parents' relationship sounds like a fairytale match made in heaven compared to mine."

"Really? That bad? Tell me."

"Well...truth is I hardly knew my dad. When I was four, he left us. He was half sailor, half cowboy at heart. He just couldn't sit still. Just not a suit-and-tie, sit-behind-a desk kind of guy. He did all sorts of things before he met my mom, and after he bailed. A chef on a cruise line. Sold yachts. Worked a couple years on a dude ranch in Texas. Traveled everywhere. Even hunted lost treasures. Indiana Jones type. Last I heard he was driving a truck for a company in the south: ARCO, my mom said, or something like that. It was after he started working there that their marriage broke up. My mom never really got over it. She loved him. Maybe he loved us in his own strange, weird stupid way."

"Did you ever see him again?"

"Not even once after he left when I was four. In fact, I barely remember him." I paused, reflecting on my past, surprised at how hard I was breathing. We gazed down at the ruddy canyon walls and the grassy fields below us. "He did leave me two of his favorite books, illustrated versions of *The Iliad* and *The Odyssey* he'd owned since he was a kid. I still have them. My father was obsessed with ancient Greece and Troy. He caught the bug from my grandpa. My dad's name was actually Ajax Diomedes Parker—Ajax and Diomedes were two Greek warriors in *The Iliad*. He went by Jack. But because he was left-handed, some of his friends called him Lefty. He wanted to name me Diomedes, but my mom refused, thankfully. So, he settled for Troy."

"Why do you go by Jaden?"

"Jaden's the name my mom wanted. My father was away on business when I was born, so the birth certificate says Jaden Troy Parker. But my dad always called me Troy. I don't even think he knew Jaden was my official first name. Once he flew the coop, my mom stopped calling me Troy." We paused at a scenic overview on the path and gazed at the valley floor.

"He did send a card on my tenth birthday," I continued. "Addressed to Troy, of course. Still have that, too. A picture of a big sailboat…the old clipper-ship type. He said he was traveling the world and thought of me. Hoped I'd grow up to be a better person than him. He actually said that. And…and he said…" I stopped and wiped my eye with my arm, struggling with a strange feeling swelling inside, filling my throat and my head.

"What?"

"Sorry…must be a vortex nearby."

"No…I understand. Please go on if you want to. I'd love to hear more."

I nodded, struggling to get a grip on my feelings. "Anyway, he wrote on the card that he loved me and was sorry he wasn't a better father." I shook my head, surprised at the emotion seizing me. "You know…he was probably drunk when he wrote it, but I wouldn't trade that card and those books for anything. Guess I'm just a sentimental freak."

"Oh, Jaden. That must've been so hard for you. Growing up without a father."

"Well, lots of people grow up without a parent…especially their dad. You too, for the most part. I *did* have some father figures in my life. The Three Stooges, for instance. Sorry, bad joke. My mom never remarried but she had some boyfriends. One was a guy named Zachary, who sorta took me under his wing. Brought me to Giants' games. Forty-niners' games. We played catch and hiked and stuff. But one day he just moved on. My mom didn't have real good luck with guys. I think what finally broke her spirit was when she heard my dad was living in New Orleans with some chick, a year after living with another gal in Amarillo. I think it just broke her heart. She really loved the guy. Even though he was a total jerk."

We sat on some boulders in the sun until it grew too hot, then slowly made our way back along the trail. Once in our room, I risked a quick dip in the pool, never removing my Ray-Ban's, giving Viva time to shower.

As I toweled dry, the concierge texted me that flowers had been delivered for us, so I stopped to get them. Strolling through the lobby with the cluster of red roses, my attention was drawn to a seated, muscular chap in a plain T-shirt and sunglasses. Another man in sunglasses and wearing a blue Hawaiian shirt sat near him. Although ten feet away, I caught the unmistakable scent of Captain Darko's cheap, obnoxious cologne.

Damn! He's here…playing plainclothes cop.

Pressing the roses to my face, I pivoted and made a detour through the large swinging doors leading outside.

CHAPTER 16

Viva's Gift

I snaked my way around to our room along the back route, deciding not to tell Viva I spotted (and sniffed) our nemesis. The fellow with him in the Hawaiian shirt looked like the driver of the white van we'd seen in Machiavelli's parking lot. Despite my concerns, I pushed aside all troubling thoughts. I had other things on my mind and didn't want to spoil the evening mood.

"I know it's not your birthday yet, but it's coming up, so I'd thought I'd surprise you in advance," I announced as I entered the room. There was only one bed, a queen. Viva was sitting on it when I handed her the bouquet of roses and a card with a poem I'd written.

"That's so sweet of you." She placed the flowers in a vase, sat on the bed again, and read the card and poem.

> *Stars in the sky like fire,*
> *Tiny jewels so bright.*
> *Moon bathes the earth with silver,*
> *Glowing through the night.*
> *Lovely is their luster*

Yet my love outshines their light.
I love you.

"That's so lovely." Viva's smile and the light in her eyes were intoxicating.

"Thanks. It's how I feel." There was an awkward silence as she gazed at the roses and read the card again. "What are you going to do when this is all over?" I asked. "When things get back to abnormal?"

"Not sure, really. Don't have much of a life in Phoenix."

"What brought you there in the first place? You never told me."

Viva's smile vanished. "Oh, stupid stuff. Boyfriend stuff. It didn't work out. My astrology was starting to take off, and then Luca got me the job with the police. You know, sometimes life just happens around you when you don't even intend it. Right?"

"Right. Like John Lennon said, 'Life is what happens when you're busy making other plans.'"

Viva nodded. "What about you? What'll you do?"

I shrugged. "Get on with my road trip, I guess." I paused, hesitant to ask the question on my mind, afraid of her answer. "Would you like to come along? You'd be a good navigator. And my Jeep Cherokee is super classy. I could use a traveling gypsy fortune teller."

Her eyes glistened in the dim light. "I'm really enjoying your company. Despite the bizarre circumstances. You're fun, and you're funny. You're sweet and you're attractive, and all that. I'm just not ready for that kind of commitment. Not yet anyway."

"Me neither. It's just that when you meet the most gorgeous and fascinating woman of your life, it's hard not to be swept away."

She smiled. "We've barely known each other two weeks. Is that really long enough to be sure about your feelings?"

"I loved you the moment I saw you. And I love you more now."

"Oh, stop it! I'm not sure I even really know what love is. Michaela says love isn't just an emotion. I mean, it *is* an emotion, we all feel it. But it's more than that… like a cosmic emotion or something…I can't explain it the way she does. It's something that emanates from our true nature. Our spirit. She says *feeling love* is what makes us happy. Love is divine magic, a heavenly feeling. It's a light from our hearts that never stops shining. She says light and love are everything. Without them you have nothing."

"I guess I'm in love with love itself," I said. "Or maybe *the idea* of love, the feeling of *being in it* as a kind of energy. Not just physical. But an energy that keeps on going even after our bodies disappear."

"That's why they say love is eternal. I've always believed our essence is immortal. The light of our soul lives on."

We were lying side by side on the bed and she had her arms crossed in front of her, as if shielding herself. "I'd love to kiss you," I said, touching her hand.

"I *might* like to kiss you, too. But this isn't the time, Jaden. Or the place. With all the pressure, and everything." Her hand felt suddenly cold. "We need to let things resolve. It's just madness right now."

"I suppose you're right." Despite my words, I didn't really care if it was a good time or place. To me, being with her anywhere was the perfect moment.

Viva nodded almost imperceptibly. "Anyway," she started again after a long silence. "I thought you had a girlfriend."

"You did?" I was surprised by her words because I'd never mentioned a girlfriend.

"Yeah, of course…Lyla. You two seem so perfect together. Like it's a real fit. And she seems to really like you. I thought it was obvious."

"Oh, Lyla! Sure, she's super. We're just friends. I've only known her a couple weeks. Since I got to town."

"Sounds like you and me." Viva tilted her face slightly away from me and tightened her folded arms. Her words hit hard, and I didn't know how to take them. Was there jealously in them, or just matter-of-fact indifference? Regardless, they were a jolt, and the special mood I'd hoped to create with the flowers and the poem collapsed like broken glass.

"Tell me about you and Luca," I said, realizing it was time to steer the conversation a new direction. "You seem really different."

"Day and night," Viva said, relaxing and sitting up on the bed, her back against a pillow. "Luca was a good big brother growing up. Kind to me. He was always really grounded and practical, and he thought my interest in spiritual stuff was weird."

"When did you realize you had this clairvoyant gift, or have you always had it?" With all the questions, I felt like a talk show host.

Viva shook her head. "Not always, but I was always kind of psychic and intuitive, even as a kid. I often knew what my mom was about to say…teachers even. But it was actually recently, with Luca, that I realized I had a special clairvoyant knack." She paused reflectively and examined the little red rose tattoo on her wrist.

"Anyway, after I wound up in Phoenix over a year ago," she continued, "he took me to lunch one day, and told me about a case he was working on, an unsolved murder. That is, they assumed it could be murder…a missing boy. Right there at lunch Luca described the little boy and showed me his picture. I'd heard about it on the news." She paused again and breathed deeply, her eyes glinting in the light.

"When I saw the photo, I felt tightening in my heart. He looked so young and sweet. At the same time, a series of crystal-clear images appeared in my mind. And I just blurted out, I'll never forget, 'He's in the woods by Lake Mary, on the north side. Less than fifty feet from the water's edge.'"

"Luca looked at me like I was crazy, then called the police station, right there at the restaurant. They found his body next morning. Exactly where I'd seen it in my mind."

"That's incredible," I said. "How could someone do something so evil? Pardon me for asking, but did that make you a suspect?" Viva shook her head.

"Not really. Being Luca's sister, and all. Although it probably crossed some of the cops' minds—they're professionals, after all. Anyway, they already had a suspect who later admitted the crime. DNA tests supported it."

"It's so amazing. You're not kidding when you say you have a gift. Do you see stuff like this all the time? I mean…when you do horoscopes, even?" I was wondering what images might have popped in her head when she was doing my chart.

Viva laughed. "It's not something I'm able to control. When I'm doing astrology, I guess I'm using another hemisphere of my brain, or something, because these sorts of images rarely pop up. They come when I read the cards or go into deep meditation. When I'm in that flow, like you saw the other day at Jenna's at the breakfast table, the images just stream out. The hard part is interpreting the riddles." *That's an understatement!* I kept my thought to myself.

"Anyway, Luca got me a job with the cops. At the police station they'll show me pictures of missing people, and often I'll see an image or series of images. They just stream through my mind as I look at a photo or piece of evidence. It just happens. Lots of times what I say is more cryptic and riddle-like...like the other day at Jenna's, that weird line about finding Marisa in the eighteenth century. And the bow and arrow bit. I never know what will happen. I've been involved with them over the past ten months, and I've helped them catch a few perpetrators. They matched my description almost exactly...that is, the images that flashed in my mind."

"You're not the only one with a gift," I said after a pause. "I can read your palm."

"Really? I didn't know you could do that that."

"Let me take a look." She held out her right hand and I took it gently in both mine, examining the lines in her palm, pretending to comprehend what I was seeing.

"You're the kind of person who likes to be happy," I said.

"Oh, stop it!" Viva pulled her hand away. "You're such a joker!"

"Well, you can't say I was wrong. Right?"

"As if anyone doesn't like to be happy."

"You also like to shop. You have a natural talent for it."

"Brilliant interpretation. You'll go far," said Viva.

I lay close to her, hearing her breathing. We talked about what to do next. Should we go to Vegas? Take Marisol? It was a huge risk. Our bodies touched, as well as our minds, but it seemed a superficial contact. She wasn't feeling what I was feeling.

She let me squeeze her hand before she fell asleep. I lay awake, pondering. To be this close to Viva, to be sleeping beside her, in itself was a kind of victory. *Progress*, you could say. At the same time, she still seemed impossibly distant. Our backs touched as we lay there.

Lyla's image sprang to my mind, and I pondered my attraction to her. My bookstore friend exuded sensuousness from every pore, yet with an innocence that was beguiling. Her physical magnetism was palpable. She possessed that sultry mixture of sexuality and wacky playfulness most men find incredibly alluring, whereas Viva had a kind of emotional purity that made her seem slightly unattainable and aloof. Much as I liked the charming bookshop clerk with the goofy sense of humor and fun personality, my affection for her lacked the special unique intensity of *being home* that I felt for the one who lay beside me. My heart's axis synched with Viva's unique pole star.

Was it love at first sight? Undeniably. I found her strikingly attractive the moment I saw her at Coronado's. No doubt Viva would turn the heads of most guys, though she was a bit slender by the standards of many. Her captivating features could grace the cover of fashion mags, and her striking, deep brown eyes would stop a runaway truck. To me, her physical charm was matched by her inner beauty. And I loved her changing mannerisms and facial expressions, matching the flow of her thoughts and moods. Even just now, the combination of amusement and exasperation that flashed across her features as I teased about reading her palm.

Both Lyla and Viva were funny, charming, and smart, but in different ways. "I'm a triple Scorpio," Lyla had told me matter-of-factly. "I know how to have a good time." No doubt she did. In contrast, Viva projected an almost goddess-like unattainability, which made her even more of a prize, because of the challenge. I suppose it boiled down to the simple fact I really *liked* Lyla, but I *loved* Viva. No point in trying to analyze it. Feelings are what they are.

A sinister image kept breaking through my reveries: the menacing face of Darko. What confused me was how Seth's investigative discoveries might be tied to the police captain's apparent trafficking operation. I suspected a link. The fact the big cop appeared at Seth's apartment after his murder made me think my friend's death and the twins' abduction might also be connected. I figured we'd soon stumble on more puzzle pieces.

I pushed away all pressing thoughts and rested my mind on the enchantress beside me. My breathing slowed till it matched hers, heartbeat to heartbeat. A blanket of quiet fell over me that felt nearly like being at peace. Sifting through blurred and broken feelings, and the ominous murmurs of an uncertain future, I finally drifted off.

CHAPTER 17

Madame Lucretia

Saturday dawned magically, with sunlight streaking over the Sedona hills. I awoke with a renewed sense of adventure. Bizarre and perilous though it was, I was on my road trip with a beautiful companion. *Things could be worse.*

Rising before Viva, I built a fire despite the fact the temperature would likely hit high nineties by mid-afternoon. I handed her a mug of steaming coffee as she leaned against the headboard, a pillow propped behind her.

"I'd love to know what you see in your crystal ball today. Get a sense of the future. What you said about my horoscope sure turned out to be true, right?"

"Right. Dramatic changes. I didn't tell you, but my chart has some of the same planetary transits. Crisis and opportunity."

"Mayhem, I'd say. I feel as if I've fallen through a crack in the fabric of space and landed in an alternative universe. It's been a house of horrors."

"It's a karmic rough patch, Jaden. You'll get through it. At least *I think*, you will." She smiled and winked mischievously. "You'll be a different person when it's over."

"I'm a different person now! I just want to make it through alive." Viva sipped her coffee and didn't respond. "Does the snake show up today? What d'ya think?" I still couldn't bring myself to tell her I'd seen the chief of police.

She shrugged. "Darko? I wouldn't doubt it. He wants the girl. We're just accessories in his way." *Is it time to tell her about Seth's article?*

"True. I can't believe Luca trusted him."

Viva drank a second cup of strong coffee and devoured two strawberry Danishes, then chilled in silence for a few minutes on a chair by the fireplace, getting centered. To some attendees at the psychic fair, a card reading might be simply fun and games, but I knew Viva treated each one earnestly. She told me the first reading she gave was to a fifty-year-old woman, a lawyer, a complete skeptic who did it as a lark. Within minutes the woman began sobbing uncontrollably at Viva's words. The layout revealed exactly what was going on in her life, including suppressed secrets. Combined with my friend's stunning intuitive gift, the cards probed a nerve in the lawyer's unconscious psychic makeup.

"The cards never lie," Viva told me. "We can hide from the truth, but it eventually hunts us down."

I drained the last of my coffee and examined my appearance in the mirror. I didn't have the luxury of wearing a mask, but my new blond persona gave me confidence. Viva tied my hair in a short ponytail. With my Ray-Ban's and a baseball-style cap I'd picked up in the hotel gift shop, I seemed reasonably incognito. Darko didn't know me well anyway. Nonetheless, I was determined to avoid him. *Besides, his cologne reeks.*

"Classy," Viva said, as I adjusted the cap. "And it'll hold your brains in."

She put on her gypsy fortuneteller's costume, replete with a partial veil over her mouth and nose. Originally the veil had been to conjure a sense of mystery. Now it was for subterfuge.

As she twirled theatrically, I inspected her outfit. "You look stunning, and you're the perfect gypsy." She laughed and gathered her bag with card deck, crystal ball, and a purple cloth for the table.

"I'll swing by in a bit and check things out," I said. "Not gonna let looming catastrophe spoil my day."

Viva giggled. "Great. See you there. Wish me luck." She kissed me on the cheek, smiled, swiveled on her heels, and headed out the door.

That was our first kiss. To say it thrilled me would be a dramatic understatement.

On my way to the lobby, I swung by Jenna's room and stuck my head in to say hello to her and Marisol. The young girl who was the object of the big cop's hunt rarely left the room, and never unattended. Her attire was now completely that of a typical American pre-teen. And with her hair in a ponytail, she would've blended inconspicuously in almost any setting. Still, knowing Darko's radar was primed to locate a young girl her age spelled, *Take no chances.*

The psychic fair began at ten and was in a low-lit, medium-sized room with eight small tables spread apart with several feet between each. Conference attendees moved around casually, checking out the readers: a palmist, numerologist, astrologer, and five assorted psychics and card readers, Viva among them. I strolled into the room to say hello, but she was already engaged in a session with a middle-aged woman dressed in a blue business suit, wearing a Dolly Parton-style wig. Viva sat at a small round table with her back against the wall. A purple cloth covered her table, and on it shone a clear crystal ball resting on a purple velvet cushion. Beside her elbow was a small, framed picture of Lakshmi, Indian goddess of beauty, abundance, and good fortune. Printed signs on the tables and on the wall above the readers indicated each one's specialty. Viva's read:

Madame Lucretia
Romanian Gypsy Extraordinaire
See Your Future in the Cards

In the corner of the room, not far from Viva's table, stretched a gray curtain behind which were stacked a dozen or so folding chairs. I thought of slipping behind the curtain to take in the proceedings, and maybe surprise her when the coast was clear.

A burly man in a brown leather jacket and blue jeans appeared at the doorway, accompanied by a policeman and the man in the Hawaiian shirt I'd spotted in the lobby the night before. A birthmark was visible on the big guy's forehead. It was Darko, out of uniform. To my dismay, he stepped right up to Viva's table just as the blond-haired woman got up to leave.

Does Darko know?

I ducked behind the gray curtain as the plainclothes cop sat at Viva's table and asked for a reading. I wasn't more than ten feet away, his back to me, and I could hear their voices clearly. If Viva was shocked or frightened, she didn't show it as far as I could tell. I stood, mesmerized, focused, commanding myself to prepare for any scenario.

"What would you like to know?" Viva asked, her voice artificially low. "Any questions or issues?" Her nose and mouth were covered by the thin violet veil, leaving only her eyes visible, and she'd put on tons of eyeliner and mascara. Her lips, glossed with shiny red lipstick, were barely perceptible through the gauzy fabric.

"Well, you're the psychic, Madame Lucretia," the police captain laughed. "You tell me."

"It's always helpful if you have some questions," Viva said calmly. "The cards reveal your subconscious in any case, but if you have a special query in mind, it helps to focus things. That way you connect your conscious mind with the subconscious, which makes for a more accurate reading."

Darko shifted slightly in his chair and folded his hands on the table. For the first time I noticed how large, muscular, and veined they were. "Okay...very well. I'd like to retire in couple of years. Tell me what you see."

"All right. Choose three cards and place them face down on the table." She held out a portion of the card deck and the officer chose three and set them down. Viva then shuffled the remaining deck and placed ten more cards in a pattern, face up. Then she turned over two of the three Darko had chosen. She pondered the cards before speaking.

"You may be retiring earlier than you thought," Viva said.

"The cards suggest that. Also, some big events are on the way. Momentous events, soon to come." She gazed intently at the cards, keeping her hands beneath the table. Darko watched her silently. "It looks as if you're going to be traveling. You'll be on the road. Possibly visiting some large establishments or institutions. Hotels perhaps. Or hospitals."

"Ha!" He seemed to think it was funny. "That's pretty good. You scored a bullseye. Hotels sound about right. I'll stay away from hospitals."

"Yes," said Viva. "The hotel is big and has thousands of guests. Some are important people. It's like an entertainment center. The building has a letter on it. *M*, I believe it is."

"You can see that? That's pretty striking."

Viva went on. "Sometimes the details are remarkably accurate. I see an *M*… and I see water on the desert, like a mirage."

"Nah, not the Mirage. Nice hotel, but not that one. It's close though…starts with an *M*." He stopped and stared intently at Viva. She dropped her glance, avoiding his eyes, and I feared the worst. *Thank God for the veil!*

"You know…you remind me of a gal who's got quite a psychic gift. She works with cops, solving murder cases."

"Some people do have gifts," Viva said, her face tilted downward, staring at the cards.

"I guess so. Well, she's got a gift, that's for sure. She helped crack some tough jobs. What else do you see?"

"I see a couple of girls. Twins."

"That so?"

"Yes, they're visiting someone. Someone important. He seems

to be expecting them. He's connected in some way with the hotel. A guest, maybe."

"Really? That's fascinating. You're pretty good, Madame Lucretia. Tell me more."

"Umm...the girls have dark hair...they're possibly Indian or Hispanic. They've run away from home. Or maybe been taken against their will." For the first time I detected nervousness in Viva's voice. Darko squirmed. "And you are trying to help the girls. Help them get to where they belong."

"Hmm. That's interesting. Fact is, I'm looking for one of the girls who's missing. One we know about. She's safe. The other one's been abducted."

"Where's the girl who's safe?" Viva asked. "That might help me see where the other one is."

"Funny you mentioned a hotel. She's in a hotel...in Vegas. The one that starts with an *M*. But what the hell do you need to know that for?"

"Like I said, the more we know, the more the subconscious aligns with the conscious mind." Viva paused and closed her eyes. "I do see a picture. The girl you're looking for, the sister, is far away, out of state. Traveling with a small group, it appears. And they're headed east. Maybe New Mexico. Possibly even back to Mexico." She was lying now, throwing a red herring on the trail, leading Darko astray.

"Back? Why back? What makes you think she's from Mexico? You can see that?" Darko's voice grew testy.

Viva opened her eyes. "A hunch. Umm...though I do sense you may be in some danger. You might want to take a few weeks off, take a break from work. Stay out of harm's way. Let's look at the last card."

The gypsy fortuneteller lifted her hands from under the table. The shawl covering her arms fell away. She turned the last of Darko's cards over, and I could plainly see the tiny, red rose tattoo on her right wrist.

"Fuck! It *is* you!" Darko shouted. "Bitch!" He swiped all the cards off the table and stood, turning the table over onto Viva. The cards flew everywhere, and the crystal ball rolled across the carpet. All the readers stopped cold, and the room hushed.

"Fuckin' bitch! Where is she? Where's the girl?" His voice was loud and threatening. "Where's the girl?" he demanded again, pulling a revolver from inside his leather jacket. His deputy came in from outside the room and stood a few feet away, hand on his holster. People screamed, knocking over tables and chairs, and rushed from the room.

I froze, uncertain what to do. Had the second cop not been there, I might have tackled Darko on the spot. That would have been a dumb move.

"I don't know what you're talking about!" Viva pleaded, her voice high and nervous. She backed toward the door.

Darko laughed loudly. "Watch where you go, *Madame Lucretia*. You're under arrest."

"Do as he says!" I shouted, rushing from my hiding spot to Viva's side. "It's okay, officer." I stared Darko in the eyes. "I know where the girl is. I'll show you. Follow me." I turned and dashed through hotel lobby, fearful of getting a bullet in my spine.

At the side entrance, I paused and yelled back at him. "She's hiding on the trail. I'll take you there." I rushed out the door, through the parking lot, and hurried along the footpath leading to the edge of the canyon. Reaching the trailhead, I stopped to see if anyone followed. I saw Darko, but not the other cop or the man in the Hawaiian shirt. They must've stayed back to keep an eye on Viva.

My goal was a place I'd seen on our hike the day before. An unlikely maneuver, a roll of the cosmic dice, but the only thing that sprang to mind in the chaos.

I paused to catch my breath and let Darko catch up. "She's just up here on the trail!" I shouted. "She'll be better off with you." The big cop lagged fifty feet behind me as I reached the desired location on the path. The sun hadn't yet risen over the high canyon wall and the way ahead was obscured by shadow.

Darko sprinted up almost beside me, breathing heavily, and stopped at my chosen spot, a trail fork where the path split in two directions. I feared he might shoot me but gambled he'd wait till he found Marisol. "She's hiding right there!" I said pointing. "A perfect hideout, but the game's up. Let her go home with you."

The police captain gasped for breath, his chest heaving, and I detected the tawdry scent of his cheap cologne. He glared at me as I pointed down the path and his eyes followed my gesture. "If we don't have the girl within the hour, you're a dead man," he growled. The rage in his eyes showed he wasn't bluffing, but in this arena of massive red rocks and enormous canyon walls, he didn't seem invincible.

Though muscular and powerful, Darko was exhausted by

the run and appeared almost vulnerable out of uniform, a small figure dwarfed by the monumental landscape. He rushed forward a few steps, his eyes scanning the shadowed trail ahead. "About fifty yards farther!" I shouted. "Marisol!"

Darko lunged forward on the path and stopped abruptly, his arms swinging wildly, looking like a crazed human windmill. Desperate to stop his forward motion, the big cop hung for a moment at the edge of the path, which ended abruptly above a chasm. He hovered, flailing the air, appearing to lose his balance.

He let out a weird sound. Not a scream, but more of a squeal. Then silence as he disappeared from view. I raced to the cliff edge and glimpsed over. Darko lay face down on the rocks about thirty feet below, motionless.

I heard footsteps behind me and turned to see Viva.

"What happened? Where is he?" she gasped, breathing hard.

"He fell over the edge. Might've slipped on a rock." I paused, nearly breathless, celebrating in my mind, even as my body trembled violently from the shock of adrenalized fear. "Or maybe it was a vortex."

"They can make people do strange stuff," Viva said. We stared over the ledge at Darko's still and lifeless form. I was elated my risky scheme had worked, knowing full well the dire consequences if it hadn't.

"I think he's dead," I told her. "Probably hit his head on a rock. Good riddance. Have the hotel call an ambulance. We've got bigger fish to fry."

We turned to traipse back to the hotel when we saw an astonishing sight. Ahead on the trail, between us and the hotel,

Michaela stood on a rock, facing the sun, just as the rays of the celestial orb broke above the canyon top. Her face shone with sunlight, serious, focused in deep concentration. There was a radiance about her. An aura. I wondered if she knew what had just transpired. Had she, through some invisible mechanism of the spirit, aided and protected us in some mysterious way?

We reached the hotel and told the waiting cop that his superior had fallen on the path. "He's with the girl," I lied. There was no sign of the man in the Hawaiian shirt. Michaela arrived moments later and spoke softly to the officer. She touched his arm and offered to take him to where the police captain lay. The cop nodded and moved with Michaela toward the door, abandoning any attempt to arrest Viva.

Michaela stopped abruptly and turned to a stunned member of the hotel staff standing nearby. "Call an ambulance," she said. "He may be hurt."

Better a hearse, I thought. The curandera then touched my arm and handed me an object—a miniature, metallic flashlight, about five inches long. Peering into my eyes, she held my hand and said, "In a battle of light and dark, light wins." Then she turned and stepped rapidly away with the policeman.

I crammed the flashlight into my pocket, and Viva and I hurried through the lobby. "What now?" she asked. Her veil had fallen off and her skin was flushed from the feverish events and her sprint along the trail. With her wind-blown, raven hair and her exotic gypsy outfit, she radiated otherworldly beauty.

"Pack up. We're heading out. To Las Vega with Marisol." I stumbled by the room where the readings took place and glanced in. Tables and chairs were overturned, and it looked as if a storm swept through.

Spotting one of Viva's tarot cards on the floor, face down, I snatched it up on the half run. "What's in your hand?" she asked, following a few steps behind.

"One of your tarot cards. Picked it up on the floor just now."

"Which one?" Viva asked seriously.

I flipped it over. At the top was the Roman numeral eight. Below, rode a skeleton in black armor on a white horse and holding a black flag in its left hand. In the center of the flag was a white, five-petaled flower against a black background.

"Umm…it says DEATH."

We hurriedly gathered our things from the room and met Jenna and Marisol in the parking lot.

"It's a ten-day rental," Jenna said as we threw our belongings in the trunk and piled into the red Chevy Malibu. "May God go with you."

As we pulled away from Enchantment Resort, a dark cloud swallowed the sun, precursor of a monsoon on its way. A swirl of angry leaves hit hard against the windshield. With Viva in the back seat, her arm around Marisol, I wheeled onto the road leading out of Sedona.

PART THREE

"If we are related, we shall meet."

— RALPH WALDO EMERSON

CHAPTER 18

Double Jeopardy

We drove north through gorgeous Oak Creek Canyon to Highway 40, heading west. The road from Sedona to Las Vegas is three hundred miles of changing terrain, passing through several climate zones. From the forested, high mountain plateaus of Flagstaff, down into the desert wastes of southern Nevada, the road winds through majestic evergreen groves, pastoral fields, and scenic, desert rock formations framed by distant majestic peaks.

I'd never been to Sin City. Odd that Maxie should live there, and odd that it should unexpectedly become for us another vortex. Not the kind created by intersecting, subtle-energy lines of force, but by the intense pressures of our lives abruptly colliding with the corporate elites who trafficked Marisa.

From Viva's reading with Darko, we gathered she was being kept at a hotel that started with the letter *M* but wasn't the Mirage. Of course, Darko could've fabricated that, but we figured he was telling the truth. Viva searched on her phone for info about Vegas hotels that started with the letter *M,* and we concluded it was likely the Mandala and agreed we'd check it out as soon as possible. Staying there, or at any hotel, was another matter. Too risky. With networked reservations systems, the police could track our location if we checked in using our real names. In fact, we only used cash for purchases, knowing our credit cards could be used to track us.

So, I texted Maxie from our first rest stop on Highway 40 and told him we were on the road to Vegas and needed a place to stay. I also told him to keep his mouth shut about it, but we might have to show up at his door.

He called back before I reached the car.

"When do you get in?" he asked.

"Tonight. We're in hiding, understand?"

"Believe me, I get it. You can stay at my place."

"Great! Thanks. How's Karina doing? Any idea?"

"We've been in touch. She just got back here, in Vegas. Tying up loose ends at her apartment."

"Tell her hello. See you tonight."

I told Viva we could stay at Maxie's, and she looked relieved. "Tell me about your friend Seth," she asked when we were on the road again. She still sat in the back seat beside Marisol.

"Just a super great guy. Smart, fun...he'd do anything for you." I shook my head as I recalled the circumstances surrounding his death. "It's not easy to talk about it, but Seth was murdered because of what he discovered. He found out about child trafficking. But more than that—and this is what got him killed—he uncovered a pedophile ring of elites. He had names. The elites he was set to expose arranged his murder so he couldn't publish the dirt he had on them."

"I gathered that from all you said before, and from my reading at Jenna's. It's so tragic!"

"There's more, if you want to know."

"I'm all ears."

"He sent me his final unpublished article the day they killed him."

"You're kidding! *You* have it?" Alarm oozed from Viva's voice.

"Yep. The article they didn't want published. I have it and might be the only person in the world who does. Other than the psychos who killed him." I didn't mention the incident at the Tempe Mission Palms as I checked out: the men looking for me. I didn't want to put even more of a scare into her. Besides, she was capable of filling in the blanks. If it was obvious to me, it was obvious to her: if they killed Seth to stop him from publishing, they'd do the same to me.

"I'm not sure what to do with it," I continued, "but I think I'm gonna send it out everywhere. In tribute to Seth, if nothing else. That'll also get the heat off me."

"Do that, Jaden. Send it out everywhere. And soon. Get the truth out, and it'll get the pressure off you."

"You know my motto, Safety Third," I said.

In the mirror I caught Viva flash a grim smile. "Third? You'll have to tell me first and second some time."

We fell silent and I could tell she was absorbing the double danger we were in. Not only for escorting Marisol, as if that weren't enough, but due to Seth's article.

"So, Seth named names?" Viva finally asked.

"Mostly he named corporations. He implied the individuals

by saying the leadership of these companies were involved. I can't recall names. I skimmed the last part...will have to read again more closely."

We fell silent again, and when it came time to talk, I changed the subject.

"By the way, that reading you gave Darko was amazing." She knew I'd hid behind the curtain a few feet away and witnessed the entire drama at the psychic fair. "How exactly can the cards be so accurate? I mean, intuition aside, what's the principle involved? It's uncanny."

I was aware of the Jungian concept of synchronicity, which explains the rationale behind the accuracy of Tarot card readings, as well as other divining systems such as Nordic Runes and the ancient Chinese I Ching.

Jung arrived at the idea through his work with a client, a cerebral, highly intellectual woman, remote from her own feelings. He tried to get her to work with her dreams, to help her get in touch with the emotions of her inner life. In his office one day, she described a dream she had of a butterfly. As she related the dream to Jung, a butterfly came in through the open office window and flitted around, hovering between him and the woman, who was completely oblivious to the butterfly's presence. In contrast, Jung was in a state of wonder. From that incident he coined the term *synchronicity*. Simply put, a simultaneous connection between what's going on in your mind and how that's reflected in your environment.

"Good question," said Viva. "I'd say it's the idea of synchronicity. What happens outside of you, on the external, reflects what's going on inside, in your psyche. The world is a mirror, and we see ourselves reflected in the people and events that make up our lives in the daily motion."

"I must be insane then. Feel as if I'm locked in a madhouse."

"It's a destiny transit. Saturn, remember? It won't last forever. Synchronicity is a bit different. It's like when you're thinking of somebody, and they text you. Or a book pops into your head, and you see it lying on your friend's coffee table."

"I'm aware of the concept," I said. "Carl Jung coined the term." In the rearview, Viva nodded.

"Michaela explains it a bit differently," she said, "but it's the same idea. She says nature is a living book of wisdom and we're always receiving messages and guidance. Most people are oblivious to the fact that life—the universe, God, whatever name you give it—communicates to us through people, events, signs, and so forth."

As Viva spoke, I recalled an incident in a bookstore when a volume literally dropped off the shelf into my hands. I bought it and discovered powerful messages. "Right. We send out signals through our thoughts, feelings, and actions, and the universe signals back. It's like light on the path."

Viva continued, "That's a good way to put it. Synchronicity is just the way the world works. The universe is constantly sending us messages. What happens around us mirrors what's going on in our own minds." As she spoke, I thought of a book I'd read on animal symbology. It explained how many ancient cultures viewed the four-legged as keys to our own psyche and as indicators of coming events.

"Animals are also a key," she added, as if capturing my thoughts.

"Right. Totems. Power animals. I understand birds especially are often signs. Like God texting you."

I glimpsed Viva nodding from the back. "According to Michaela, the world is alive and conscious. I'd say a sign of psychological maturity is when you begin to realize the universe is talking to you through all the events of your life."

"Some of the new quantum physicists would agree. And I like the way Michaela puts it: nature is a living book of wisdom that conveys messages in the form of signs, events, and people."

"And that's why the cards work," Viva continued. "And why all oracles and systems of divination work. The runes, the cards, the hexagrams of the I Ching. These are organized systems designed to accurately reflect the messages of the moment from the universe to you. Or you could say, from your deepest self to your conscious mind."

"Makes sense to me," I said.

"The cards reflect hidden feelings, as well as your subconscious," Viva explained. "It's then only a matter of interpreting the symbolism. And of course, that's the hard part. It usually requires serious study to get good at it. I've been at it since I was a teenager."

"And you've got that clairvoyant thing."

Viva smiled. "I suppose I'm lucky, but I'm not so sure."

"It's a gift from God, if you ask me."

She gazed out the window. "I'm grateful, but sometimes it scares me."

We pulled over for a break at Love's Travel Stop gas station and convenience store and I chose a parking spot beside a couple of Blue Palo Verde trees, so common in the dry Arizona landscape. As Viva escorted Marisol inside, I thought to seize the moment to contact Lyla.

Only days had passed since our frantic escape from Phoenix the night Luca McCloud told us about the attempt on his life. Since the moment we fled Lyla's apartment on the run with Marisol, I'd asked my bookstore friend not to call. Yet we exchanged texts almost daily. Our messages were brief and sketchy, as she knew we were in danger.

Our communication felt normal to me until my recent conversation with Viva and the awkward moment she said she thought the charming, sexy, slightly giddy bookstore clerk was my girlfriend. Now I felt almost guilty texting her. But Lyla said she missed me, and I was anxious to preserve our connection, however it should unfold. *Never burn bridges.* Besides, to me it was a natural friendship. The last thing I wanted was for my bond with Lyla to be a stumbling block between Viva and me, but I also felt I had to be honest regardless of any awkwardness. And the fact Hunter French was ex-Special Forces and ex-FBI seemed most auspicious. With his connections, Lyla's dad might prove valuable in freeing Marisa. Possibly indispensable.

Lyla answered and we spoke for the first time since our frantic escape. I swore her to absolute confidence, then explained we were on our way to Vegas where we believed Marisol's sister was held captive. On the spot she asked permission to let Hunter in on the unfolding circumstances. I hesitated, but knowing Hunter's background, I agreed. Seeing Viva and Marisol exit Love's, I abruptly ended our call.

To my astonishment, Lyla texted back almost immediately and said Hunter wanted to help us rescue the girl. She hadn't seen her dad this excited in years.

Viva and Marisol arrived with fries and a plate of tacos as I responded to Lyla's text with a thumbs up. Two hummingbirds flitted in the Palo Verde branches above. Someone had placed hummingbird feeders there.

"Ah, hummingbirds!" I said, as I awkwardly stuck my phone in my pocket. "One of my spirit creatures. According to Native American tradition, hummingbirds mean happiness."

"True," said Viva. "They also mean love." She avoided my eyes and walked with her arm around Marisol toward our car.

Damn that clairvoyance. This is surreal. It's as if she *knew* I was speaking to Lyla and disapproves. *Is Viva really jealous?*

On the road again we were silent for a time. Marisol was humming and singing to herself, and I enjoyed listening. The young girl seemed accustomed to her new life and appeared reasonably happy under the circumstances. Between Viva, Lyla, and a brief excursion to a consignment shop with Jenna, she had a bundle of new American clothes, and she seemed to enjoy traveling—the meal stops and the conversation with Viva, who she adored. She even seemed to like me! She'd been impressed with the beauty of Sedona and told us she'd felt one of the vortexes. Said it made her arms tingle.

Marisol was starting to pick up some English. Jenna had given her a Spanish-English dictionary with common phrases, and I taught her a few words, such as days of the week, and how to count to a hundred in English. Our little Mexican exile was smart, pretty, and determined, and she caught on fast. We could sense her gratitude—she knew we were on a quest to find and free Marisa. She was excited and understandably nervous.

At times I tried to joke and tease with her in Spanish, which she found amusing. Not the jokes, but my fracturing of her language. "Care for a milkshake?" Viva asked me as we pulled into a shopping area in Kingman. I knew she was thinking of Marisol's tastes.

"No. *No me gusto mucho,*" I said, winking at Marisol. "*Prefiero los tacos! ¡Siempre tacos! ¡Vamos a la taquería!*"

Marisol giggled from the back seat. "*Por mi parte, me gustan las* milkshakes." she said.

"*Muy bien. Vamos aquí.*" I pointed to a greasy spoon eatery where we could probably get a milkshake. On our road trip I shoved aside my own nutritional preferences and deferred to Marisol, who with typical pre-teen enthusiasm, loved fast food.

"When this is over, I'm going to write a book," I said to Viva as the three of us ambled into the roadside cafe.

"No doubt," she said. "What'll you call it? *Innocents Abroad*?"

"Sorry, that's been taken."

"How about *My Claim to Fame*? Or…*Holiday Road Trip from Hell*?"

"The latter, more likely. But my working title is *My Super Fab Summer Vacation.*"

"Should be a major hit."

"It'll be a movie, no doubt."

"Who'll play you? Tom Cruise is too old."

"The guy who plays me is probably unknown at the moment. Kinda like me."

"I hope you stay unknown, not..." Viva cut off in mid-sentence. I couldn't interpret her expression as she stood in line to order, but her mood was somber. Oddly, it struck me she'd stopped herself from adding, "not like your friend, Seth."

There were a couple of hours of daylight ahead of us as we hurtled past Hoover Dam and Lake Mead across the Nevada desert into Casino Land. Cruising into America's throbbing, glitzy capital of the senses, it seemed ironically fitting that a city founded by mobsters would become one of the nation's favorite playgrounds.

Our GPS led us directly to Maxie's place, a surprisingly upscale apartment a couple of miles from the town center and famous hotel strip. Not more than six hours after my confrontation with Darko on the red rock trail in Sedona, we pulled into the parking lot at Maxie's.

CHAPTER 19

Dante Ferraro

I awoke to the comforting smell of strong coffee. The morning sun spilled radiance through the windows of Maxie's luxury apartment.

Exhausted by the drive and the events at Enchantment Resort, we'd crashed shortly after arriving. Marisol slept with Viva in the guest room. I took refuge on the couch.

I'd dozed fitfully, harassed by the recurring nightmarish dreams of ancient warriors clashing beneath the walls of fortress Troy. Strangely, this episode featured my father, clad as a Greek warrior, sword and shield in his hands. Though his bronze helmet concealed his face, I knew in my dream's omniscience it was him.

As Maxie poured me a cup of dark-roast Colombian, I pushed aside the unsettling nocturnal imagery and brought him up to date on the events since we'd been in Phoenix at Seth's funeral, a mere handful of days before. My old Monterey buddy seemed more muted and subdued than I'd ever known. As we caught up, he told me Karina was coming by later that day.

"I've been doing some research," he said. "Seth was onto

something huge, or they wouldn't have killed him." *Maxie, you're a master of the obvious.*

"Obviously," I concurred. "A no-brainer."

"I excel at no-brainers. But honestly, I've learned so much. I mean, the news...they, like, fornicate information."

"I think you mean *fabricate*."

"Right. That's what I meant. Need to brush up on my Latin." Maxie sipped his coffee and gave a half-hearted smile. "I'm different now, Jaden," he insisted. "What I've learned...Seth's murder. You know. It's changed me. Maybe not much, but I've sworn off drugs. Well, maybe not totally. Maybe I'll allow myself a joint, or some THC gummies now and then. But I cut way down on alcohol. One beer per night, max. At least that's my goal."

"Really? I'm impressed."

He hesitated before continuing. "Well...maybe two beers. By the way, how's your friend, Lyla? Man, that babe is hot! Quite a pair of headlights she's got." As he spoke, Viva entered the room. *Damn, Maxie! Do you have to say things like that out loud?* If she heard him, she didn't let on. My old high school bud may have changed, but he still had *obnoxious* on tap.

"Tell you later," I said, discreetly pressing my finger to my lips. Viva greeted us and I gave her my best smile. She'd been distant since the previous day. On our arrival, I'd introduced her to Maxie simply as my good friend, and nothing in our behavior suggested more than that. Maxie poured her coffee in a green mug with a red *S* inscribed on it, probably for his girlfriend, Sheila. She was away till next week, so he had the place to himself. My high school comrade set a cold croissant with a slice of cheese and some green olives on a ceramic plate beside Viva's coffee.

"Sorry it's not the Ritz, but the croissant is less than a week old." Maxie seemed amused at himself. "There's cereal and milk for Marisol when she gets up." Not one to complain, Viva ate the modest breakfast slowly, then joined us in the living room, taking a seat at the opposite end of the couch from me, gripping her coffee mug. She wore a sleeveless, beige blouse, khaki pants, and had her dyed-black hair tied in a ponytail. First time I'd seen her do that. Her cool manner and studied distance were like freezing wind on my back.

Maxie explained that he worked in security at the Golden Nugget, one of Las Vegas's famous casino hotels. My friend agreed that Mandala was likely the object of our search. But he said it could also be the MGM Grand. "If the girl you're looking for *is* at the Mandala, it's certainly convenient," he said, "I've got a friend who works there. Dante Ferraro. Smart as hell. He's lived in Vegas forever and knows just about everyone and everything. In fact, if I recall correctly…Dante used to work at the *Vegas Sun*. He's an information technology guy and also a hacker. One of the best, so he says, and I believe him. Guy's a genius."

Maxie texted Dante, then followed with a phone call. He paused in his chat and told me his tech buddy confirmed that Mandala was hosting a conference next week with the Arkom Corporation.

"Arkom!" I practically shouted, jumping to my feet, recalling what I'd learned from Seth's articles. "That's one of the main companies mentioned by Seth! He believed they're deeply involved in trafficking minors." Maxie stared at me silently, then nodded. He asked his friend for more info about the upcoming Arkom conference. They conversed several minutes, and Maxie invited him over, declaring it urgent.

"Dante'll be here within the hour," he said, ending the call. "He told me the conference starts on Friday and goes through Sunday afternoon. They've reserved the entire top floor. There's an activity center where the kids can hang."

"Kids? What do you mean, *kids*?"

"You know…small, young, immature humans. Even corporate execs have children."

"Why would they bring their kids to a Vegas conference?"

Maxie paused and thought a moment. "Okay, I see what you're driving at. Does seem strange. We'll ask my techie friend what he thinks."

"What do you know about Arkom?" I asked.

"Nothing, really. Dante says the CEO is a guy named Frost."

His words jolted me like a punch to the gut and I recalled Viva's reading at Jenna's. When talking about Seth's killers, she clearly described a frosty winter scene.

"Frost! Viva, do you remember?" I looked at my clairvoyant friend for confirmation. "Your reading at Jenna's house. He was *in your reading!*"

Viva sipped her coffee and pondered a moment.

"You were describing the people responsible for killing Seth. You described a winter scene with frost on the ground. You said the word "frost" at least twice. You were saying…in symbolic pictures…that Frost was responsible. Frost gave the order to kill Seth!"

"I remember. You and Michaela said I'd mentioned a frosty winter scene."

"That's uncanny!" Maxie said. "Proof you shouldn't take things too literally. Like the first time I went to a strip mall. By the time I put my clothes back on, they'd already arrested me."

I shook my head at Maxie's stab at comic relief and noticed Viva smile.

"Viva's amazing," I confirmed. It occurred to me that Frost must have requested through his crime network that preadolescent twin girls be at his conference. It repulsed me to think what he had in mind for them.

"Okay, Maxie," I said. "Your assignment over the next twenty-four hours is to find out all you can about Arkom Corp."

"I'll do that," Viva said, looking intently at me. "And it won't take twenty-four hours. May I borrow your laptop? Left mine in the car."

My cell buzzed as I nodded to Viva.

"Oh, hi Lyla! What's up?"

With my MacBook under her arm, Viva took a step toward the guest room and paused when she heard it was Lyla on the phone.

"That's great news," I said. "Let us know when you check in." Lyla told me they were driving into Vegas and asked me if I could recommend a hotel. I told her there was a strong chance the event would be at the Mandala. The call was brief and when it ended, I turned off my phone, set it on the coffee table, and glanced at Viva.

"That was Lyla," I said, announcing the obvious. "She and her dad are in Vegas."

"Lyla?" Maxie said. "That sexy babe you introduced me to in Phoenix? How are you two doing? Man, she sure has got the hots for you."

Maxie being subtle.

Viva's eyes flashed. She took Marisol's wrist, and with my laptop in her free hand, hurried into the guest room.

Damn! Way to throw a wrench in the works, dude.

"She'll be a better investigator than me," Maxie said, gesturing toward Viva. "Never was good at homework. But tell you what...I bet Dante already knows tons about Arkom." I was going to say something about Lyla not being my girlfriend, but Maxie's phone buzzed at nearly the same instant the doorbell rang.

"Speaking of the devil. That's him now." Maxie answered the door and a tall, thin man sauntered in the room. The IT expert wore a white T-shirt with a palm tree on it and sported several days of stubble on his chin and upper lip. He had a hawkish nose, a dark ponytail, and a broad smile. He radiated intelligence and humor.

"Dante, this is my bud, Jaden...Jaden, this is Dante Ferraro, hacker extraordinaire." I stood and extended my hand. Dante grinned broadly and we bumped fists. He seemed more sociable than most of the computer nerds I'd known.

Dante sat in a puffy armchair and Maxie brought him a mug of coffee. The tech wizard was a piece of work. He'd lived in Vegas about twenty years, having come originally from Silicon Valley where he'd been a tech guy at Apple and Microsoft. Made a ton of money but burned out and fled to Vegas. He kept extending his holiday and eventually decided to stay in the desert gambling mecca. He'd worked at the Vegas Sun for almost a decade prior to his current position as the Mandala tech guru.

Dante seemed excited about the prospect of helping us. He told us he'd known Seth when they both worked at the *Sun*. Being the former website manager at the paper, he promised some surprises.

"They don't know it but there's a back door into their site," he explained. "I know because I created it. I could hack into it in five minutes. We could really have some fun."

Dante confirmed that the CEO of Arkom was a man named Ethan Frost. "It's their twentieth anniversary gala," he said. "And they're celebrating the launch of a new business division of their company, Arkom Bank."

"That'll make it easier for them to launder money," I said.

Dante nodded. "No doubt," he said. "Even the dark side's got to pay its bills."

When Maxie and I told him our plan to free a trafficked girl, he got visibly excited. And angry.

"Damn!" he said. "I hate those fuckin' pervs. I'm all on board with you guys. I'm gonna screw these psychos over. Damn pedophile junkies…should stand before a firing squad. Or worse."

When Viva returned about an hour later, her manner had changed, and she was smiling with enthusiasm, like a teenager who'd just learned she made the cheerleading squad. Maxie introduced her to Dante, and they shook hands. She slid back onto the opposite end of the couch from me, her face alight.

"You look as if you found the Holy Grail," Maxie said.

"Not quite," she began, "but nearly as fascinating. Arkom's an arms manufacturer and dealer. Started in Texas. Been around a couple of decades. They sell rifles, ammo, and small arms weapons to the US government. It's rumored they have covert deals with the Mexican cartels. That's more confirmation that Mandala is the hotel we're looking for and Arkom is the conference."

"That would explain a lot," I said, thinking of Darko's trafficking operation. Through him Frost had a conduit for trafficked minors directly from the cartels. Arkom supplied the cartel with weapons. They supplied him with kids and drugs. Darko was a go-between, no doubt paid handsomely.

"And this is where it gets really interesting," Viva continued. "Frost has two companies he's heavily involved in. Arkom and Sagitta. He calls them '*The twins!*'"

"That's insane," I said. "He's really into some weird symbolism."

"Absolutely. But this is the clincher…" She smiled at me with a look of triumph. "Arkom and Sagitta are Latin for *bow* and *arrow!*"

"Unbelievable!" I said, sitting up with a start, grinning at my clairvoyant friend, recalling her confusing word enigma: "Follow the bow and arrow."

"Riddle solved!" I said.

"And that explains why he wanted twin girls," Viva added. She glanced at the guest room, then stepped across the carpet and gently closed the door so Marisol wouldn't hear. The young girl's English was rapidly improving, and we never knew for sure how much she grasped.

"So, bows and arrows mean something special to you?" Dante asked, eyebrows raised.

"It's a long story," I said, "but yes, it's confirmation that Arkom is the corporation we're looking for. Frost is the guy and Mandala is the hotel."

"Arkom and Sagitta…bow and arrow. Appropriate names for an arms manufacturer," Maxie said. "I understand they use the image of an archer as their logo."

"Amazing. It's all falling into place." I looked at my friend and she nodded, her coolness vanishing in the light of her discoveries. Viva's confident expression broadcast her feelings of vindication.

"Frost wanted twins for his conference and his network hired the cartel to get them," she said.

"Right," I affirmed. "Seth mentioned there was sex trafficking going on, and he named Arkom as a culprit."

Dante told us he and Seth had crossed paths a few times, and he'd read his articles in the *Vegas Sun*. The tech expert was furious when we told him who we believed were the suspects in our friend's murder. He didn't for a second think it was suicide.

"I read somewhere," the prodigy said, "a saying from some intelligence guy…CIA dude. 'Anyone can commit a murder. It takes a professional to commit a suicide.' So, it doesn't surprise me. These elitist bastards are the worst people on the planet. Probably fuckin' criminal satanists. I'm all in with you guys. We'll make 'em squirm. Hang 'em by the balls."

It appeared Dante could do even more than we dreamed of and was thrilled by the prospect. Not only did he possess ability to hack the *Vegas Sun*, but he had digital keys to the entire Mandala computer network. It was clear the success of our operation to rescue Marisa relied heavily on his participation.

"Won't this compromise your position at the hotel?" Viva asked.

Dante scratched his head. "No doubt," he said. "It could even get me killed. But it's time to move on. I'm ready to retire; in fact, I'm overdue. I'm giving notice tomorrow. Leaving the country. This'll be fun."

"I found out a few more things about Frost and his operations," Viva continued. "Seems Sagitta is a front or shell corporation, veiling other activities," she explained. "Possibly illegal drugs, as well as trafficking minors. Apparently Arkom and Sagitta supply arms to rebel groups internationally, along with Central American drug cartels."

"Running an illicit trafficking operation," Maxie said, shaking his head. "Dragging minors across the border. Fuckin' creeps."

"This is what Seth uncovered and got him killed," I said. "He named names and Arkom was one of them. They're probably protected in Washington by bribed politicians."

Dante was listening intently, hands folded in his lap. "Aren't all politicians bribed?" he said.

"We need to make things happen Friday night," I continued. "If we wait beyond then, they might do some horrible things to Marisa."

"Marisa?" Dante said, eyebrows raised.

"Marisol's twin sister. The girl we're trying to rescue. We think she's in the hotel already."

Dante's face creased with a frown, and he pressed his lips together. Abruptly clapping his hands, Maxie's hacker friend stood up to leave. "Four days to prepare," he said. "Not much time, but if you focus, it's an eon. I'll check into a few matters to make things go smoothly. See you tomorrow."

Despite Dante's seeming total commitment to our cause, I couldn't bring myself to fully trust him. At the same time, I realized that without him our chances of pulling off our sketchy plan were dreadfully slim.

As the tech wizard was leaving, Karina showed up at the door. Though happy to see her, it brought back an avalanche of distressing memories of my friend's murder.

"What *is* this? Grand Central Station?" Maxie said, hugging Seth's widow. I did the same, then introduced her to Viva, aware of the perfect round bump on her belly. A painful thought struck me: the murder of Seth carried a double crime, snatching away not only Karina's husband, but also the father of her child.

It was a somber reunion. Maxie spoke gently to her, with a tenderness that surprised me. It was a side to him I'd never seen. Karina was dressed in brown pants and a blue sweater, her blond hair tied in the back. Her eyes had dark circles around them, and she looked emotionally drained. Nonetheless, she smiled warmly and seemed relieved to see us. I sensed beneath her sorrow a prodigious emotional strength, and the fire in her eyes hinted at a desire to avenge her husband's murder.

"Tea or coffee?" Maxie asked as Karina settled into a comfortable, upholstered armchair.

"No thanks, I'm feeling a bit nauseous." She touched her

belly. "Not sure if you knew, but I'm expecting." Soberly, I remembered Seth and Karina had probably intended to announce their expected child when Maxie and I visited them on the day of the murder.

"Congratulations," Viva said, standing up and hugging Karina.

We all smiled, veiling mixed emotions, our cheerfulness dampened knowing Karina would welcome her child into the world without her husband beside her.

"You know," she started after an awkward silence. "Seth knew tons he never told me. There's much more on his laptop…the one they stole from the apartment. The unpublished article was only on that computer. Not on the one at home. So, nobody but the murderers have that information. Which is too bad because it would probably incriminate them and lead to the suspects. Other than the creeps who killed my husband, nobody has that article, not even me."

Viva was staring at me, and I sensed her thoughts.

"There's something I need to tell all of you," I began. "Fact is, there's someone else who has Seth's unpublished article." Maxie and Karina eyed me intently.

"Yeah, who?" Maxie asked.

I pointed at my heart. "Seth mailed his unpublished research to me after our meeting at his apartment. I've got it, and the dirtbags know." I paused to let my words sink in.

"I'm on their list," I continued. "They're looking for me."

Maxie's frown morphed into a wide grin, and he exhaled noisily. My Monterey buddy stood up, leaned toward me, and stretched out his hand, as if to congratulate me. I wasn't impressed by his gesture, but we shook hands.

"Welcome to tonight's episode of *America's Most Wanted*," he said with a theatrical air. "Our featured desperado this evening is Jaden Troy Parker…America's number one fugitive from the law. And from the lawless."

Karina and Viva were silent as Maxie glided toward the window and drew the shades. He ambled over to the coffee maker on the kitchen counter, gripped the half-full glass carafe, and held it in the air.

"Cold brew, anyone?"

We declined Maxie's offer. He poured himself a mug, took a swig, then sat down again.

CHAPTER 20

A Traitor Among Us

I described to them the incident at the Tempe Mission Palms as I was checking out of the hotel—and the two CIA types who confronted the receptionist about me. Hearing it for the first time, my clairvoyant friend raised her eyebrows.

"Sorry, Viva," I said. "Meant to tell you earlier, but the timing wasn't right." Expressionless, she nodded slightly.

We filled Karina in on the details of our plan to find Marisa and what we knew about Frost and the Arkom gathering. Seth's widow listened intently and finally spoke, confirming what we knew. "Seth only told me a few things about his findings, but he did mention Frost. He believed top executives of Arkom and Sagitta were among several corporations at the center of the trafficking." As far as she knew, he'd mentioned Frost by name only to her.

"I realize how dangerous it is for you, Jaden," she added, "but I'm relieved you have the article. Seth wouldn't let me have it. He wanted to protect me from everything. But I searched his computer and I've got the email addresses of over a hundred media outlets he planned to send the article to. Not just mainstream, but independent media—here and abroad."

"You're amazing," I said. "We can use those contacts. Listen, I have a crazy plan."

"Yeah? What?" Maxie clutched his mug, eyeing me skeptically.

"Friday evening at the opening of the conference, we make our move," I explained. "Karina, you be ready at your computer. I'll email you Seth's article, and when you get the signal, you send it out to all those media outlets. Just as Frost begins his keynote address."

Viva chewed on her lip. "Excellent. That needs to happen," she said, "but I think big media will protect the elites. They'll try to squelch it."

Karina nodded. "Seth always said mainstream mouthpieces would try and bury the truth. Say it's fake news. But people are starting to see through the lies."

"True," I agreed. "And who knows? Maybe some intrepid editors will go rogue and publish the news. Anyway, the alt-media will run with it, and it'll seep into the mainstream. Seth will be vindicated."

"If I can see the light," Maxie offered, "there's hope."

His cell rang. "Hey Jaden, it's your hot girlfriend Lyla!" With Maxie's permission, I'd given Lyla his number as an alternative if I couldn't be reached. *Shouldn't have turned off my cell!* Avoiding Viva's glance, I flashed Maxie a disgusted look.

Grinning, he handed me his phone.

"Hi, what's up?" Embarrassed by Maxie's tactlessness, I put the phone on speaker so Viva could hear.

"The cavalry's arrived," Lyla said. "We checked into the Mandala."

"Fabulous!"

"Hunter doesn't waste time. You know, he really liked that kid. The girl...Marisol. Dad's got a big heart."

"I'll say. What room are you in?"

"We actually have two rooms. Eighth floor, 853 and 851."

"Why two?"

"It's a Hunter thing. I'll let him explain." With the phone on speaker, we heard her father clearly.

"One thing I learned in the FBI," he said, "is you've got to have an operations room. So, I got two rooms. One for Lyla and me and one for operations."

"Sounds good," I said. "Stay tuned...we'll be in touch soon. Meanwhile, find out all you can about the Arkom conference. It starts Friday night."

"Will do," Lyla said, coming back on the line. "Can't wait to see you, Jadie," she added fondly. "I miss you. Hugs and kisses!"

"We've got allies," I said, avoiding Viva's gaze. Her voice was subdued when she spoke again.

"Speaking of allies," she said. "Dante's awesome. And if he's as brilliant as you say he is," she looked intently at Maxie, "maybe he can hack their website. Arkom's site, I mean."

Maxie nodded. "I bet he'd do it as a prank. He's a genius, but also crazy."

"And he's head of security at the hotel," I added, quietly jubilant at our good fortune. "I'm sure he's got a bag of tricks." It was clear the success of our operation to rescue Marisa relied heavily on Dante's cooperation.

"Speaking of security...what about the girl?" Karina asked,

nodding in the direction of the guest room where Marisol was leafing through magazines. As if on cue, the dark-haired refugee entered the room and stood beside Viva at the end of the couch.

"What do you mean?" I asked.

"Maybe she shouldn't stay here. I noticed a couple of vehicles parked outside with some weird-looking dudes inside. Do you think they're surveilling your apartment?"

"Hadn't thought of that," Maxie said.

"To be safe, she can go with me," Karina said. "I speak some Italian and French and can get by in Spanish." Her words made sense, though she too was a target. "By the way, don't mean to be nosy, but who's she?" Karina pointed at a framed picture on a shelf by the television of a smiling young woman in a soccer uniform.

"That's my girlfriend, Sheila," Maxie replied. "She's away till next week."

"Is that so? Well, as I was coming into your apartment, I saw a woman the spitting image of her in a parked car out front with two guys. They were pointing something at your door. Now I'm thinking it was probably a video camera."

My stomach felt as if I'd eaten another tamale from hell. I stared at Maxie. His mouth fell slightly open, and his eyes widened. He looked as if he'd just learned his pension was dissolved. Viva glared at Maxie with a dagger gaze as Karina's words sank in.

"Shit!" he muttered.

"Damn!" I said.

"Oh, God," said Viva.

Marisol nervously followed the conversation, seemingly more with her eyes than her ears. She slid between Viva and me on the couch, a frightened look on her innocent, young features. Viva put her arm around the dark-eyed girl and squeezed her gently.

CHAPTER 21

The Runaway

Karina's words dashed the hope and optimism I'd felt at our remarkable gathering. Things looked so promising till reality intruded. Reality does that.

"Damn Sheila!" Maxie said. "She can't keep her mouth shut. And she'll do anything for money. Well, almost anything. She's not a hooker."

At least, not that you're aware of, I thought to say, but checked myself.

"Do you think someone recruited her?" I asked.

Maxie shrugged. "She's been weird since I got home from Phoenix. I should never have told her about Seth and everything. She accused me of acting strange. Going bonkers. Becoming a conspiracy theorist."

"That's a compliment," I said.

"If you say so," Maxie replied, shaking his head and grimacing. "Honestly…I should've known better than to trust her. When God was making her brain, he ran out of clay."

"Look out the window," Karina suggested. "Make sure it's her." Maxie nodded.

"I'll do more than that," he said, and immediately strolled outside, headed directly toward the black Pontiac Cruiser where Karina had spied the Sheila lookalike. My Monterey friend reappeared minutes later, tense and angry.

"It's her. I'm sure of it. She hid her face as I went by, but I'd know her curly brown hair anywhere. And the two guys she's with look like perfect spooks. Short hair, sunglasses. Like they stepped straight off the set of *The Matrix*. And her car's parked down the street. There aren't many red Mustangs around these days. Stupid bitch."

"If we're under surveillance," Viva said, gazing at Karina. "You can't just leave with the girl. They'll track you."

"We'll go at three in the morning," Karina said. We fell silent, considering her words.

"Probably the safest thing to do," Viva said. "But are you and Marisol any safer at your place? To be honest, I'm surprised they haven't already raided you, considering they might be concerned about what Seth stored there."

Karina nodded solemnly. "Believe me, I've thought a lot about that."

We agreed it best for Karina to take Marisol with her early that morning. We also decided our fugitive shouldn't stay at her place more than a day. We'd need to come up with a Plan B.

"Probably should remove Seth's computer," I said. "They'd want that."

There were still several hours of daylight. We ordered pizza and attempted light chatter through the evening. Viva noticed an acoustic guitar in the corner of the living room and asked

Maxie if she could play it. He nodded and she strummed some chords. Marisol was enthralled and Viva entertained her with a couple of Mexican folk ballads. Her guitar playing was more than adequate and her soft, lilting soprano voice was enchanting. At least to my ears.

After we devoured the pepperoni pizzas, Maxie taught Marisol a card game and we all played, eager for something to distract us from brooding over the dangerous web into which we'd fallen. At dusk, Viva and our Mexican protégé headed to bed to give the girl a chance to sleep. Maxie let Karina use his room while he unrolled a sleeping bag on the floor. With phone alarms set for 2:30 in the morning, we tried to drift off.

Unable to fall asleep, my mind raced as I recalled the events of the past weeks and tried to tie it all together. Darko was in on the trafficking and provided high-level police protection and security. His network teamed up with the cartels to supply a steady stream of trafficked minors. These kids commanded a high price. Apparently, Marisol and Marisa were worth at least a hundred thousand dollars, of which Darko and his associates got a big cut. That explained why the dirty cop was so anxious to get hold of Marisol, to get paid. And also, to protect their whole scheme.

It was this network that Seth uncovered—and the fact that Frost's "twins," Arkom and Sagitta, were involved in the trafficking. No doubt my murdered friend knew much more and had been anxious to reveal it. He'd only hinted at pedophilia. Yet when underage kids are being trafficked to corporate execs, it doesn't take much imagination to fill in the gaps linking sex to the crime network. Obviously, the editors at the *Vegas Sun* were either paid off or otherwise pressured to smother the article. But it was unlikely they were directly involved in Seth's murder. The blame for that likely led directly to Frost himself, or some others of his elite ring of corporate criminals. The *Sun* could kill the article, but they couldn't prevent Seth from releasing the info and making it public. That was why the corporate big shots wanted him dead.

And now they knew I had the article, too.

With Lyla, Viva and me having serendipitously intervened in their scheme and rescued Marisol, the entire covert racket was compromised. Prior to his demise at Enchantment Resort, Darko must've tipped off corrupt elements of his law enforcement network about the girl's likely whereabouts. In turn, they signaled Frost's corporate security apparatus, and they too were on her and my trail.

The fact Maxie had been at the scene the day of Seth's murder made him an obvious target to surveil. Clearly, the Arkom security team could have approached Sheila and bribed her to provide info. She knew via Maxie that we were on our way.

Of course, with the media to front for them, it was possible nothing permanently damaging would come from Seth's or our accusations, but it obviously caused them serious concern. If the public got wind of a criminal scheme involving Central American cartels, elements of law enforcement, and high-level business executives, the crime syndicate would face a damaging scandal.

We'd stumbled into a rat's nest of frightening possibilities, and the circle was closing in on us. Our enemies were ruthless, implacable, and beyond deadly. And they were committed to our destruction. We were targets, and Maxie's place was no longer a refuge.

~

EARLY THAT MORNING, I awoke with a start, my fitful sleep once again disturbed by my periodic dream of ancient warriors battling. Sweating and shaking from the violence, I felt myself in the center of the gory combat. This time, again, I saw my father, gripping a shield and wielding a short sword in the thick of the fight. In the crazy surrealism of dreams, he'd lost his helmet. Growing up, my mother had removed all the obvious photos of him in our home—there were no pictures on the walls or framed snapshots on night tables. But I'd found a few pics of him when I went through her things after she died. I was struck by how closely my features matched his. This particular dream was especially shocking, not so much by my father's presence, but by an inscription painted on the breastplate of his armor. In a truly disturbing twist, in bold red letters I beheld the word ARKOM.

My agitation multiplied as I recalled the face of the Hawaiian-shirted man I'd seen in the Enchantment lobby with Darko, apparently the same individual I'd seen pull up into Machiavelli's parking lot—the driver of the white van that was supposed to pick up Marisol. The fact he so closely resembled an older version of me was beyond disturbing, and my imagination ran riot with a horrible possibility.

My father had last worked for a company I thought my mom said was ARCO. But now, I wondered if I'd mis-heard. Could it be that my father was driving for Arkom? If so, might he have been drawn into the insidious job of trafficking? Was he possibly the driver of the white van? Was this the message my surreal dream was attempting to convey from deep unconscious layers of universal mind?

My own father!?

I resolved to keep the depressing thoughts to myself.

The insolent ringing of phone alarms dashed my melancholy reflections, and I arose with the conviction we'd have to remove Seth's computer from Karina's apartment immediately and that meant Viva and I should leave that morning.

I told Viva and she agreed. Looking at her as she yawned and rubbed the sleep from her eyes, realizing how her connection to me and loyalty to Marisol had derailed her life, made me respect her even more.

We scrambled to collect our things and assembled at the door. Karina and Marisol would lead. Viva and I would wait a few minutes before exiting. Maxie grumbled he was calling a locksmith as soon as they opened—to change the locks. Sheila would never set foot in his apartment again, he swore. She'd have to pick up her stuff from the sidewalk.

Squeezing Karina's hand, I said we'd be by shortly for her husband's computer. Viva and I hugged Marisol and waved as the two of them fled the apartment by the back stairs that led to a grassy area behind the complex. From there they'd make their way to street parking and Karina's car.

Viva and I waited ten minutes after we heard her engine start before hurrying stealthily to our rented Chevy Malibu and driving off. *Thank you, Jenna!* A half hour later we pulled into an all-night eatery, the Badger Cafe, and ordered breakfast.

Fugitives again!

Food at Maxie's had been sparse, and I was famished. A heavyset waitress with the forearms of a wrestler, half-inch-long, fake black eyelashes, thick red lipstick, and the name tag Gladys, took our order: a grilled cheese sandwich and coleslaw for me, tuna melt on rye for Viva. And strong coffee.

We sat quietly and focused on our food as if it were our first restaurant meal after seven years at sea.

"I miss Marisol," I said, shattering the silence. I meant it, but mainly just wanted to say something to break the ice.

"Who wouldn't?" Viva responded. "She's adorable."

"I also miss you," I added, suspecting something I said or did irked her.

"Really? What about your hot babe girlfriend?" *Oh, so that's it.*

"Lyla likes me, okay? Something wrong with that?" Viva shrugged dismissively. "We're just friends. We've never even kissed."

"Missing out, are you?"

"What? You think I want to?" Viva was silent. The air felt like ice.

My cell phone rang; it was Karina.

"You guys better come early," she said. "I have a bad feeling. I'm gonna take Marisol and go to a hotel this afternoon. I've got Seth's computer ready for you. I'll take my laptop."

"Got it," I said. "We're having a bite and will be there within the hour." I asked Gladys for a pen and scribbled something on a napkin, then handed it to Viva. She glanced at it and stuck it in her purse.

We paid for our meal, thanked Gladys, and hurried to our car. There were still no signs of dawn in the inky Vegas sky as we drove toward Karina's.

"Any word from Luca?" I asked, breaking a cold silence.

"As a matter of fact, yes. I heard from him yesterday. He's been texting since we arrived in Vegas. I hesitated to respond, not a hundred percent sure it was him. He must've suspected that, so he mentioned something...the name of our first pet Golden Retriever. So, I texted back. He's still in hiding, but possibly heading to Vegas. Which is curious because he doesn't even know we're here. He says he's uncovered a ton of stuff about Darko's operation. I told him Darko's dead."

We pulled up to Karina's apartment and met her at the door. Her brow was creased, and her anxiety was palpable.

"Everything all right?" I asked.

"Maybe not. I just noticed someone tried to force the bedroom window open. Not sure when. Might have been last week while I was away. I don't feel safe here... with the girl...I'm not sure she should stay." Marisol appeared and stood beside Karina. I sensed she wanted to go with us.

I exhaled slowly, thinking. "Listen, take Marisol with you to the hotel. We'll come by tomorrow and pick her up. We've got to figure out where we're going. Maybe the Mandala. We've got friends there already."

I put my hand on the girl's shoulder. "You stay with Karina today and we'll get you tomorrow, okay?" Viva repeated in

Spanish, though I'm certain Marisol clearly grasped my words. Our young refugee flashed the gorgeous, innocent smile I'd grown to love.

I stepped inside and grabbed Seth's heavy iMac desktop. Glancing around, I saw on the mantle a framed picture of my murdered friend, along with some of their wedding photos. I winced to think of the heartbreak afflicting Karina.

We waved and headed to our car. Moments later we were on the road, unsure of our destination. Viva dozed off as I drove on Highway 15 for ten miles and then back into downtown Vegas, cruising slowly with the dense early-morning traffic. As red clouds streaked the dawn skyline, I pulled into the Mandala parking lot.

My phone rang. It was Karina, panicked.

"Everything okay?"

"No! No! No! It's awful. Horrible! Three men came just after you left. They wanted Marisol. There was no place to hide. There was nothing I could do!"

"They got her?"

"No! She ran away! She climbed through the back window and ran. I have no idea where she is or where she went. There's no sight of her anywhere. She just vanished!"

I was crushed. "It's…it's not your fault, Karina. It's okay. We'll figure out what to do."

"They left me alone. They wanted the girl. And Seth's computer. Thank God you took it. I'll be at that cheap hotel. Bye."

Defeated, I turned my face from Viva and stared out the window. She'd awoken from her slumber and heard everything.

"It's over," I said, despondent. "I failed her. It's my fault. I never should've let her leave us."

Viva put her hand on mine. "You did everything you could. *We* did everything we could. You're Marisol's hero. She adores you."

I closed my eyes and slumped in the seat, unable to face the truth.

Marisol was gone.

CHAPTER 22

Missing Time

There were no words. I was devastated. Our efforts were in vain. I'd failed Marisol and our plan was annihilated.

"What now?" I finally said, my voice a feeble whisper.

"We can still try to free Marisa," Viva said softly. I knew she was shattered and was putting on a brave face. "Marisol will find her way to a safe spot," she persisted. "She's a smart kid."

I wanted to believe her, but my spirit was crushed. Thinking to look for our runaway, I started the engine and headed toward Karina's neighborhood, but after a half hour of fruitless driving, scanning for any sign of the girl, a fog of hopelessness engulfed me.

I drove to a nearby casino parking lot, killed the engine, slumped in my seat, and didn't move for an hour. Only now, with Marisol gone, did I realize how deeply attached to her I'd grown. Her disappearance was a saber through my heart. Despite my heartache, I realized it was better that she'd run and not been nabbed by the agents. Small consolation in that anguished moment.

Wanting to stretch and give me space, Viva left the car and explored the environs of the casino hotel. Time to come to terms with the harsh new reality. Difficult as it was to accept, we'd have to find a way to move forward.

"I need to drive," I said, when Viva returned. "Are you all right with that?" She nodded and slid into the seat beside me.

"You need a navigator, right?" She gently touched my hand. The way she looked at me, her deep brown eyes full of sympathy, was more healing than any remedy. I keyed the ignition and pulled onto the street.

"Any idea where we're going?" she asked.

"Going?"

"As in, *destination*?"

My vague goal was to head for a desolate place at top speed. *Why let misery and heartache spoil a fun road trip?*

"Extraterrestrial highway," I muttered.

"What? Are you serious?"

I nodded. "Area Fifty-One. It's legendary. Top secret military base near Groom Lake. Ask Siri."

"Whatever you say, captain. Damn the torpedoes. Full speed ahead."

Racing along Interstate 15 to the turn off on Route 93, we drove the two hours to Area 51, urban legend and aeronautic wonderland hidden in the desolate Nevada landscape. The stuff of myth, mystique, and hyperbole, Area 51 is a military test site for stealth technology, and a celebrated epicenter of UFO lore and legend. I'd always been curious about the top-secret base.

We pulled off the road near a large, foreboding sign that read:

WARNING
Top Secret Research Facility
Use of Deadly Force Authorized

AREA 51
Restricted Area
Photography Prohibited

I said, "Makes you feel all warm and cozy, right?"

"Like being home for the holidays," Viva sarcastically agreed. "Where's my teddy?"

We stalked around a bit, discreetly taking photos despite the warning, and climbed back in our car. With nowhere to go, we drove a few miles to Rachel, Nevada, population forty-nine, to the "Little A 'Le 'Inn," a famed shop and cafe catering to curiosity seekers. We browsed through their eclectic selection of postcards featuring alleged photos of little gray aliens and strange disc-like aircraft supposedly spotted in the vicinity.

An earnest, friendly young man with a trim, reddish beard was happy to talk and told us he'd lived there five years—moved from Florida to be near the UFO action. There were all kinds of aircraft overflights, he said, day and night at any hour. Warthogs, troop transports, low-flying stealth jets.

Standing in the nucleus of the extraterrestrial cult, I hoped Area 51 would provide the dose of weirdness I needed to get my mind off Marisol and our colossal failure. But even the Extraterrestrial Highway couldn't completely distract me.

Reminded of the weird tales of alien abductions featured in UFO literature drove home the realization that Marisol and Marisa were *in fact* abductees. Victims in a horrific criminal enterprise that took place beneath the negligent scrutiny of government authorities and public figures. I was nauseated, wondering where our precious refugee might have wandered in the dense urban wilderness of one of the world's most notorious metropolitan pleasure dens.

We bought some postcards and left Rachel, this time driving slowly. "How are you feeling?" Viva asked.

"Terrible. Too much anguish for one day. Anguish isn't my native lingo."

Viva paused a long moment. "I know the feeling," she said, her voice soothing and sympathetic. "Anguish as a second language. It's the hardest to learn."

Unwilling to return to Vegas, I drove some more until creeping fatigue overpowered me. Viva hadn't slept much in two days, and I'd slept even less. We came upon a flimsy motel well off the beaten path, that looked as if it was built in 1950 and forgotten. Exhausted, we decided to quit for the day.

Too weary to talk, Viva showered and put on a robe. I showered after her. The mattress of the queen bed had a disagreeable hollow in the center, and we leaned into each other. Under normal circumstances, I would have grasped this opportunity for intimacy. But my insane weariness, shock, and sorrow at losing the young girl at the heart of our mission left me despondent and emotionally paralyzed.

Strangely, the cryptic words from Viva's reading at

Jenna's house sprang to mind. The odd riddle about Marisa's whereabouts: "You'll not find her in this century, but in the last year of the last decade of the eighteenth century." If we needed a time machine, I mused, Area 51 would be a good place to find one. Knowing that both twins were now lost was too much for me to bear.

When Viva got up to use the bathroom, I dozed off and didn't wake till ten the next day. Pushing aside my heartache, I rolled from the bed, wiped the sleep from my eyes, and for no sane reason began laughing.

"You okay?" Viva asked, eyeing me with concern. She was lying on the bed with her head propped up by her elbow.

"I'm fine," I shrugged. "For a moment I thought I'd call in sick but there's no one to call and I'm not even working."

Viva's eyes were sympathetic. "I get it," she said. "It's just the crazy wisdom of life that sometimes you have to laugh at the things that make you cry."

I nodded, resolving to embrace our new reality and head back to the city. Sleep is nature's daily miracle.

We drove toward Vegas through the paranormal Nevada bleakness, ate breakfast at a gloomy diner an hour from Area 51, then coasted into the Neon Capital in early afternoon. Still unsure what to do, I parked at the Mandala and turned on my phone while Viva stretched her legs in the parking lot. There were nearly a dozen messages from Maxie and Lyla, and with no response from me, the tenor of each grew more alarmed as the day progressed. I texted Maxie and told him we were parked outside the Mandala. Seconds later he called me.

"What the hell, bro! Are you alright? I thought you'd been abducted by aliens."

"That's not far from the truth. Definitely logged some missing time."

"I haven't heard from either you or Karina. What the hell's going on?"

I told him everything. That Marisol ran away to escape capture. That Seth's widow had gone to a hotel to get away from her apartment. And that we had cruised the Nevada desert for a day, trying to recover from the blow. Offering words of encouragement, my friend said we needed to move on, for Seth's sake if nothing else. We needed to get our murdered friend's article out, no matter the cost.

"You did everything you could," he told me, echoing Viva's words. I thanked him and said we'd be in touch soon.

Then I texted Lyla and told her we were parked outside the hotel but got no response. Maxie called back a few minutes later and said he'd contacted Dante and to expect his call. "And the good news," my Monterey bud added, "is he wants to try and hack the Arkom website. If anyone can, he can."

The tech wizard buzzed moments later.

"Listen," he said. "I know you must feel terrible, but we can still move forward. You've got friends staying in the Mandala, right?"

"Right."

"Well, I'm in the hotel now. I can shut down the security cameras for ten minutes while you go inside with your lady friend. Go to your friend's room and we'll make up the next step as we go. We can still rescue that Marisa girl. I've got some tricks up my sleeve I'm itching to try. We can expose this trafficking ring and kick these psychos in the balls. Trust me."

I thanked Dante and told him we'd enter the hotel that afternoon between three o'clock and ten after. I called Lyla but she didn't answer. We'd make our move regardless.

Viva arrived at the car, and I filled her in on my conversations. "You're back on track," she said and squeezed my hand. Despite our failure, I was determined to keep on keeping on. With Dante's help and a big dose of luck, there was hope. If Marisa was in the Mandala, we might still rescue her. It was a big *if*.

Realizing Lyla and Hunter's rooms were the safest spots for our computers, we put them in our luggage. Seth's desktop barely fit in my suitcase, so I abandoned half my clothes in the car. Viva lugged our laptops in her shoulder bag.

I'd stopped wearing my Hawaiian shirts in Sedona, but they seemed appropriate in Vegas. I changed in the parking lot, donning the gaudy, red floral one. With my baseball cap and Ray-Ban's, I looked like a random casual tourist, eager to hit the casino. Viva was gorgeous in a blue, tight-fitting blouse, white shorts, and tennis shoes. Computer-laden suitcase in tow, my free arm around Viva's shoulders, at three minutes to three we strolled toward the front entrance of the Mandala.

I studied my phone, and at one minute after the hour we cruised through the big glass doors of the celebrated casino resort.

CHAPTER 23

Central Command

There were people everywhere. The oddly soothing, seductive ringing of the gambling machines filled the atmosphere. One armed bandits, my mother called them, referring to the old slot machines in operation a century ago. You pulled down on an arm-like lever, spinning the reels, appealing to Lady Luck. The modern generation of slots have no arms and are all high tech and glitzy—designed to keep players in that hazy addictive zone where it's just you and the machine. *They're still bandits, though.*

Viva and I had no interest in the games and had no need to stand in line to check in with reception. Our goal was Lyla's and Hunter's rooms on the eighth floor, and we made our way to the elevator core without stopping.

Cramming in the conveyer, there could be no doubt we were in Vegas. Nearly half the occupants still had on sunglasses, despite the darkness of the cavernous casino. The elevator reeked of perfume and cologne, mixed with the overpowering scent of sweat and liquor. I imagined if remorse and fear-of-losing had an odor, they were there too. The expressions on faces ranged from exhilaration to beyond jaded. I'd hoped that people, seeing us burdened with our luggage, might give us room. That was a fantasy. Pushed to the back of the elevator, I faced off with an exceptionally large, middle-aged woman in an undersized bathing suit. I gazed at the ceiling to avoid staring at her massive breasts, though she probably wouldn't have cared. Viva seemed amused; at least her smile suggested it.

Reaching the eighth floor and being at the very back presented a logistics problem. Fortunately, like Moses parting the Red Sea, we were able to push ourselves through the crush of bodies. Stumbling onto the eighth floor with our possessions, I felt like we'd reached our Promised Land. Then I remembered Marisol, and my momentary euphoria dissolved again into disappointment. I couldn't shake the depressing feeling of failure. We'd made it this far on our bizarre desert odyssey, only to lose our prize companion.

Rooms 853 and 851 were almost at the end of the corridor. As we trundled our luggage down the hallway, I wondered why Lyla hadn't responded to my texts and calls, especially since she'd texted me steadily yesterday. We knocked on 853 and got no response. Maybe they were at the pool or playing slots. I couldn't imagine Lyla gambling, but perhaps that was Hunter's thing. He certainly wasn't risk-averse and had a pension or two to fall back on.

We tried 851 and waited.

"Who is it?" I was relieved to hear Lyla's voice.

I thought to say "room service" but held back. "You've got a surprise visitor," I said.

The door swung open, and Lyla stood there in a white bath robe, smiling serenely. She wore her dark-framed glasses and had her hair tied back in a ponytail, the way it was when I'd first met her in Tattered Pages. She embraced me and shook Viva's hand cordially as we entered the room. Seated on the chair by the window, Hunter tossed us a wave and a smile, but didn't move. I recalled his bad back.

"Great to see you guys! I can't believe we're here," I said. "It seems an eon. Unfortunately, we've got bad news. It's a long story, but Marisol ran away." I paused, shaking my head, and sat at the edge of one of the two queen beds. "We left her with a friend here in Vegas and the bad guys came after her. I'm devastated… just hoping her twin sister is in the hotel so it's not a total loss." For the first time since Marisol's disappearance, I nearly choked with emotion and had to check myself. Viva sat beside me and put her hand on my back. "I…I was going with the idea I was unstoppable. Forget that."

"Jaden, you're amazing," Lyla said. "I can imagine how awful you feel. I've got to say, though, you're not the only surprise visitor today." She swiveled her head toward the bathroom and called out. "Sweetheart!" The lavatory door swung wide, and we heard a gleeful squeal. A dark-haired girl burst from inside and raced into my arms.

"Marisol!" I shouted.

Our runaway was home.

I lifted the precious girl above my head, spun her around, then slowly set her down beside Viva, who embraced her and held her tightly for a long time. Marisol laughed with delight and happiness.

"Qué pasó? What happened?" Viva asked her.

Breathlessly, Marisol explained in Spanish how she'd run away from Karina's to escape the creeps who'd come to apprehend her.

"How in the world did you know where to go?" I asked, heart pounding with excitement.

"*Sabia el nombre del hotel.* Mandala. *Y los números,* eight-five-three. *También,* eight-five-one." Marisol knew the name of the hotel and the room numbers.

"You taught her English numbers, remember?" Viva said.

"Amazing. Brilliant *chica!*" I said, hugging her, recalling how intently she'd followed our conversations at Maxie's. Obviously, she'd grasped far more than we realized.

We learned that Marisol had hiked the four miles from Karina's apartment to the Mandala. She found the route by asking some Mexican workers for directions. Once she knew the hotel's distinct appearance in the Vegas skyline, it was relatively easy to make her way.

Reaching the massive structure in the evening, she waited by the entrance till a big group of casino patrons approached, slipped in among them, and simply strolled in. No one stopped her, and she made it to the elevators. The rest was easy. She'd slept the night in Lyla's bed. Hunter used the other room.

"It was the surprise of my life when she knocked," Lyla said. "Not hearing from you, we hesitated to text or call to let you know she was here in case you were in trouble—on the chance your phone was confiscated. But when I got your last text saying you were on the way up, I couldn't resist surprising you. And Marisol loved the idea."

"*Una sorpresa!*" the girl beamed.

"I'm stunned," I said, giddy with happiness. "This may be the best day of my life."

"And mine," Viva said. She and I sat on the edge of a bed with Marisol sandwiched between us, her hands in each of ours. Our runaway looked up at me with joy and pride. It was the first time she'd shown me much affection, and I basked in it, feeling as if I were a parent reunited with my missing child.

"This calls for a celebration," Hunter announced from his seat in the corner. "I'm ordering pizza." Lyla's dad ordered room service as we compared notes and stories.

"Amazing," said Lyla, after hearing our exploits since leaving Phoenix a week before. "Sounds like a paranoid fever dream."

"It's been nightmarish, but at the moment it feels transcendent," I said. "And the real action has yet to begin."

"That's why we're here," said Hunter, standing and stretching his arms over his head. "Time to set up the command room and figure out the plan."

"I'm making this up as I go," I conceded.

"So far, so good," Lyla said, smiling gorgeously.

The food arrived and we divvied it up. Three New York-style pizzas, spicy shrimp tacos, and "Border Guacamole" with chips.

"Courtesy of the US government," Hunter said. "Via my pension, that is."

"Three cheers for Hunter!" Viva, said, holding up her paper cup filled with surprisingly bold hotel coffee. Tomorrow held danger and uncertainty, but we'd lived to see another day. And we still had our most precious cargo...Marisol.

"You three young ladies sleep here," Hunter said, handing

a room key to Viva. I wondered how she and Lyla would get along. "Jaden and I will take the other room. Time to work out our plan." The two rooms were connected by a door that locked from either side, so we didn't have to use the hallway. *Ingenious set up,* I thought. *Hunter's no slouch.*

We set up Seth's desktop in my and Hunter's room—which he christened "CENTCOM." It was comforting having Lyla's dad with us. Despite his bad back and slight limp, he projected that ex-Special Forces, ex-FBI confidence we sorely needed, even if it was just an old guy blustering.

I texted Dante and Maxie to say we were safely in the hotel. Utterly drained emotionally, I had no clue what to do next. My brain was fried.

My phone rang. It was Dante.

"Kudos on getting in, man. The security cameras were off so everything's cool in that regard. Not that it probably mattered, but the devil is in the details."

"For sure," I concurred. I wanted to project an aura of confidence to Dante but was so spent it was all I could do to keep my eyes open. I decided not to mention Marisol's miraculous reappearance. "We'll have to make our move Friday night," I offered. "We'll need you to do some hacking tricks."

"Wait till you see what I've got in mind," Dante said. "You'll be stoked. I need someone to write some short articles about Frost and Arkom. Something along the lines of an exposé of his crimes. Something to embarrass him."

"I think we can do that," I said. "Let me get back to you in the morning."

No sooner had I ended Dante's call than my phone buzzed again, this time Maxie. I figured he also didn't need to know about Marisol's return just yet. Even among friends, some secrets are worth keeping.

"Congrats, man!" he said. "You made it! I was worried, let me tell you. Lady Luck loves you."

"Maybe so. Maybe I should play the slots."

"No time for that. Listen, Karina got in touch. She feels awful about the girl, but she's keen on sending out Seth's article. You should contact her and decide when to email it to her. She said those hundred media contacts are on Seth's desktop, which she said you have. Maybe you can get in touch with her and figure out how to make things happen."

"Where is she?"

"The Star Motel. Room 212. You got her phone number, right?"

"Right. I'll call her now."

"Oh, and one more thing," Maxie said.

"Yeah? What?"

"Send the articles to me, too. All of them. Everything Seth sent you."

"You sure?"

"Positive. I want to do my part."

"Will do, my friend." *Maxie really has changed.*

Ending the call, I texted Seth's widow. The message came up: *Karina has notifications silenced.*

I poked my head into the adjoining room and was surprised to see Viva with Tarot cards laid out before her on the bedspread. Lyla was seated opposite her with legs crossed, watching every move. Marisol was stretched out fully on her stomach, hands to her face, observing carefully. Viva was reading Lyla's cards.

"Another psychic fair," I said. "I'll leave you gypsies to determine our future." They waved but were absorbed in the card layout, so I ducked back into CENTCOM.

Despite his recent bravado, coming off like a general in the war room, Hunter was asleep on the bed, snoring softly.

We look like a bunch of wimps. I don't think we could rescue a puppy from the pound.

The insulation between rooms left much to be desired and I could make out some of Viva's words. I heard her say *lovers*, and *relationship*, among a few other snippets, and I imagined her telling Lyla that she and I were lovers, despite the fact we'd never taken that step. They were laughing and I could hear Marisol's giggles punctuating the conversation; I wondered how much of the dialogue she followed.

After eavesdropping for a few seconds, I flicked on the remote and found NFL highlights featuring Super Bowl flashbacks. Zoning out, I evaded reality for a brief interlude. My mental hiatus was interrupted by a knock on the door. It was Viva. She was taking Marisol for a stroll and some fresh air. Our refugee girl looked almost comical in a blonde wig and sunglasses Lyla had procured for a disguise.

"When you get back, I need you to compose some short pieces for Dante," I said. "Spoofs about Arkom and Frost. Fake news to make them look bad, but also actual stuff about their trafficking. Stuff that will embarrass them if Dante hacks their site. Just a paragraph or two each. Can be taken directly from Seth's articles."

"Got it. I'll start as soon as we're back." Viva smiled and tossed me a kiss, which lifted my mood. As she left the room with Marisol, Hunter roused himself and said he was hitting the lobby to stretch his legs.

Moments after he left the room, a gentle knock came again, and I opened the door for Lyla. For the first time since our fateful lunch at Machiavelli's, when we miraculously received Marisol, it was just the two of us. Smiling seductively, she took my hand and pulled me beside her on the edge of the bed. We were alone.

"It's so great to see you, Jaden," she began. "I've missed you!" She'd changed out of her bathrobe and was wearing loose-fitting purple yoga pants and a tight-fitting, burgundy-hued, spandex workout top that hugged her breasts. Ponytail down, her tresses seemed thicker than when I'd seen her last and framed her attractive features in a beguiling brunette softness. Lyla oozed the implicit confidence of a woman who could instantly attract nearly anyone if that was her intent.

"I know! So great to be together again. Feels like a lifetime."

"Wow! You know, Viva's amazing! She read my cards and said she'd do my horoscope at some point. After the dust settles. I told her I'm a triple Scorpio and she laughed. I really like her."

"I'm glad. Me too. She's amazing."

"She's gorgeous. Well, I thought you two were maybe together, but when I asked her, she said you were just friends."

"She said that?"

"Yup. You know, Jaden, honestly…that made my day. I never told you this, but I've never met a guy like you. You're half humility and half bravado, and I like both halves. Viva said my signature card for the reading was The Lovers. She told me I might be entering a new love relationship. And she said I'd probably already met him…and when she said that, like, I confess, this may sound crazy, but I thought of you. Of us." Lyla smiled and squeezed my hand. My charming, funny friend transformed before me into the goddess Aphrodite.

"Whatever happens the next few days, I want you to know I…I think you're awesome and special and I really like you and… well, I'd just love to really spend some serious time with you. If you're open to that." I couldn't speak. My mind raced, registering the implications of her words.

Lyla leaned into me, threw her arms around my neck, and kissed me hard on the mouth. We held the kiss for several seconds before she let go. It was overpowering and my head spun, and I felt as if the room was shaking.

"Umm…thanks, Lyla, I think, I mean, I think you're awesome, too. Let me…let me just get my head screwed on right. With everything that's happened, I feel as if I've been hit by a Mike Tyson uppercut. Just need to get my bearings and clear my head. And we've got some heavy-duty priorities to deal with next two days. Okay?"

She smiled and held my hand. "Oh, I understand. Totally. No hanky-panky or anything. Not here. Not now. Lots to deal with, for sure. And we're not alone, obviously. My dad's so funny. I feel like I'm being chaperoned." She giggled and squeezed my hands again. "Just want to let you know how I feel."

She got up from the bed, threw me a dazzling smile, and sauntered out of the room into the hallway, letting the door close loudly behind her. I sat for a moment, mesmerized. Stunned and giddy, I got up and stumbled around the room, finally collapsing back on the bed.

CHAPTER 24

In the Belly of the Beast

If Frost and his network didn't kill me, the off-the-rails trainwreck that was my life surely would.

My brain was on fire, and I wanted to melt into the bed. My joy at Marisol's return dissolved, replaced by anguish at Lyla's revelation. Not by her display of nymphlike affection—certainly as powerful a dose of love medicine as I'd ever experienced. What hurt me were Viva's words to her. My heart felt as if struck by a dart soaked in curare poison.

Viva *seemed* to enjoy my company. We synched on most things and shared mainly upbeat chemistry. There wasn't much friction. Except for her annoyance at my *already having a girl-friend,* the notion of which I'd tried to erase. Was I simply delusional? I'd nursed the belief she'd reciprocate the feelings I projected onto her. But obviously she didn't. I'd have to accept the fact she simply wasn't interested in an intimate relationship. A classic case of unrequited love. Clearly, I was deceiving myself. *What a naive idiot!*

I suspected Viva saw something in my horoscope that bothered her. Or perhaps in relation of her chart to mine. Astrologers call it "synastry," comparing the horoscopes of people to see if they're a good match. It's been practiced in Asia for thousands of years. In some circles in India, families wouldn't think of arranging a marriage without consulting an astrologer for compatibility. Possibly Viva spotted a red flag in our chart comparison that led her to back away. A lack of affinity, perhaps.

Viva was a pro at reading other people: astrologically, with the cards, and through her clairvoyant gift. Yet she herself was hard to read. At least, I couldn't get a clear sense of her feelings. Knowing the acute dangers involved in our efforts, she could've flown any time. Yet she chose not to. No doubt she felt a measure of loyalty to Marisol and to "our mission" to save her and rescue her missing sister. But she wasn't *required* to stick her neck out and put her life at risk. She *seemed* to like me…laughing at my jokes and smiling as we talked. We had many similar interests, though we were also very different. She was a mystery. And she showed signs of jealousy. Yes, it was unmistakable. She was jealous. Maybe that explained her being so stubbornly noncommittal. She'd likely been recently damaged in a close relationship. She'd hinted that, so maybe she was on the rebound and distrustful. She wasn't interested in amorous flings; she wanted true commitment or nothing. Yet she inspired feelings in me I'd never known with any other woman. I concluded she didn't trust me. No doubt there was more to it than that.

Regardless of the reasons, clearly it was time to move on. I had to shove other considerations aside and focus. We had to find Marisa and send out Seth's article. Everything else was a distraction.

The prospect of locating the missing twin was slender at best. I truly was delusional. A certified idiot. It was all wishful thinking. What could we really do? Against all odds. But that was precisely it! We'd accomplished all this so far *against all odds*. Here we were, in the belly of the beast. In the hotel where Frost's conference would start in a couple of days. Against all odds... we'd made it this far, and miraculously, Marisol was still with us. According to Darko's words, Marisa was here, too, in the hotel. We *could* find her. Especially having Dante's help. That alone was astonishing. Incredible, really. That Maxie should work at The Golden Nugget and just happen to know the head of security at the Mandala. There was some invisible hand at work, some miraculous intervention. Michaela's otherworldly presence on the path at Enchantment Resort—after Darko plunged to his death—symbolized it.

In the end, it didn't really matter if I lost Viva. All that mattered was the cause, the goal, the striving. The effort we make to love, to seek truth, and to stand up for that truth. Our deeds live on in eternity. If I died tomorrow, so what? Everyone dies. Only by dying can you live forever. *Wake up from your slumber, Jaden. Your choice matters now...and it matters always.*

My reveries were interrupted as Viva and Marisol returned from their excursion to the pool. I rolled off the bed and walked into their room to greet them. Moments later, Lyla sauntered in, a bouquet of red roses in her hand. "Just want to make the place festive," she said, winking at me. She'd acquired several board games from guest services and she and Marisol began playing checkers. Hunter returned to CENTCOM and began working on

Seth's Mac. At least, he said he was working. I supposed he was just wasting time web-surfing.

My mobile buzzed. It was Maxie. "Listen, I've had visitors at my apartment," he said, his voice low and troubled. "Law enforcement types. Asking questions. They wanted to know if a young Mexican girl was here. And they asked about you and Viva. I told them nothing. Not a word."

"You better be careful your phone wasn't bugged," I said.

"I understand. I'll only use my cell. I want to be of help to you guys, but I don't want to jinx you."

"Lie low," I said. "And by the way, thanks for recruiting Dante to the cause. He's proving to be indispensable."

"Glad to know. I knew he would be. I'm thinking of asking him if I could stay at his place a night or two."

I ended the call with Maxie and focused on helping Viva. She'd started to write the articles Dante needed for his hack. Figuring it was now or never, I emailed Seth's article to her.

"There you go," I said. "Now we're both doomed."

"Thanks for sharing," she said, managing a smile. She spent several minutes scrolling through the pages of the article before she spoke.

"This stuff is amazing! He says the trafficking and pedophile activities go right up to the top of the global food chain. Politicians, business leaders, Hollywood personalities. Even some religious figures and elements of the clergy. This is the most explosive stuff I've ever read. Yet lots of it's suggestive. For the most part, he doesn't name individuals' names. He keeps it to organizations. And yet it still got him killed."

"He hit a nerve," I said. "I think they were worried what he'd write next. He was laying the groundwork in this article for even more explosive and damaging material. It's probably all on his computer if we had time to search."

Reading on, Viva's face hardened. "It's really sick," she said grimly. "Seth claims the goal of these elitist psychopaths is to normalize pedophilia, so their crimes are no longer viewed as criminal."

"Perverts. Let them hang," I muttered.

"They're criminal psychopaths," Viva said, shaking her head.

"I keep hearing that word," Lyla said, looking up from her game of checkers. "What's the difference between a psychopath and a sociopath?"

"The difference," I volunteered, "is that a sociopath will hire someone to kill you. A psychopath will do the job himself."

As Viva continued to work on the articles and Lyla went back to her board games with Marisol, I moved next door to CENTCOM for a breather and to think. Hunter had gone out again. Sitting at the little desk, I scribbled notes on a hotel message pad, listing the goals we had to accomplish. Number one on the list was locating Marisa. Ditto for numbers two and three. I circled numbers one through three, crumpled the note and tossed it at the wastebasket. I missed and it landed in Hunter's open suitcase on his bed. I shuttled over to recover it and my hand touched cold, hard metal. Brushing away a pair of socks, I noticed a handgun. *Hunter is deadly serious about all this, after all.*

Going back to the adjoining room, Viva and I spent the next three hours cutting and pasting sections of Seth's article. We lifted entire paragraphs verbatim, making minor edits, and formatted them into simple stories with bold headlines. Sometimes Viva would read aloud a portion she'd written to get feedback. Headlines included:

C.E.O. Frost Admits He Traffics Kids.
Arkom Conference Shelters Child Abductees.
Are Corporations Involved in the Trafficking of Minors?
The answer is Yes.

She shared a statement she'd just written: "Frost says he's in it for the thrills more than the money."

"Whoa! Better be careful, even if it's a prank," I said. "Let's keep the wording close to Seth's. They can't kill him twice."

"We're sure putting a lot of trust in Dante," Lyla said, looking up from the checkerboard. "Maybe too much. What if he can't hack in? Or it backfires?"

"Those are the risks," I said. "That's the way it is. Thankfully, he's on our side. At least, I *think* he's on our side. If he knows enough to hack them, he'll know enough to hide his tracks."

"We'll see," Lyla said. She turned on the television and started surfing the network wasteland, stopping at a local news station.

After the talking head reported on a local crime spree, the image of a white-haired man in a business suit flashed on the screen. "Wow! Get a load of this!" Lyla said.

I glanced up from my laptop in time to see the televised image of Ethan Frost, holding an enormous publicity check on oversize poster board, made out to the Las Vegas Police Department. The newscaster said words to the effect that Arkom CEO Ethan Frost is bringing his company to its annual convention in Las Vegas and is contributing to the local police chapter of Boy's and Girl's Clubs of America. "Giving back to our community is an important part of our corporate outreach," Frost said. "In other local news, two men robbed a convenience store on Market Street…" Lyla clicked it off.

"Can you believe it!" she said. "Public relations crap."

"I'd call it bribery to keep the police and local government in line," Viva said. "Smart dude, though."

"It's typical PR," I said "Winning the war of public opinion. But it's really just putting lipstick on a pig. Wipe away the PR cosmetics, Frost is still a pig."

"He's obviously in town," Viva said. "Perhaps at the hotel already."

"Gives me the creeps," said Lyla. "Maybe Dante knows."

Another call came on my mobile, this time from the tech guru. "We were just talking about you. What's up?" I asked.

"I need to introduce you to an extremely important person. Can you and your two lady friends be ready at eight tomorrow morning?"

"We'll be ready," I said. While Dante tried to pump me up, saying I'd love what he had in store for Friday night, I wondered what *extremely important person* he had lined up. Still not trusting him fully despite my words of assurance to the others, I even imagined it could be Ethan Frost, supported by a contingent of police. The pressure of external events on my overloaded mental landscape created a surreal reality, and my imagination tilted between visions of jubilant celebration and Hieronymus Bosch hellishness.

"By the way," I continued when he'd finished. "We noticed on local news that Frost is in town. Has he arrived at the hotel yet?" Dante hesitated, then said he'd try and find out. I ended the call and turned to Lyla and Viva.

"We meet with Dante here at eight," I said. "Arkom guests start arriving in earnest tomorrow. We've got to figure out how to find Marisa."

Viva was still glued to her laptop. I put my hand on her shoulder and told her it was time to quit. "Better get some sleep," I said.

Hunter appeared through the door and made a beeline for the fridge.

"We're up against heavy odds," I said to no one in particular. "If we fail, we're toast. Whatever happens, this'll make headlines."

Hunter pulled a beer from the fridge, popped the cap, waved the can at each of us in turn, as if saluting. "Congrats. We're about to be famous," he said.

"Let's hope it's not posthumously," I said. "Dying has long-term consequences."

"Don't be morbid," Viva protested.

"No point worrying," Hunter persisted. "Nobody's immortal forever."

"Right," I said. "Enjoy the show. Go out with a bang."

I lifted my water glass and saluted my friends, opened the door to my and Hunter's room, backed in, and let it close hard behind me.

CHAPTER 25

Glock 44

"This is Elsie," Dante said, introducing us to a small, plump woman with dyed, auburn hair covering all but a gray streak visible at the roots. She wore the dark beige work dress of the hotel staff. "Elsie is head of housekeeping."

Viva, Lyla, and I were gathered in room 851, while Hunter was making coffee next door. "I suggest you introduce your runaway girl to Elsie and tell her what you're trying to do," Dante continued, while escorting Elsie into our chamber. "She'll be discreet, I assure you."

Everything was risky so there was no point in resisting. If we couldn't trust Dante now, our efforts were futile. We shook hands in turn with Elsie as she sat down on the most comfortable chair in the room, and we gathered around her in a semi-circle.

Dante insisted we needed Elsie to pull off our plans, and he'd convinced her that meeting us was *muy importante*. The two of them were on casual speaking terms, having both been employed at the hotel for many years. She was Guatemalan, had lived in the US for three decades, and had worked at Mandala for most of them.

Viva spoke in Spanish to her, introducing Marisol. She told

her the young girl had been kidnapped in Mexico by agents of a drug cartel, and that her twin sister, Marisa, had also been snatched away, and might be at the hotel. Our goal was to rescue her sister. Marisol then explained to Elsie how the abduction took place.

As the girl spoke, Elsie's eyes filled with tears. She pulled out a beaded, silvery rosary from her uniform pocket and began touching the beads. *"Madre de Dios!"* she said, and hugged Marisol when she finished her story. The head of housekeeping promised she would do all she could to help us.

We had another essential ally.

An hour later, Elsie toted three housekeeping uniforms to our room for Lyla, Viva, and me. Two of the uniforms were standard garb for hotel staff who cleaned guest rooms, and mine was general maintenance. She produced three name tags as well. Darlene, Sophia, and Lionel.

Elsie then advised us to tell any hotel staff who asked that we'd just started work and were training. We arranged to meet Elsie in the early afternoon in the housekeeping staff room on the first floor so she could show us around. The meeting ended and Dante and Elsie left the room.

"Now what?" Lyla asked.

"Maybe try on the uniforms," I said.

"Good idea," Viva agreed.

The uniforms fit decently well. "You look so fashionable," Lyla said.

"Always trendy," I replied. Hunter asked me if I would please remove the trash from the rooms. I declined.

For his part, Hunter spent a lot of time moving between the several hotel bars and didn't seem at all focused on our goal. When I gently brought up the subject, he became defensive, saying he'd been texting and emailing for much of the past two days, and assured us he'd been in touch with some old law enforcement colleagues. I assumed he meant FBI. He said their response was encouraging but offered little else. Despite his assurances, I began to doubt Hunter was the strong asset I'd imagined.

That afternoon, still wearing our hotel uniforms, Viva, Lyla, and I waited by the door for Hunter's signal. When the ex-Special Forces fighter saw no one in the corridor, he gave us the all-clear, and we took the freight elevator down to the staff area on the first floor and met Elsie and Dante.

"I only have a minute," Dante said. "Listen. Arkom has its own plainclothes security, so be on your guard. If they see something that strikes them as suspect, they might question you. Frost isn't here yet, as far as I know. He'll likely arrive tomorrow. I'll check in with you about that later. Meanwhile, you're in good hands with Elsie." He nodded at the head of housekeeping, pivoted, and hustled away.

Elsie showed us around the staff maintenance area and the break room. The nearby first aid room caught Lyla's attention. "May I look in?" she asked. "I'm a nurse, you know," she reminded us. "Well, almost."

"What're those for?" she asked, pointing to a medical kit with syringes when we'd entered the room.

"A couple of things," Elsie explained. "We keep some insulin in the fridge for diabetics in case of emergencies. There are also tranquilizers...in case we have, how you say? Rowdies? You know...*desperadoes*. Maybe crazies high on drugs...this will knock them out."

"Guess you have to be prepared for anything at a major resort in Las Vegas," Viva said.

"Absolutely," Elsie said with a smile.

"Now for the big moment," she announced. "I'm taking you up to the eighteenth floor where Arkom guests are staying. We're only going to walk down the corridor and back. Dante told me Frost reserved the room at the end, a large suite. Beside it is the workout room."

Elsie supplied us with housekeeping keys that could access any room, then led us to the elevator and we rode up to our destination. We exited the lift and headed with her down the well-lit corridor. When a couple of men walked by us, I took care to avoid eye contact, staring at the floor as we passed. Elsie pointed out the emergency stairwell and the exercise room.

When we finished the abbreviated tour, she took us back to the freight elevator and we descended to the housekeeping break room. Her day was over, she told us, and she didn't normally work Fridays, but she was making an exception, coming in tomorrow to be available if we needed her. We thanked her and took the elevator to the eighth floor one at a time to be less conspicuous.

Back in room 853, I shed my hotel uniform and hung it in the closet. Hunter was seated at the end of the bed. To my surprise, he pulled out his handgun and began checking it.

"You look the part now," I said. "Channeling your inner, Special Forces self."

"This handgun's not something I ever used in the military," Hunter said, "but it's powerful. A Glock 44. Are you a weapons aficionado?"

"Hardly. Growing up I thought a Smith and Wesson was a bicycle." Hunter laughed. "But my grandpa did teach me to shoot a .22 rifle. I was pretty good at that."

Hunter smiled. "That's a high-powered toy. This'll stop a grizzly." He held it up and pulled out the cartridge magazine. "And I have a rifle in the trunk of my car for special events." His smile morphed into an expression of grim resolve as he ran a cloth over the handgun.

"Is it loaded?" I asked.

"Not yet. I'll get to that tomorrow."

It was raining outside, and I heard the rumble of distant monsoon thunder, which added to my unease. I fell asleep wondering what it was like to fire a Glock 44.

CHAPTER 26

Where's Lyla?

Friday morning Viva and I descended to the first floor to pick up pastries for breakfast at the Seabreeze Cafe. Hunter had left early, saying he was meeting old friends. His vagueness was starting to get to me.

As we paid for our snacks and moved toward the elevators, my attention was drawn to a short, swarthy man and a tall attractive blond woman pulling light suitcases. The two swept through the doors with two children between them. Girls about twelve with long dark hair. They appeared to be identical twins. I nudged Viva and pointed. She saw what I saw. We watched, transfixed. The couple moved directly toward the elevator core. We followed them as they made their way through the crowded hotel floor dotted with restaurants and boutiques and watched as the elevator door closed behind them and the girls.

"Twins!" Viva said. "About Marisol's age."

"Damn! I should've gotten on with them," I said.

"Astonishing," said Viva. "Can't imagine who'd be interested in bringing twins here today," she added sarcastically. "I'd love to know what floor they were headed to." We took the next elevator to our room and told Lyla what we'd seen. Marisol listened with wide-eyed attentiveness. I think she recognized the word *twins*.

What immediately concerned me was that Frost or his executives were no doubt frustrated by the fact the second twin hadn't arrived as planned so they possibly substituted these for the missing pair, meaning Marisa might not be in the hotel after all. I kept my thoughts to myself so Marisol wouldn't overhear my fears.

Back in our room, huddled together over coffee and pastries, we shared with Lyla what we'd seen. We decided one of us should go uniformed to the eighteenth floor and walk through just to see what we noticed, particularly any signs of the twins.

"Volunteers?" I asked, feeling it should be one of them.

"I'll go," said Lyla, raising her hand slightly. "Wish me luck."

"Be back in half an hour," I said. "We want to know you're all right." I gave her thumbs up.

"Don't forget your name tag," Viva said as she opened the door.

"Dumb! Almost forgot." Lyla grabbed a tag from the table by the door before vanishing into the corridor.

Viva brought me a second cup of coffee and blueberry muffin as I texted Maxie. He called right away and said Karina was back at his place and ready to send out Seth's article tonight as planned. He wanted to know if the two of them could come to our room in the hotel. I said yes, be here by five sharp.

Viva and I sipped our coffees and shared the muffin. "This might be the perfect time to check out Seth's desktop," I said when the last crumb had vanished.

Viva agreed. "It's about time we did," she said.

She turned on the Mac and we waited for it to boot up. Karina had given us the username and password so we could access the info on Seth's hard drive.

Sitting close beside Viva, waiting for the programs to load, I feared I might never have this opportunity again, so I put my arm around her shoulder, squeezed gently and kissed her on the cheek. Her rose fragrance drew me in.

"Not now, Jaden!" she complained, her face turning a light shade of red.

"I just want you to know…I've never met a woman who touches my heart the way you do. Whatever happens today, I'll always love you."

Viva looked at me for a long moment. "Always is a long time." Our lips met and we held the kiss for what seemed a few minutes but was probably only seconds. It was the most powerful kiss of my life.

"Umm…I suppose we should look through his files," Viva said, pulling herself away.

"Of course. You shouldn't be distracting me like that," I said. She smiled and rolled her eyes.

"This one looks promising," she said, scrolling down to a file named SPECTS.

"Let's have a look," I said. Viva opened the file, and we scanned through the document. It named top people in government, the corporate world, media, and Hollywood. People Seth believed, based on his research, were involved in child trafficking.

"Oh my God…this is so explosive!" Viva muttered.

"You're telling me!"

We found a paragraph about Frost, detailing the testimony of several unnamed insiders accusing the CEO of criminal activity in collaboration with Central American drug cartels. Not only illegal drug and weapons trade, but specifically and shockingly, the trafficking of minors for sex.

"Wait!" she said. "This is amazing!"

"What is?"

"This is! Seth names Anton Darko as a suspect!"

"Why am I not surprised?"

"Here it is." She pointed to the screen. "Phoenix police, it says. It's got to be him."

"Remarkable. Seth was hot on the trail. Does he name his sources?"

"Apparently not here. I bet they're on another file." We scrolled further until Viva stopped at a file named LEADS.

"This looks interesting," she said, and opened the file to begin reading through names of law enforcement officers, Customs and Border Patrol officials, attorneys, FBI personnel, lists of journalists, and assorted private citizens. People who Seth believed were reliable sources.

"I'll say."

"By the way, Luca's been in touch again. Mostly texts, but I spoke with him yesterday."

"Is he all right?"

"I hope. He's still in hiding, but I know it's him because we have some codes we use as safeguards. Maybe I shouldn't have done this, but I told him we were in Vegas."

"Let me know if he connects with you again."

Viva nodded, never glancing away from the screen. She

breathed out a long sigh. "I think we should we send this file to Dante," she said. "Along with the articles he's using in his hack."

"That's way dangerous. Yeah, let's do it."

Viva emailed the file to herself. Then she moved to her laptop in the next room and pasted several incriminating paragraphs we'd just discovered into the manuscript we'd prepped for Dante. The headline she created for it read:

EVIDENCE ARKOM CEO FROST IS LEADER IN CHILD TRAFFICKING

"I'd love to watch Frost's face when he sees this," I said. "Make the monster squirm." *If it doesn't get us killed first.* I called Dante for the fifth time that day and this time he answered.

"What's up, man?" he said.

"We've got the articles ready to send you. It includes stuff taken directly from Seth's computer."

"Cool. Send it anytime. I'm working from home today. This isn't something you do on a hotel computer."

"No doubt. You should have it in five minutes. By the way, how's it going? Think your hack will be successful?"

"So far so good. The *Vegas Sun*'s a piece of cake. Could hack that baby with my eyes closed. Arkom and Sagitta are tough nuts to crack. But I've got a network. Can't say much about it, but we help each other. Trust me, these guys are from all over the world and they're the best. Absolutely tops. With some time and focus, they could hack the Pentagon. Anyway, when I told 'em what it was about, they were seething. They hate these weapons bastards. Merchants of death. With their savvy, I'm pretty sure we can pull it off. Can't talk about it over the phone, though. Already said way too much."

"I understand. We're pulling for you."

"Awesome. I'm aiming to do this thing at quarter to six tonight, as planned. A bit later I'll stop by the Mandala and see how you guys are doing. Break a leg, man."

I cut off with Dante as Viva sent him the file we'd created with the stories he needed for his hack.

"Done!" Viva said. "A major hurdle crossed."

"A landmark event in world history. Right up there with Caesar crossing the Rubicon. And Diego Maradona scoring the winning goal against England in the World Cup. But where the hell is Lyla?" By this time, nearly two hours had passed with no word from our friend.

"Something's not right," Viva said. "She'd have called or texted if she was hung up for any reason. One of us needs to go up there." I nodded and pointed a finger at her. "I know," Viva said. "I volunteer." At that moment we heard the door latch click. Lyla stumbled in, clutching a medical kit, breathing hard.

"Hey guys, miss me yet?" She waved at us and flopped in a chair by the window, dropping the medical kit on the carpet beside her.

CHAPTER 27

The Last Year of the Eighteenth Century

Viva and I leaped up and rushed to Lyla as she kicked off her shoes and stretched her feet on a small table.

"What the…are you all right?" I asked. "You look like someone slipped hemlock into your drink. And what's with the medical kit?"

"Damn near catastrophe," Lyla whispered. She closed her eyes and rested the back of her right hand on her brow.

"Tell us."

"You won't believe it. I tell ya, I'm not cut out for this life-style!" She abruptly took her feet off the table and adjusted her position in the chair.

"That's my line," I said. Lyla's uniform dress was disheveled, and half her buttons were undone. I was relieved Marisol had stayed in CENTCOM watching a Spanish TV channel.

Viva handed Lyla a cold cup of coffee and she drank half of it in one swallow. "So…I go up there and all is well," she started, studying the cup in her hands. "I'm just strolling down the corridor like I work here when this geeky corporate guy in a suit and tie asks me my name. I'm embarrassed to admit it, but I had the name tag upside down! Did you notice, Viva? I took yours by mistake!" Lyla looked up and stared at her.

"Oh no!" Viva checked her uniform pocket and confirmed they'd somehow switched tags.

"So, like a dimwit I said my name is Darlene," Lyla continued, "but I was wearing the one that said Sophia. Upside down, no less. Freaking dumb." She paused and shook her head before continuing.

"So, I said, 'Oops, picked up the wrong tag today.' He goes, 'Sure you did, honey.' He says, 'Just a little identity crisis you're going through, huh?' I'm thinking he's one of Arkom's private security. A secret agent wannabe. And I've just blown our cover. I thought, *Oh, no, I've really screwed up. Jaden'll be ballistic.*"

"*Terrified for you* is more like it," I said. "Talk about a predicament! What happened next?"

Lyla took another swallow of cold coffee. "Now he's suspicious and makes like he's going to apprehend me, or something. So, he grabs me hard by the arm and says, 'You better come along with me, sweetheart. We'll check with the authorities to see if you really are who you say you are.'"

"So, I'm saying to myself, *Think fast, Lyla*. And I said, 'Listen. I'm diabetic. I need to go down to the employee room and take a shot of insulin.' He's staring at me like I'm an idiot. And then I said, "You can come with me.' And then I said, 'You know… there's nobody down in the break room now.' And I start to look him up and down like he's really hot, and said, 'You're a real cute guy. We could have a little fun you'll never forget.' So, he starts laughing and I could tell he's kind of attracted to me, if you know what I mean. So, he says, 'Okay, let's go downstairs.' I guess he was in the mood."

Viva and I looked at each other and shook our heads. I was in awe of Lyla's ability to think on her feet.

"So, we take the elevator down and I go to the first aid room. He's with me every step. I get out the medical kit." She pointed to the kit on the carpet beside her. "And I got out a syringe and filled it with the tranquilizer stuff. The dude didn't pay close attention. That's maybe because I pulled my skirt way up and unbuttoned my top first." She threw us a devilish smile. "I slid over to him real close and told him how handsome and sexy he was. And the guy couldn't control himself. It's a bit embarrassing…but he, like, starts playing with my boobs and doesn't notice I've got the syringe in my hand when I put my arms around his neck. So, I shoot him up in the neck and he shouts and pushes me away. Meanwhile, the syringe is still stuck in his neck. I thought, *It's all over now. I'm a goner. I've blown everything.*"

"Oh my God," Viva said, covering her mouth.

"He jumps up, shocked and everything," Lyla continued, "then takes a few steps toward me and sinks to his knees. So, I squeezed the syringe all the way and made sure he got the full load. Just then a coworker comes by…a big dude named Darius, and I told him this guy tried to assault me, but I had everything under control."

"So, Darius helped me tie him to a chair. The creep's out cold by this time. Man, this tranquilizer stuff really works. Would knock out an elephant. So, Darius asks me, 'Are you new here?'"

"And I said, 'Yeah, just learning the ropes.' He laughs cause he thinks I'm talking about tying up the guy. Then he goes, 'Stay out of trouble.' I said, 'No worries, I'll call Elsie.' I told him I'd be all right, and he said he works the night shift and was going home. 'Night shift sucks,' he said. He laughed and left, so I tied a bandage around the dude's mouth. The tranquilizer lasts about four hours, so we'll have to give him another shot. He's in a corner of the first aid room, facing the wall."

"Unbelievable! You're amazing!" Viva said.

"I'll say! Incredible," I said. I didn't know if I was more alarmed at the danger she'd evaded or impressed at her remarkably cool-headed response to it. "Damn close scrape, though. Thank God you're all right."

"Sure starts our day with a bang," Lyla said. "I could use a shot of that tranquilizer stuff." She got up, took a few steps, then dropped onto the bed, propping two pillows behind her. Viva brought more coffee, but she pushed her hand away.

"You rest," Viva said to her. She turned to me and asked, "Now what?"

"Good question," I said. "We need to get hold of Elsie to see if she knows what room Marisa's in."

Viva sighed. "Better find out soon. Clock's ticking." I flinched at the discouragement in her voice.

Elsie didn't answer my calls, so I left a message to get in touch. I glanced at my phone; it was almost two o'clock.

"I need to think things over," I said, and dejectedly opened the door into CENTCOM. I nodded to Marisol, and we exchanged rooms.

Depressed and discouraged, I collapsed on the bed. The

oppressive shadow of doubt in my brain grew into a black cloud of anxiety. Thinking that maybe I too needed a Glock 44, I impulsively reached into my open suitcase. Brushing aside the copies of *The Iliad* and the *The Odyssey*, my hand touched cold metal, but not a handgun. My fingers curled around the miniature flashlight Michaela had given me in Sedona and which I'd forgotten. I flicked the switch, but it didn't come on.

Twisting the cap, I shook it to retrieve the dead batteries, but none fell out. Instead, an object wrapped in white tissue dropped on the bed along with a pack of matches. Curious, I unwrapped the tissue and retrieved two small white candles about three inches in length. The candles were fused together, as if melted. I thought back to the moment in the Enchantment lobby, minutes before we escaped toward Las Vegas, when Michaela gave me the flashlight. She'd said, "In a battle of light and dark, light wins." She'd obviously replaced the batteries with the fused candles, but why? I opened the match pack and a small piece of folded paper fell out, on which I made out a few words hand-written in blue ink. "Act with boldness and the two will again be one."

I set the candles on a ceramic plate. With a match, I lit the two small wicks. They flared for a moment and the two lights joined together as one flame. I was awestruck by the symbolism. It appeared Michaela was telling me we'd reunite the twins if we acted with audacity.

I blew out the candles, stuffed them back in the flashlight and tightened it shut, then tossed it into my baggage. Shaking my head in wonderment at the strangeness of it all and the bizarre methods of the curandera, I strode across the carpet and entered the adjoining room.

"Any brainwaves?" Lyla asked, sitting upright on the bed, pillows at her back.

I shook my head. "Not really. I've got a plan, but we need to have at least reasonable certainty of Marisa's whereabouts."

Viva was lying on the bed beside Lyla, her hand over her eyes. She abruptly sat up and glared at me.

"I know where she is," she announced.

"Oh really? The Oracle of Delphi whispered in your ear? Tell us." I sat at the end of the bed.

Viva's features were stern. "Tell me again the riddle I spoke at Jenna's place. It holds the answer."

"Oh right, the part about time travel." I pulled out a folded piece of paper from my back pocket. Jenna had typed the words spoken by Viva in her meditative state and given each of us a copy. I knew the riddle by heart but felt it appropriate to read aloud.

"You'll not find her in this century, but in the last year of the last decade of the eighteenth century." After a pause I added, "Time machine, anyone?"

"Time machine not needed," Viva said, her eyes intense with light. "It really couldn't be more obvious."

"Go on," Lyla said, throwing her feet over the edge of the bed, ready to stand.

"Well…Frost and his cohorts are on the eighteenth floor… as in eighteenth century. The last year of the last decade of the eighteenth century is—"

It dawned on me before Viva spoke the answer to her riddle.

"Room 1800!" I practically shouted. "Leave it to Viva!"

"Wow! What a gift you have!" Lyla exclaimed, jumping to her feet. In that instant, Elsie buzzed us. Lyla picked up the hotel phone and turned it on speaker.

"We think Marisa's in room 1800," the head of housekeeping said. "Staff told me they saw a young girl there." Lyla, Viva, and I stared at each other in gleeful, wide-eyed amazement.

Elsie went on to say that the woman in charge of the girl was named Stephanie White. She also confirmed Frost was in room 1804.

"Incredible synchronicity!" Viva said when the call ended.

"We're in tune with the infinite!" Lyla exclaimed.

"I'll say," I added, thunderstruck by Viva's cracking of her own coded language, and the timing of Elsie's call. "Talk about a smooth move! You're vindicated, Madame Lucretia!" I smiled and winked at my intuitive companion, who flushed with pride at the accuracy of her cryptic utterance.

"But we can't just go barging in," Viva said.

"Why not?" I asked, Michaela's words fresh in my mind. "If she's not there we can just say, 'oops...sorry.'"

Lyla nodded. "You could make a Room Service delivery," she said, looking at me. "Even to Frost's room. Might be revealing."

"Also dangerous," Viva cautioned.

"Everything's dangerous," I said.

"Let's do it, then," Viva said, moving to the closet.

She and I donned our housekeeping garb while Lyla freshened up. I called Elsie back and arranged for a service cart with Spanish tapas to be delivered to our room. The head of housekeeping said she'd meet us on the eighteenth floor.

When the Room Service cart arrived, Marisol poked her head into the corridor and gave us the all-clear. With me pushing the food cart, we left and took the elevator to the top. There was a steady stream of personnel changes in hotel staff so a few new faces in the mix would not seem out of order.

Elsie met us at the top floor. While she, Viva, and Lyla approached the door of room 1800, feigning they were there on a housekeeping visit, I pushed the service cart to 1804. Taking a deep breath, I pressed the bell.

"Room Service!"

Moments later, the door opened and in front of me stood a man of about sixty, with a full head of snowy white hair and bushy white eyebrows. He was trim and athletic-looking, and sported blue jogging pants, and a blue T-shirt with the Arkom logo: an archer holding a bow. His jaw tensed and his forehead creased in angry lines, signaling his annoyance at the intrusion.

"Here's your food, sir," I said, barely able to get the words out. The short muscular man and attractive blond woman Viva and I'd seen entering the elevator that morning were both in the room with the twin girls they'd brought along.

"You've got the wrong room, moron," the snowy-haired man said. His voice was gruff and slightly Southern. "We didn't order anything. What the fuck's wrong with this hotel?"

"Oh...so sorry, sir." I backed away and the door slammed. As I started to push the cart away, the door opened again. Without glancing back, I moved faster to avoid another confrontation.

"Hold on a minute!" an irritated voice commanded. I recognized Frost's peculiar gravelly twang. *Crap. Should never have pulled this stunt.*

I stopped and wheeled around, bracing for the worst. "Yes, sir. Anything I can do for you?"

The Arkom magnate stared at me with cold, stony contempt. "Yeah. Take these damn dishes with you." He handed me a tray of plates covered with food-stained cloth napkins. Our eyes locked and I felt a wave of icy hatred emanate from the depths of his soul. "And tell the idiots in your goddam kitchen not to use so much fucking salt. Fucking trying to kill people with condiments."

"Absolutely," I said, trembling as I took the tray from the angry exec. "Less salt. Got it."

I shoved the cart down the corridor and took the freight elevator to the eighth floor. Hurrying to our room, I let the door slam behind me and gave Marisol a weak smile. *Maybe knocking on Frost's door isn't the brightest way to act boldly.*

CHAPTER 28

The Lost Twin

The plan was to meet back in our room, and I didn't have long to wait.

Viva and Lyla rushed in together, with Elsie a few steps behind. Their excited expressions telegraphed they'd discovered something. "We saw Marisa!" Viva exclaimed. "In room 1800." Marisol gave a little squeal as she ran to her, and they hugged.

"She was alone, other than one woman with her," Lyla said, beaming.

"Darko told the truth," Viva said. "She *is* here."

"A liar you can trust," I said, elated to have located Marisol's missing twin. "And to top it off, I saw Frost in his room. The twins we saw come in this morning were there as well." I looked at Viva.

"Incredible!" she said, bursting with enthusiasm. "What's Frost like?"

"Not at all like his TV image." I felt my courage returning. "He's about three feet tall with long pointy ears and long white hair, with a white beard to his knees... and...and he was dressed all in green."

"Just as I pictured," Viva said, rolling her eyes.

"He'll be easy to spot, then," Lyla added.

"The conference begins in less than three hours," I said, getting back on track. Michaela's words still echoed in my mind. "We've got to do something bold. A brazen, in-your-face act."

"Like snatching a banana from a gorilla," Lyla said. Viva gave her an odd stare.

"I've got a plan," I said, "but to pull it off we need someone who reeks of importance. Someone who will command respect by his presence."

The door opened and Hunter stepped in, limping slightly. His breath smelled of liquor, and I noticed a mini flask of Jack Daniels in his coat pocket.

"I think we have our man," I said. Lyla smiled and Viva suppressed a chuckle.

"What's up?" Hunter asked.

"Where've you been? Playing slots?" I asked.

"Actually no. I don't gamble, at least not in that fashion." He winked at his daughter. "I did have a drink," he continued. "The bars here are excellent. Truth is, I attended a remote business meeting. FaceTime is amazing."

"Do you have a business suit?" I asked him.

"Yes, of course. I thought I might need it for the conference. Ya gotta plan for all contingencies."

"Great. This is risky and it'll involve Marisol...it's a huge gamble." We told him about our trip to the eighteenth floor and that we'd discovered the room where Marisa was held.

"So, what's your plan?" Viva asked, fixing me with her chocolate brown eyes.

"It's simple," I said. "Well, sort of. Hunter dresses as a conference attendee. Someone who knows Frost." I locked eyes with Lyla's dad.

"I see where you're headed with this," he said.

I continued. "With Marisol, you go to the room where her sister's held. According to Elsie," I nodded toward the head of housekeeping, who was seated by the window, "the woman in charge of the kid is Stephanie White. We converge on the room...and Hunter...you say you're Marisol's guardian escort. If Stephanie White asks, say it took a while, but we tracked her down. If things get dodgy, you can mention Darko's network... that might give you leverage. And Lyla...make sure you've got the tranquilizer and a syringe."

"I don't know about this," Viva said after I shared a few more details of my makeshift plan. She nervously touched the leather pouch on the cord around her neck that Michaela had given her.

"Our story is that we want to surprise Frost with both twins," I continued. "We say he doesn't even know about Marisol yet."

"This is making me nervous," Lyla said.

Elsie snatched a rosary from her pocket and began praying the beads.

"It's a roll of the dice," Hunter said. "But I'm game."

"And...if it doesn't work?" Viva asked. "What if there are others in the room, besides this Stephanie White lady?"

"If there are other people, then we leave," I said. "We'll have to come up with Plan B. Something even more radical and dangerous. What do you think?" I looked at Lyla and Viva.

No one spoke for several seconds. "It's risky, but we've got to do something," Viva said. Lyla nodded.

"When do you propose we do this?" Hunter asked.

"We want to go as close to six as possible because the floor will be mostly empty. But we can't wait too long...we don't know what they plan to do with Marisa."

"Let's say five forty-five then," Hunter said. "That gives us two hours. Rehearse your parts. This could be our finest hour... or maybe our last."

"I'll prep Marisol," said Viva. "So she knows what to do."

As Hunter put on his suit, Maxie and Karina showed up. Maxie was dressed less casually than usual. He had on black slacks and a blue, long-sleeve shirt with a collar. And to my surprise, he'd cut a couple of inches off his hair. It was still longish, falling over his ears, but it made him look less boyish. Karina was dressed in a smart, blue dress suit that came just below her knees. She could've passed as a business executive. She brought her laptop but insisted on using Seth's computer for the email blast. The plan was to send out her husband's article at a few minutes till six. Maxie had printed a hundred copies of Seth's article and put them in unmarked manila envelopes. His idea was to distribute them that night to conference attendees.

Maxie and Lyla hadn't seen each other since our trip to Zipp's Sports Grill in Tempe more than two weeks earlier. They hugged, and Lyla gave him a peck on the cheek.

Elsie's day was over, but she said she'd stay an extra hour in case we needed her. At five thirty she took the elevator up to the eighteenth floor and texted that most of the guests were downstairs for the start of the conference. Maxie descended to the first-floor ballroom and messaged that the place was bustling. We decided it was time to make our move.

"We go in two groups," I said. "Hunter and Lyla take the elevator directly to eighteen. Viva and I take the elevator to seventeen, then the stairwell up a flight. Marisol comes with us. Viva escorts Marisol to Marisa's room. I'll enter from the freight elevator, pushing a food cart. When we're all there, we knock on the door."

"Maybe Viva ought to stay in the stairwell," Lyla suggested, "ready to contact Elsie on her cell if something goes wrong."

"Maybe," I said, "but Marisol is most comfortable with Viva along."

"If anyone knows any prayers, now's the time to say them," Lyla said.

"Would be nice if Michaela was here," I said, glancing at Viva. It was my turn to touch the leather pouch on the cord around my neck.

"I think she *is* here, in her own special way," Viva said. She and Lyla closed their eyes and Hunter bowed his head. I thought of Seth and silently called out to the highest power in the universe to aid us now. If anyone ever needed help, we did.

We put our ragged plan into motion. When the ex-Special Forces fighter was ready, he and Lyla left. Viva and I waited with Marisol till our refugee twin signaled the corridor was clear, and the three of us hurried out.

In the elevator we confronted several substantially built, middle-aged women and one well-dressed man who looked like a member of Arkom's security team. *Damn! Why didn't we take the freight elevator? What were we thinking!?*

"What a sweet little girl," a woman said. "How are you doing, sweetie?" Marisol smiled shyly.

"Having fun in Las Vegas, sweetheart?" she continued. "Where are your parents?" I flinched and hid my grimace, noticing Viva wince slightly.

"She loves it," I said. "We're taking care of her. Kids get lost, you know."

"I wish I could take you home with me," she gushed. "Oh, here's our floor. Bye-bye sweetheart." The three women smiled at Marisol and left the elevator. The man in the business suit stared at us.

"Here's our floor," I said, and hurried from the elevator with Marisol and Viva at fifteen to avoid the scrutiny of the dude in the business suit.

"Damn stupid of us," I muttered to Viva. We hustled to the freight elevator and went the rest of the way to the seventeenth floor.

From there we took separate paths. Viva and Marisol walked the stairs to eighteen. I continued up on the freight elevator. We met Hunter and his daughter by the stairwell. From there, Hunter, Lyla, Viva, and Marisol strolled down the corridor.

The food service cart with now-cold Spanish tapas and Frost's tray of dirty plates stood where I'd left it at the end of the hallway. Following a few steps behind the others, I trundled the cart to room 1800. Hunter knocked and a well-dressed woman in a gray pantsuit answered. She appeared to be in her fifties, with reasonably pleasant features but for an unfortunate slight curl on her upper lip that cursed her with a perpetual snarl.

"Hello," Lyla said, beaming a confident smile. "We have a surprise guest for Mister Frost. The missing twin has been found... the sister of the girl in your care. I believe her name is Marisa. This is her sister, Marisol." She nudged Marisol to the doorway so the woman could see her face.

The woman looked them over. "Oh? I thought a new set of twins had arrived since this girl's sister was detained."

"As you can see, her sister's been found," Hunter said, stepping forward slightly. "We've got it all under control. Let me introduce myself. I'm Charles Wheeler. I'm with US Steel. Old friend of Ethan's...went to school together. You must be Stephanie White."

"I am," the woman said. They shook hands curtly.

"I've arranged this little surprise," Hunter continued.

Stephanie White stared at Marisol with obvious astonishment. "A surprise indeed. Marisa's twin. Very well. But I'll have to come with you, of course. I won't let the girl out of my sight."

"Of course," Hunter said, flashing a smile. "Ethan will be pleased that our people have upheld their part of the bargain and delivered the missing twin. And we'll bring the girls back in a few minutes, unless Ethan has something else in mind."

My heart raced with excitement as I spoke loudly from the corridor. "Someone ordered Room Service for the kid." The strangeness of it all was palpable.

The woman raised her eyebrows. "Really? They should've asked me first." Without waiting for her permission, I wheeled the cart into the room. A young girl looking like a replica of Marisol was seated in a chair in the corner, watching the events, wide-eyed.

When Stephanie White turned around, Hunter grabbed her by the mouth from behind. Lyla snatched the tranquilizer syringe from the pouch in her uniform pocket and plunged the needle in the woman's neck. The Arkom employee sagged, and Hunter eased her onto a chair. With one hand clamped tightly over her mouth, he yanked a handkerchief from his coat pocket and gagged her. As if they were one person in two bodies, the ex-Marine and his daughter tied Stephanie to the chair and adjusted her gag. Marisol raced in and embraced her lost sister, unable to conceal her joy. Marisa seemed stunned and docile, and I wondered if she'd been drugged. Still, she smiled and hugged her twin.

"They teach you that in Special Forces?" I asked Hunter.

He shook his head. "Nah...Boy Scouts." Stephanie White was soon sleeping like a baby.

The fateful Wheel of Fortune had mercifully paused at a most auspicious point. But that fickle wheel never stops for long.

We moved with measured haste to the stairwell. The abducted twin girls, holding hands, stumbled between us. Hurrying down two flights of steps to the sixteenth floor, from there we rode the freight elevator to the eighth.

Giddy with excitement, we rushed along the hallway to our room. Closing the door behind us, the celebration began.

CHAPTER 29

Revenge of the Cabal

I t was all too easy.

We had rescued Marisa and reunited the twins.

Back in our room, we exchanged hugs and joyful slaps on the back as the rescued sisters collapsed on the bed. They held hands and giggled, though Marisa was subdued. Lyla did a cursory exam in the bathroom and whispered that there were no obvious signs she'd been sexually molested.

Karina entered from the next room to congratulate us and meet Marisa, who she hugged warmly. "I want to announce we have another accomplishment to celebrate," she said triumphantly. "I've mailed out my husband's article…to every organization on his list."

It was another milestone, and we cheered and applauded.

"And look at this," she added. "Check out the *Vegas Sun* website."

Viva opened the web browser on her laptop and brought up the newspaper's home page. A large photo of Seth graced the screen. The caption read: "In honor of the courageous *Vegas Sun* reporter who died under mysterious circumstances."

On the front page a bold headline declared:

Seth Rosen's Article on Child Trafficking

The article began with the words, "Deceased journalist who wrote for the Sun is vindicated. Proof of corporate involvement in child trafficking"

Several abbreviated teaser stories appeared with bold headlines—the short pieces composed by Viva using Seth's article, also published in its entirety.

We cheered and hoisted coffee cups. "Seth's vindicated!" I whispered, raising my fist in the air. Karina's eyes shone with happiness and her resolve was evident.

"Check out the Arkom and Sagitta sites," Viva said. "Let's see if Dante pulled it off."

We anxiously hit the websites of Frost's two enterprises. Seth's photo stood out on the home page of each. They too had been hacked.

In much the same format as for his hack of the newspaper, Dante had hijacked the Arkom and Sagitta sites. Seth's article was posted in full length, along with a half dozen short stories created by Viva with large headlines designed to embarrass and incriminate the leadership of Frost's two corporations.

"It's Seth's revenge!" I said, pumping my fist in the air. "Make the freaks squirm!"

"Bravo!" Viva exclaimed, clapping. "I wonder if they've gotten wind of it yet at the conference?"

"If not yet, any minute," I said. "And Dante called the *Sun* journalists to tell them to show up here tonight."

"We've done what we came here to do," Viva announced. "We need to get the girls to safety. To the custody of US Customs and Border Patrol."

"We should leave now," Lyla said. "Mission accomplished."

"I wish," I said. "But there's still unfinished business. Get all of it done and we can leave tonight."

Viva shook her head and folded her arms. "Jaden…please! We need to get the girls to safety and get ourselves out of harm's way. Now!" I'd never heard her raise her voice before.

Lyla stepped across the carpet and stood beside Viva, as if in support. "Jaden!" she almost shouted. "Get real! Time to bust out of this place!" Both of my guiding goddesses were practically yelling at me.

I nodded, trying to calm them. "I agree," I said. "We'll leave tonight. Just a few loose ends to tie up. I've got to check out the conference and meet Maxie." I didn't mention my obsession with seeing Frost's face when he discovered the hack.

"You're making a mistake!" Viva insisted. "I have a *really bad feeling* about this. We need to leave now!"

"We'll be all right," I said, pushing aside a nagging intuition that Viva's clairvoyance was kicking in. Hunter's phone buzzed, and I glanced at him.

"My friends are here," he said. "The fun's only beginning. Time we go downstairs." *Nice to have someone on my side.*

We'd come to a crossroad. Our destiny hung in the balance and circumstances were more dangerous than ever. Everything now hinged on a series of interrelated acts, and like the precision mechanism and timing of a Swiss watch, all actions were geared to one event: the impending reaction from Frost and his group. This decisive mainspring would lead to our deliverance or our destruction. And it would likely take place in the next several hours as the instant blowback of our deeds to hack the company websites, release Seth's article, and snatch Marisa from their jaws. Fury and vengeance were guaranteed.

Hunter took a sip from his mini flask, embraced and kissed his daughter, hugged Viva, put his arm around Karina and squeezed, then shuffled to the door. I knew he had his Glock 44 inside his coat. He smiled gallantly and shut the door behind him.

"All right," Viva sighed. "Have it your way. But what about the girls? Someone's got to stay and protect them."

"You three stay here with the twins," I said. "We'll be back in a heartbeat."

I put on my street clothes, deciding to wear my Hawaiian shirt. *Time to let go and unwind.* I hugged Marisol, waved to Marisa, and gave a thumbs-up to Viva, Lyla, and Karina.

The conference ballroom was called the Phoenix Room. I tarried outside the entrance to the big conclave, gazing at the logo on the wall, a large orange-yellow Phoenix bird perishing in a roaring fire. I recalled my conversations with Lyla and Viva about tests and trials by fire. I'd already had enough of those.

Maxie waved me over and pointed to several long tables on which he'd placed a stack of articles in unmarked manila envelopes beside a folded card that read, "Please Take One."

"Man, you're bold," I said.

"It's for Seth," Maxie said.

"For Seth," I repeated.

We gazed at the stage where a podium was positioned beside a big screen. The twin girls Viva and I had seen escorted into the hotel earlier that day were on opposite sides of the stage, each with a silk cloth pinned at an angle over their dresses. One said *Arkom*, the other *Sagitta*, Frost's twin companies. The Arkom twin held a wooden archery bow, the Sagitta girl a feathered arrow. *The guy loves perverse symbolism.*

"Did you notice the hotel lights?" Maxie said. "Is that awesome or what? Dante's incredible." He was referring to the lighted electronic signboards located at various points throughout the hotel lobby and gaming areas that streamed a constant flow of flashing announcements and items of interest for hotel guests. As the conference began, the flashing signs announced the Arkom gathering, calling it an International Symposium on Child Trafficking. Subtitled, "Putting a Stop to Pedophilia in High Places."

"Frickin' unbelievable," I said beneath my breath, astounded at Dante's skill and audacity. "Now we have to protect ourselves." I had a sudden feeling an invisible noose around us was tightening. *Maybe I should've listened to Viva.*

An announcement came over the loudspeaker. "The Arkom Corporation conference on child trafficking is underway in the main conference room."

"That's Dante!" Seth said. "The guy has balls!"

There was an uproar in the conference ballroom. Frost was delivering his speech, welcoming guests, and showcasing the launch of their new business division, Arkom Bank and its website. On the screen in front of us, in real time, Dante's hack of the Arkom homepage appeared, witnessed by all. Seth Rosen's face was showcased on the screen, with the headlines and articles composed by Viva the day before. Attendee reactions ranged from amusement and surprise to extreme rage. Some were clearly confused by what they were seeing. Most were stunned and furious.

The Arkom CEO stopped in the middle of his speech and gazed up at the screen, unsure what people were excited about. When he saw images of the live hack appear in real time, his face reddened, and he visibly trembled with shock and fury.

Knowing that to stay longer was perilous, I tugged at Maxie's arm, but he was transfixed by the unfolding drama and didn't budge. Glancing about, I noticed two men enter and stand by the tables in front of the entrance to the conference. The silhouette of one of them looked much like me, the other seemed familiar. The broad-shouldered man sported a bandage around his forehead and moved with a noticeable limp. His left arm hung in a sling, and I detected an oddly familiar odor of cheap cologne. I turned around and looked squarely in the face of Anton Darko.

My heart froze. The Gorbachev-type birthmark on his forehead left no doubt it was him. The man the cops called "the snake" had survived his fall at Boynton Canyon. Though more gaunt and paler than when I'd confronted him in Sedona, he was still an imposing figure. I took a step back and shifted my gaze, hoping he wouldn't see me.

"Hey, Jaden," Maxie said. "Get a load of this!" He was gesturing to the conference stage and pointing. Darko looked up when he heard my name and stared directly into my eyes. He nudged his sidekick and gestured at me. I instantly recognized the big cop's companion—the driver of the white van that pulled up beside us just as Lyla and I were leaving Machiavelli's parking lot with Marisol that fateful day in Phoenix. He wore his hair as I did before I dyed it, and his features so closely resembled mine he could have passed as my older brother.

Even as I convinced myself I was safe in any event thanks to the sheer number of guests crowding the hotel, the driver of the white van came up behind me, seized my right arm, and pointed something hard in my back that felt like a gun barrel. "I'll kill you if you run," he whispered. "Move straight ahead and don't try anything smart." I had no reason to believe he was bluffing.

Darko shoved up on my left side, glaring at me like I owed him money, and grabbed my arm with his good hand, his grip like a vise. "Say anything or make a false move," he hissed, "and you're a fuckin' dead man. Understand?" Had it just been Darko, I would have pulled away, but his accomplice with the concealed object rammed in my back gripped my arm ferociously and prevented escape. My hesitation cost me the chance to run.

Darko's wingman pressed the gun in my back as the big cop pulled my arm. I stumbled forward, sandwiched between them, hoping Maxie would see us and realize something was wrong. They led me away from the conference room, weaving through guests on the crowded hotel floor.

"Careful what you say or do or you're fuckin' dead meat," the police captain snarled, his voice hoarse and filled with hate. "You angered the bosses, and you angered the cartel. We'll make you pay."

My heart pounded like a drum in triple time as I calculated how I could make a break and run. If I waited too long, we'd reach the doors. Once outside, they could kill me where few eyes would notice. I had to break away in the hotel.

We passed a cluster of guests watching a blackjack game. There was a small gap between them. The big cop slowed and pulled at my arm, timing his approach so as not to bump into anyone. There was an artificial tree rooted in a small square base close to the group watching the game. If I pretended to trip, I could push Darko's weakened left arm into the fake tree trunk, causing him to lose his balance. My timing had to be exact. Exquisitely perfect.

As we strode in tandem, I deliberately caught my right foot on my left heel and tripped hard while pushing Darko's wounded arm against the artificial tree trunk. He let out a low growl of pain. I dropped to the floor and rolled, hoping to shake the thug who looked like me. Both he and Darko lost their grip on me when I hit the ground and twisted violently. Leaping to my feet, I dashed through the crowd of astonished onlookers, provoking angry shouts.

"Hey man! Watch it! Idiot!"

I raced past the elevators and through a swinging doorway into a hall I recognized—the one Elsie had shown us on her brief tour. I ducked into the employee break room, not sure if I'd shaken them.

Damn! Should have run toward the lobby! Too late now.

The break room was outfitted with a couch, long tables with several folding metal chairs, and on the tables were paper plates, napkins, and two fruit baskets. I opened the door to an adjoining closet-like room and was shocked to see a man tied to a chair with a bandage around his mouth. The Arkom security agent Lyla had vanquished that morning made loud noises with his throat and rolled his eyes to get my attention.

The door of the break room opened and Darko appeared, limping badly, and gripping a handgun. My nemesis pointed the gun equipped with a silencer at my belly.

Practically jumping out of my skin with fright, desperate for anything to defend myself with, I pivoted hard and grabbed a flimsy towel hanging from a chair. The criminal cop had me cornered.

"Fuckin' bastard tried to kill me in that canyon!" Darko growled. I was sure he could hear my pounding heart. "You made a lot of people mad. Cost me some serious money. Hurt our reputations. You ruined my life. Now I'll ruin yours."

The only thing between me and the big cop was the heavy table with baskets of fruit. Lunging, I shoved the table toward him, and it crashed on its side as I ducked behind it. A basket of apples and oranges fell off, with fruit rolling everywhere. I snagged an apple and hurled it at his face, hitting him squarely in the mouth. It momentarily stunned him and gained me precious seconds as I fell on my hands and knees behind the collapsed table and groped for any object to use as a weapon. I touched an orange and my fingers closed around it.

Shots rang in a torrent and the table splintered, covering me with tiny wooden shards. I felt what I thought was warm juice from the orange in my hand, then realized it was my own blood, streaming down my arm. Lifting my head above the table, I hurled the orange at Darko's face, then collapsed again to the floor and rolled away. Leaping to my feet, I picked up a chair and heaved it at him, knowing in my heart if he had two good hands, I'd already be dead.

The chair struck the police captain in his right shoulder and knocked the gun from his grip. The revolver skidded across the carpet, and I lunged, grasping at it as he leaped a moment after me. The big cop fell at my side like a gasping, raging beast. Reaching the weapon an instant before him, I curled my right hand around it and rolled. I clutched the revolver as his huge hand smothered mine in a struggle to pry it from me. My rival was an imposing man, heavier than me, probably at one time stronger. But he was thirty years my senior and badly injured from his fall. His left arm was nearly useless. That was his Achilles heel and I exploited it, punching his shoulder repeatedly with my left hand.

He groaned as I pummeled him, then shrieked in pain. A squeal like the one I'd heard the moment he fell off the Sedona cliff.

Something came over me. A resolve, a conviction, a terror. Fear and courage are antipodal emotions, yet they can sit together simultaneously in the same heart. When faced with death, when there is no escape, the will to fight overpowers the instinct of fear. I possessed the energy of youth and a sudden relentless will to live. If I died, I would die fighting.

I rolled over as he squeezed my hand so tightly the handgun fired harmlessly at the wall. Still clutching the revolver, I hit him in the face with my elbow. Yanking my hand away, I smashed upward with my knee into his chin. He lost his grip on my hand and fell to his knees.

Leaping up, I stepped on Darko's wrist and kneed him in the

mouth. Trembling, I pointed the weapon at his face. In a motion so smooth and swift he must have practiced it many times, the big cop reached in his jacket with his good right hand, drew out a short dagger and swiped it across my stomach. Had he jabbed, he might have hurt me severely, but the blade cut across my leather belt. Darko arched his hand to lunge with the knife or hurl it at my face. I had no choice but to kill him.

I'd never fired a pistol. Didn't know a Glock from a Beretta. I squeezed the revolver, and a shot rang out. Darko groaned and clutched his belly inches from his heart, then slumped to the floor.

But I hadn't shot him.

The revolver's magazine was empty.

From behind me a shadow darted forward. Luca McCloud appeared, in police uniform, pistol in hand, and rushed to Darko's crumpled form. The mortally wounded police captain stared into McCloud's face. His eyes closed and he sagged, still and lifeless.

Seconds later another shot rang out. Luca staggered and fell to his knees. At the same instant I noticed Darko's, Hawaiian-shirted accomplice approach us, gripping a gun. The man who could've passed as my father had found us and shot McCloud. Now, holding the weapon in his left hand, he aimed at my heart. Through my terror, I recalled that my dad was left-handed.

He growled, "Chill, Bozo, you die tonight."

As I stared down the barrel of his gun, an image arose from mythic depths of my soul, from that nameless reservoir where memories, dreams, and visions swirl in a sea of infallible know-ing. A scene sprang in my brain of me as a little boy, held in the arms of my father. We were laughing happily, savoring a playful moment, sharing a filial bond stronger than death, a moment more powerful and enduring than the mind-blotting amnesia of time.

"Dad!" I shouted. "Don't shoot! It's me. It's Troy. Your son!"

The man pulled his gun back slightly, hesitating, staring at me with bewilderment and wonder.

"Troy? My son?"

From the corner of my vision spectrum, I glimpsed Hunter French, Glock 44 in hand. The ex-Special Forces soldier fired once, and my father collapsed.

A trickle of blood ran down my arm, gathered in my palm, and dripped to the carpet, and I realized I should probably see a doctor.

CHAPTER 30

Ethan Frost

The room stunk of gunfire. The security agent tied to the chair groaned and twisted, struggling to free himself. He must've been terrified by the violence exploding around him.

Hunter French limped to my side, pulled out his phone, and called Lyla.

"I think I'm all right," I said, searching for the source of the blood flowing down my arm.

"Lucky bastard," Hunter said. "The bullet only grazed you."

"Thanks for saving my life," I said. "I'll try and return the favor one day." I gave Hunter a weak smile.

My mind and heart were engulfed with conflicting emotions that stunned me to the core of my being, straining the bonds of credulity. Was it really my father who had just shot Viva's brother, Luca McCloud? Was this my parent lying at my feet, bleeding?

Hunter dropped to his knees beside the man he'd just shot, so I sidled over to Luca and knelt beside him.

Viva's brother looked young and noble. He was hit in the right shoulder—a nasty wound, but survivable. His eyes were closed, and he seemed to be in shock, but he was breathing, his features serene. I noticed for the first time his resemblance to his younger sister. I held his hands and whispered my gratitude to him. Told him everything would be all right. Not sure why, but I loosened his fingers and pried his handgun from him.

I set a towel under Luca's head, then shuffled over to the assailant in the Hawaiian shirt. There was a lot of blood on the carpet. Hunter mumbled that the wound was bad, but it appeared to be only his arm and he'd probably live. Lyla's father then stood up and moved to examine Luca. Kneeling beside the man who'd abandoned me as a child, I touched his forehead. I wanted to say something, but no words came. Several hotel staff appeared, and I called them over to help, then collapsed in a folding chair nearby.

Lyla appeared moments later, and wrapped a towel around my arm where the bullet tore my skin. My wrist was sore, my neck ached, and my stomach was stinging where Darko's blade sliced my belt, slightly tearing my skin. My elbow was badly bruised from the rolling fight, there were cuts on my hands and arms, and I was breathing hard. Otherwise, I seemed intact.

"Where're the twins?" I asked.

"They're fine," Lyla said. "Safe with Karina…in our room."

Viva arrived, knelt beside me, kissed my cheek, and held my hand. "I didn't know you had a gun," she said almost matter-of-factly.

"I don't. It's Luca's. He's over there." I pointed to the crumpled form of the police officer who'd saved my life.

"Luca?" Viva's voice was incredulous. I nodded.

Viva rushed to her brother's side and held his head in her

lap. When Lyla realized I was fine, she moved to Luca and checked on him.

By this time, a number of hotel staff had entered the room. I was relieved to see both Maxie and Dante appear. *Better late than never.*

Several Mandala personnel untied the Arkom security agent from the chair and removed his gag. They led him from the room, and he didn't notice Lyla.

"It's chaos out there!" Maxie said.

"It's chaos in here," I replied.

"I can tell," Maxie agreed. "Damn! You all right?"

I nodded, holding my hand to my shoulder where the bullet had grazed me. "Business as usual."

"Yeah, pretty damn routine," Maxie continued. "Frost looked like he was about to explode...stopped in the middle of his welcoming speech and stormed from the podium."

Hotel medical staff appeared and attended to Luca. Someone stretched a towel over Captain Darko's face. This time the dirty cop really was dead. Not waiting for the ambulance to pick up Luca and my father, I pulled Maxie out of the room. My adrenaline was surging, and I couldn't stay still.

"I'll be all right," I said, attempting to calm my friend.

Dante followed behind us, and we left the staff room and headed back to the Arkom conference. I forgot I was holding Luca's pistol until a woman gasped and lunged out of my way, so I tucked it in my belt beneath my Hawaiian shirt, which was stained from my own blood. Despite the gunfire, the hotel soon returned to normal, and guests resumed their activities. In Vegas, the show must go on.

Reaching the ballroom, I was surprised to see Karina—with Marisol and Marisa—hovering by a table near the entrance. I spotted Frost lingering at the edge of the stage, conferring animatedly with several men, some of whom looked like his security team.

"They shouldn't be here!" I said to Karina, touching Marisol's arm. "It's not safe."

The exhilaration had drained from Karina's face, and she looked frayed and worried. "I know, but I got a call from Elsie. She warned me our room was a target for hotel security and possibly the police. So, I had to leave, and I couldn't abandon the girls. We need to go now, but I wanted to find you first."

Frost and his men drifted up the aisle toward us, seemingly as confused as everyone else. The Arkom CEO's face was crimson, and his jaw was clenched. He stopped when he saw the girls. Apparently recognizing the twins, having seen Marisa previously, he grabbed the girl closest to him as he pulled a small handgun from his suit jacket.

He'd chosen Marisol.

His arm around her, Frost pushed through the crowd with two of his security team. Maxie and Dante each took on the two security bouncers, shoving themselves in their faces, asking questions and distracting them, enabling me to follow Frost. Yanking Marisol by her arm, the company exec made his way swiftly through the crowd toward the elevator core.

I could barely make out Frost's white-haired head above the

crowd. Reaching the elevators, I heard Marisol scream for help as the doors closed in my face. Shaking with anxiety, the wait for another car seemed interminable but was only seconds. Dashing into the lift, I pressed eighteen, not sure what Frost had in mind or where he was taking the girl.

I stepped off the elevator on Frost's floor and ran down the corridor, but there was no sign of him or Marisol.

My cell buzzed. It was Maxie.

"He's going to the roof!" he shouted. "Frost is going to the roof! His helicopter's on the way!"

"How the hell do you know that?"

"The goddamn agents told us!"

I bolted toward the staircase, raced to the top, and shoved open the door leading onto the hotel rooftop. I glimpsed Frost with his back turned, still holding Marisol. In one hand he held a revolver, with the other he clutched the girl's arm.

I ducked behind a wooden, shed-like structure. In the distance I could make out the sound of a chopper. There was a small area on the roof where a helicopter could land. Frost was leaning against the perimeter wall that edged the rooftop. He hadn't seen me.

If he remained oblivious to my presence, I might wrest Marisol away. *Damn! Where's Hunter French when you need him!*

I held back, fearful that if I confronted Frost, he might harm the girl. Yet if I waited till the chopper came, he'd climb on board with her and leave. I had to act.

Searching for a weapon, I found a two-by-four leaning against the wall. Grasping the weathered board, I made my way along the side of the structure as the roar of the approaching chopper surged. The flickering lights of the evening sun lit the wall with fantastic rays of early-autumn splendor.

Gripping the two-by-four, I abruptly remembered I had Luca's gun in my belt. *Idiot!* Feeling like a fool, I set down the beam and nervously removed the gun. I examined the steel weapon in the sunset glow of the Vegas skyline. *I suppose I can just shoot Frost.*

Maybe I have no choice.

The thud of the chopper grew near, and I figured it was the exec's private helicopter. I group-texted Maxie, Dante, Lyla, Hunter, and Viva that we were on the roof and to come fast.

I knew I'd have to confront Frost before he got on the chopper with Marisol, but he had other, more sinister intentions. The Arkom boss dragged the kidnapped girl and began lifting her above the four-foot wall that edged the hotel roof. Horrified, I realized he was going to push her over the edge. I dashed up and struck him hard on the shoulder with the handgun. He spun around and stepped back, still clutching Marisol's arm. He planted the gun to Marisol's temple. I froze, terrified.

Other than my failed attempt to shoot Darko, I'd never fired a pistol. Now for the second time in an hour, I intended to kill someone. The slightest error and I could hit the girl. If I waited, he would murder her. I couldn't conceive what was running through his mind. There was venom and madness in his stare.

The blast of the helicopter grew deafening. "Leave her alone!" I shouted. The tycoon laughed and squeezed Marisol to his side, using her body as a shield. I aimed the pistol at his head as he held his gun to her temple. Behind Frost, I saw—or imagined I saw—Michaela, her form like a luminous apparition, dazzling in the ethereal background of the sun-drenched Vegas skyline.

The image vanished and I squeezed the trigger. The jolt knocked my hand back and I heard a terrifying scream.

Frost grabbed his right shoulder, inches from Marisol's head. I lunged forward and hit him in the teeth with the pistol. The double shock from the blow and his bullet wound paralyzed him for an instant and I wrestled the gun away and yanked Marisol free.

A crowd appeared behind us. Viva, Lyla, Maxie, Hunter, Karina, and three men in suits pushed toward us. The men pulled badges from their jackets, identifying themselves as FBI agents. Like blue-suited cavalry in an old western, Hunter's pals from the Bureau had arrived.

"I'm Agent Chang!" one of them shouted as the din of the chopper grew closer.

The agent held up a flash drive and shouted. "Frost! We've got a solid case against you! Building it for years. We're coming after you for illegal weapons sales and criminal trafficking of minors."

With his good arm, the corporate gangster managed to hoist himself onto the side of the building. I held onto Marisol's hand, lifted her, and hugged her close. Glancing back, Frost had vanished.

"Where'd he go?" I shouted, swiveling around.

As the chopper slowly descended to the landing pad, Maxie shouted above the thunder of the engine and the blades. I couldn't hear him but read his lips.

"Didn't you see? He jumped."

In that instant something died in me, and something new was born.

Heart pounding, trembling from sudden nausea and dizziness, I nearly blacked out. The roar of the copter seemed a deafening silence, engulfing me in a comforting blanket of primordial vibration. My body ached and my hands shook in the aftermath of the violence, but a surge of relief drove the fear and rage from my mind.

I let go of Marisol and she ran into Viva's arms. I stumbled after her and the three of us embraced.

CHAPTER 31

Jack Diomedes Parker

The Wheel of Fate never stops for long, but for a brief instant in eternity, the cosmic wheel had paused at a most auspicious spot. "Men's courses will foreshadow certain ends," wrote Charles Dickens. Oddly, the awkward, nineteenth-century phrase stuck in my brain over the years and popped into my head after my showdown with Frost on the rooftop.

Our "courses," as Dickens called the paths we take in life, converged in what our little band of survivors and reluctant heroes perceived as a David-versus-Goliath clash of good against shadowy, institutionalized evil. There would be no parades or public acknowledgments, but our unlikely group of adventurers had confronted this dragon of covert villainy, and for the moment at least, we'd avoided calamity and vanquished our foe.

Following my confrontation with the Arkom boss and rescue of Marisol atop the hotel, Hunter and his FBI team stayed on the roof to update with the helicopter crew while the rest of us descended to the first floor and took in the scene. Luca McCloud's gunshot wound to his shoulder was severe but not life-threatening. As medics prepared to take him to the ambulance, Viva's brother handed her a flash drive with all the dirt he'd gathered on Darko's illicit trafficking operation. That night Viva copied the contents onto both her and my computers, then later gave the drive to Hunter's FBI colleagues. Luca was taken to Summerlin Hospital, where the doctors said he would likely make a full recovery.

News of Frost's suicidal plunge spread quickly, and Arkom management hastily cancelled their conference. Knowing there could soon be more dramatic blowback from our brazen acts to expose the leadership of Arkom and Sagitta corporations, our little band was anxious to escape from the Mandala. I'd learned my lesson about delaying too long!

After Hunter and his agent buddies came down off the roof, we made our way to our rooms where our belongings were packed and ready. Vowing to meet the next day, we fled the hotel, with Hunter and Lyla going to Maxie's, while Viva, the twins and I took refuge at a small hotel on the outskirts of Vegas, which Hunter had reserved for us.

Next morning, I visited the hospital emergency room where a nurse gave me a tetanus shot because Darko's knife blade had broken my skin. The gunshot would leave a scar on my arm, the doc said, but not be too noticeable. "Hope it doesn't leave you with a limp," Maxie quipped.

I'd earned my badge of courage and garnered a stash of antibiotics to boot. And though I felt liberated from a terrible ordeal, I figured I'd eventually have a date with the police. No doubt, they'd have some questions. But miraculously, for the moment they left me alone.

Viva spent the morning with her brother at Summerlin after

handing over the twins to Hunter and Lyla. She texted to say he was in good spirits, cracking jokes, and watching TV. Their mother was flying in from New Mexico to be there.

The man I now felt certain was my father had also been taken to Summerlin. I asked at the reception desk for Jack Diomedes Parker, saying I was a relative. He was awake and conscious when I entered his cubicle. His wound was bad, but the doctors said he would make it.

"He'll be back on his feet in a few weeks," the medic told me. Miraculously, the bullet had gone through his upper right arm, grazed his humerus, pierced his latissimus dorsi, fractured a rib, and passed out of his body without seriously damaging major organs or blood vessels.

"This is Troy," I told him, taking a seat on a stool beside his bed and gingerly pulling aside the curtain. "Troy Parker. If you're Jack Diomedes Parker, I'm your son." There was a long silence and he nodded slightly. With eyes still closed, he slowly reached his left hand out from under the sheet, and I grasped and held it for a long time. There was nothing much to say. "I missed you, Dad," was all I managed. When the nurse came in to give him medication, I decided I'd use the opportunity to slip out. My father opened his eyes and noticed me move toward the door.

"Troy," he said in a soft voice, barely louder than a whisper. I stopped and turned toward him. He lifted his head slightly and gazed at me. "Will I see you again?"

The moment seemed a lifetime as a torrent of conflicting emotions swept through me.

"No doubt," was all I could say.

I wished him a speedy recovery and left the hospital with my mind in upheaval.

Discovering my long-lost father left me deeply shaken. His place in my life—or absence, really—was an emotional black hole, an emptiness, a void. And knowing he was connected with the horrors of child trafficking left a stain on my heart.

My only consolation was the hope that he was simply an underling employee who got caught up in something he didn't comprehend. Perhaps he was just a "mule." One who transports drugs and contraband. Yet the fact he was working with Darko's operation so profoundly revolted me that before I'd reached the rented Chevy Malibu, I resolved to never set eyes on him again.

The final episode with my father was history.

Or so I thought.

CHAPTER 32

Guardian of the Sea and the Sun

The following day, with heavy clouds blanketing the sky, our tight tribe of crime-fighting adventurers gathered at Maxie's to say goodbye, and to celebrate our remarkable good fortune. For a brief flicker in the moving cinema of time, we were all together, sharing an unlikely victory and savoring a sweet outcome. Viva, Lyla, Hunter, Karina, Marisol, Marisa, Maxie, Dante, and me. Our hacker friend had phoned Elsie, filled her in on the stunning events, and she was on her way.

Most awkward was parting with Lyla. The two of us strolled out onto the small balcony of Maxie's apartment, overlooking the grassy area Viva and I had traversed days before during our early-morning escape. She grabbed me by the waist and drew me close, then planted a sensuous kiss on my lips.

"You mean so much to me, Jaden. I hope to see you soon." She hugged me tightly and we held each other in an embrace that was part friendship, part frustrated passion. I pulled away, holding her hands, and told her I missed her too. But my words lacked the intensity and sincerity of hers.

I told her I'd be in touch in a few days, though I thought weeks might be more likely. I wanted to get back on my road trip with Viva. Maybe my coolness bothered her, for as we turned to go inside, her mood shifted and she pushed away my hand.

My clairvoyant friend, for her part, had never been more demonstrative and affectionate. When Lyla and I came back inside, I sat by Viva on the couch, and she held my hand as we chatted exuberantly with everyone. I noticed Maxie focusing a lot of attention on Lyla, which was understandable. His breakup with Sheila was absolute and final.

When Elsie arrived, everyone strolled outside and across the grass by Maxie's apartment complex to an adjacent park where we spread out food and drinks on a picnic table. The head of housekeeping brought some Guatemalan dishes to celebrate the occasion. Authentic tamales were her specialty, and when she handed me one in the traditional corncob sheaf, it brought vividly to mind my bout of food poisoning from the tamale from hell I'd purchased on the street in Phoenix. Overcoming my spontaneous revulsion, I bit into the delicacy. It was delicious, and I devoured two more.

Marisol and Marisa sat side by side on the picnic bench, gorgeous in blue dresses, with pink ribbons tied in their hair courtesy of Lyla and Viva, who sat on either side of them. The twins were thrilled to be reunited and glowed in the attention we gave them. Marisa had sparked to life that morning after a long night's sleep—a sign of promise she'd recover from the trauma. Overjoyed to be liberated from her captors, she laughed and chatted incessantly with her sister.

During our meal, Karina put her hand on her belly. "I'm

halfway through my second trimester," she announced. "Doctors say it's a boy. His name will be Seth."

"A toast to Seth Junior!" Maxie announced, getting to his feet. We hoisted our glasses in the air in a salute to our deceased friend's unborn son. Karina told us she was flying to Milan in a week and would stay with relatives there.

Dante also announced he was leaving that night and might never set foot in Vegas again. He'd already bought his plane ticket to Madrid. "After that it's either Thailand or Vietnam," he said. "I'm ready for some easy living on the beach."

The tech wizard's hack of the *Vegas Sun* and Arkom websites had stirred a hornet's nest. Big events make big waves, extending in far-rippling circles. In the days following Frost's final plunge and the exposé of covert trafficking, we heard of rumblings and fallout in Washington, DC and other power centers. Several Congressmen abruptly retired, and a rash of resignations and suicides made news in the corporate world.

Dante had also set up a GoFundMe account for Karina, sent an email about it to a robust mailing list explaining she'd been widowed under suspicious circumstances, igniting an instant, huge response. Nearly fifty thousand dollars collected in just forty-eight hours, with more likely to come. On the spot, Karina wrote checks for five thousand to both Viva and me, and I thanked her profusely. I could use the money.

Marisol and Marisa listened and watched everything intently, and it seemed they understood much of our conversation. Elsie asked the twins what they wanted to do when they returned home, and after a moment's silence, Marisol answered in surprisingly beautiful English. "We want to live with *familia* by the sea and the sun." No one spoke for a moment, struck by the poetry of her words.

"You know," Elsie said, gazing at Marisol. "Your name means 'sea and sun.' And yours, Marisa, means 'born of the sea.'" She repeated her words in Spanish. Marisol nodded and Marisa smiled and giggled.

"Amazing," said Maxie, slapping me on the shoulder. "Jaden, my friend…I guess that makes you guardian of the sea and the sun."

"It's an honor," I said, smiling at the rescued twins.

"What an incredible journey for you two," Lyla said, touching Marisa's hand.

"Epic," Viva added, putting her arm around Marisol. "A liberation odyssey." Radiant with happiness, the rescued twins basked in the sunlight of our admiration.

The FBI agents notified Hunter that they'd contacted US Immigration as well as Border Security. The twins would spend the night with Maxie and Karina. Tomorrow a team from Customs and Border Protection would come to Maxie's to take custody of them. The girls would be returned to their parents, who'd been contacted in their village outside Guadalajara. As happy as the twins were to be reunited, I sensed Marisol was sad to leave Viva's and my company.

"*Tenemos algo para ustedes,*" Viva told the girls. *We have something for you.* We each gifted the twins the leather pouches Michaela had given us at the little ritual she performed for us in Sedona.

"To remember us by," I said, as we placed the leather cords over the girls' heads. They beamed with pride, and I realized again how deeply attached to Marisol I'd become.

Saying farewell to the twins that day was one of the saddest things I've ever done. We promised we'd try to visit them in Guadalajara for their thirteenth birthday. When Marisol hugged me goodbye and said, "*Muchas gracias* for everything, Mister Jaden," I could barely hold back the tears.

~

BIDDING OUR COMRADES FAREWELL, Viva and I drove to the little town of Mesquite about an hour away to escape Vegas, and at dusk we found a reasonably tranquil motel.

Still shocked by the stunning revelations concerning my father, I decided to keep silent on the matter. It was all too new and sudden and crazy, and I needed time to digest and process it all. The realization that he'd shot Viva's brother was too appalling to deal with. And the horrifying fact he had unwittingly nearly killed me—his own abandoned son—was a twist of fate beyond my capacity to fathom. I'd have to let the dust settle before even considering approaching these things in conversation with anyone, even Viva.

In the room, my companion fished from her purse the napkin I'd scribbled on in the Badger Cafe in Vegas, where we'd eaten the morning Marisol ran away.

"I'm glad you think I'm a hot babe," she said.

I'd forgotten about the note. On it I'd written: "You're the only hot babe I ever want in my life." Probably the corniest thing ever, but I had to say something at the time, and the written approach seemed best in that awkward moment at the breakfast joint.

"Well, it's true," I said. "But it's your intellect that drives me crazy with desire."

Viva laughed. "No doubt. What gets my engine going are your Hawaiian shirts."

We held each other close, and I kissed her gently on the lips, softly, almost hesitantly, a kiss I hoped transmitted every ounce of my love for her.

Viva showed no sign of her former defensiveness. She held both my hands and kissed me for a long moment, then drew her head back and gazed into my eyes. We were both smiling, and I quietly exulted in perceiving her playful readiness. I put my arms around her, and we embraced for a long time, talking about our group—Hunter, Maxie, Karina, Dante, and the twins. At last, she mentioned Lyla.

"I can see why you like her," she said. "She's beautiful, smart, and sexy. And she obviously has strong feelings for you."

I paused a moment before responding. "She's all that, but I've said it before, and I mean it…Lyla is a friend. I have feelings for you I've never had for anyone else."

She smiled and held me close, putting her hand on my heart. We kissed again.

We made love that night for the first time and it was for me transcendent. Her touch, the softness of her hair, and the scent of her perfume were intoxicating. The caress of her hands was like fire and velvet and moonlight. Our bodies fit together perfectly, and merged in a love embrace that seemed like a forgotten memory brought to light, a dream made real.

I fell asleep many hours after her. Listening to her gentle breathing, savoring her closeness and warmth, I didn't want the night to end. I had never felt such happiness and fulfillment.

Next morning, we drove for a while toward Saint George, then reversed course, deciding to return to Sedona. Viva texted Michaela, to let her know of our return, and my companion's mentor reserved a room for us at Enchantment Resort. Despite driving leisurely, we completed the trip in less than five hours.

As we drove up to the resort hotel nestled below the red rock canyon walls, we spotted Michaela standing outside to greet us. The curandera smiled radiantly and hugged us.

We strolled together on the grounds of Enchantment and made our way along the path I'd led Anton Darko just a week before. Michaela took us to a fork in the path and we found ourselves on a ledge overlooking a dramatic view of the valley floor. I realized it was the exact spot where she'd stood when I saw her resplendent form on the path after Darko had plunged off the trail.

"You two have been through a lot," she understated in a serious tone.

"Bent and broken, but hopefully into a better shape," I said, paraphrasing a line from Dickens.

"Trial by fire," said Viva.

Michaela nodded. "A test of character, to be sure," she confirmed. "Sometimes you have to walk through fire to become a new person."

"Thanks for the flashlight," I said, winking. "It came in handy."

Michaela smiled. "I trust you found it illuminating." The curandera's eyes shone brightly, and I got the impression she knew far more than I imagined about all we'd endured since our hasty flight from Sedona just a week ago. I recalled the flashing vision of her presence I'd seen atop the Mandala in those terrifying moments when Frost held Marisol's fate in his corrupt hands.

"As a sign and token of all you've been through and all you've learned," the curandera continued," now stamped into your cellular chemistry and engraved in light in your imperishable souls, I give you these gifts." Viva's mentor drew from her purse two small, silvery metallic figurines suspended from leather cords. These necklaces were more elaborate than those she'd given us several weeks prior, and which we had bestowed on our rescued twins.

"This figurine comes from Hopi elders, blessed by them," she began, looking intently at my companion. "A Hopi kachina—a supernatural being that protects you. Consider it a talisman imbued with a sacred force." With these words she placed the kachina over Viva's head. I noticed a tiny turquoise butterfly inlaid in the silver.

"And for you, Jaden," she continued, extending the second corded object, also a silvery figurine, less than two inches long. A helmeted goddess holding a shield and a spear. With it she handed me a letter-sized envelope with my name written in elegant calligraphy: *Jaden Troy Parker.* I thought it odd she'd included my middle name. Though not sure what to make of it all, I felt privileged to be part of the curious ceremony and sensed I'd received a blessing.

We made our way back to the hotel parking lot and

said farewell to Michaela, who I now considered to be, in a mysterious way, my mentor as well. When she hugged me good-bye, she traced her fingers across my forehead and I felt a distinctive jolt of fine energy fill my mind, as if she transmitted some secret potency. She appeared to do the same to Viva. We waved to her as she drove off, then returned to our room.

~

THE NEXT MORNING VIVA awoke early and made coffee. She spent some time making phone calls and texting while I lay in bed, watching the autumn rays dance on the curtains. After a light breakfast of pastries and strong coffee, Viva announced that Jenna had arrived in the parking lot. She'd driven my Jeep, and we exchanged vehicles.

Jenna brought Viva's guitar along for some reason and handed it to her. My elfin companion seemed abruptly distant and acted strangely. I didn't grasp what was happening. With guitar in hand, we strolled into our room and closed the door.

"What's the guitar for?" I asked. "You already passed the audition."

"Jaden, I need to tell you something." My skin froze in a chill that swept over my body.

"What's up? Cold feet?" I asked. "It's the Grand Canyon tomorrow, then Santa Fe and Taos. The fun's only beginning."

Viva took her guitar from the case and strummed some chords.

"Umm, I can tell this'll be a solo," I mumbled, my voice barely audible. *Is this really happening?* The lovely clairvoyant who'd stolen my heart began to sing. One of my favorite songs, written and recorded by Dolly Parton and made famous by Whitney Houston. "I Will Always Love You."

> *If I should stay*
> *I would only be in your way.*
> *So I'll go, but I know,*
> *I'll think of you each step of the way*
> *And I will always love you.*
> *I will always love you.*
>
> *Bittersweet memories*
> *That's all I'm taking with me.*
> *Goodbye, please don't cry,*
> *We both know that I'm not what you need.*
> *But I will always love you.*
> *I will always love you.*
>
> *I hope life treats you kind,*
> *And I hope that you have all*
> *That you ever dreamed of.*
> *And I wish you joy and happiness,*
> *But above all of this, I wish you love.*
> *And I will always love you.*
> *I will always love you.*

Tears streamed down my cheeks, and it was all I could do not to sob uncontrollably. I got hold of myself and gazed into the eyes of the woman who'd just torpedoed my lifeboat.

Viva's eyes were wet with tears. It was like a dream. Or a nightmare. I could barely hear her. She said we'd talk soon. She needed time to get her life together. I followed her outside, mumbling about helping with her bags. But she seemed to have everything planned and didn't need my help.

She slid into the rented Chevy Malibu beside Jenna, smiling and waving as if we'd just met for the first time and exchanged business cards. *Pleasure to meet you. Let's keep in touch.*

The two drove off, leaving me standing in the Enchantment parking lot, staring at my feet.

I ambled about for a few minutes, confused and anguished. It felt as if my soul was bleeding, and I couldn't stop the flow. In the distance the sun illumined the red rock canyon walls where I'd led Darko on the chase that ended in his plunge over the cliff. Now it felt as if I was the one falling into the abyss.

For the first time in my life, I knew what it meant to have a broken heart.

CHAPTER 33

Road Trip Revisited

Love is the theme song of the human spirit. It's a light shining in us. I discovered it can also be an aching emptiness.

I spent the day hiking the red rock monuments, climbing picturesque Bell Rock with its magnificent views, snacking at Oak Creek Espresso, grabbing some pastries to go. I texted Lyla. She and Hunter were still in Vegas, at Maxie's place. Thinking to connect with my playful, foxy bookstore friend and maybe enroll her as my traveling companion, I called Maxie and told him I'd changed my plans and could I visit him for a day or two. He said yes, but I heard reluctance in his voice. *What? Do I smell bad, or something?*

I pulled up at my friend's apartment in Vegas about the same time of day Viva, Marisol, and I had arrived the week before.

I strolled in and froze. Lyla and Maxie were together on the couch. Her red lipstick was on Maxie's collar and face. My old Monterey bud's arm was around her shoulder, holding her tightly. Their body language left no doubt about the depth of their new, intimate connection. I smiled and waved to conceal my pain, hoping they didn't notice me flinch when I saw them.

I spent the night and tried to be nonchalant and friendly but was deeply hurt by my double loss and heartbreak. Losing Viva, and now discovering Lyla's hookup with Maxie, I'd lost out on everything.

"Love is the only gold," wrote Tennyson. If so, then I was a penniless vagrant. *What a damn fool I am.*

Lyla planned to stay a while at Maxie's. Hunter, I learned, had left the day before. The only uplifting moment of my visit was when he called to let us know that Marisol and Marisa's parents were being flown to Tucson to take custody of their daughters.

It was unbearable for me to remain longer, so I said goodbye the next morning and left Vegas. I toyed with the thought of going along the Extraterrestrial Highway and on to Lake Tahoe but decided to take Highway 40 east toward the Grand Canyon.

"Marriage is both a joy and a torment," states the Grimm's tale of *Three Little Men in the Woods*. The saying is true for intimate relationships of all kinds. The pendulum had swung for me to the torment side, and I was resigned to take a more solitary path. I'd pick up the scattered threads of my destiny and continue my desert odyssey.

Alone.

I stopped in Flagstaff and wandered around the mile-high downtown, figuring I'd head north to the Canyon next day. Stumbling upon Firecreek Coffee Shop, I ambled in and stood in line, enjoying the aroma of their fresh-ground blends.

The barista making my espresso sported a little red rose tattoo on her arm, in almost the exact spot Viva had hers. Too many synchronicities for me to deal with.

Come on, God! Stop messing with my mind! Haven't you heard? Breaking up is hard to do.

I found a seat at a table by the window. Even that reminded me of the first day I saw Viva in Phoenix at the Coronado Café.

As I sipped my coffee and gazed idly at my phone, a young mother came in with her baby. The child, maybe eight or nine months old, stared at me with astonishingly bright blue eyes.

The infant and mother were for a moment the center of attention as several customers congregated to smile and wave at the little one. Children are the only people who achieve celebrity status without trying.

I gazed at the infant and smiled and winked and threw her a kiss. Our eyes met for a long moment, and she uttered an endearing belly laugh. My heart opened for an instant of joy as I beheld the pure, otherworldly light in the smiling baby's eyes. "Heaven lies about us in our infancy," wrote Wordsworth. He was right.

"She laughed!" the mother cried out. "It's the first time she's ever laughed!" The woman's eyes filled with tears of joy.

I recalled the Navajo belief that these beautiful newcomers to earth, our children, keep one foot in the world of spirit, holding back, until they laugh for the first time. That's the sign they've decided to enter fully into our madhouse of a planet. This innocent being before me, seemingly with one foot still in the world of spirit and one foot in this new and dangerous and frightening place called Earth, had decided to join us. According to Navajo tradition, the one who causes the child to laugh throws a welcoming party for her.

I lifted my coffee cup and toasted the child, offering to pay for the mother's coffee and croissant. She was thrilled, and it warmed my heart to honor the child, her mother, and the ancient Navajo tradition.

I shook my head as I thought of Marisol and Marisa and how their precious childhood had been nearly stolen from them. And the hundreds of thousands of trafficked children whose lives are torn, and their innocence hijacked by this hellish world of ours, this insane asylum of the universe, where we come for a time to learn...what? If Michaela was right, we were here to gather wisdom and grow the light in our souls. Had I passed the tests Viva had warned me about? I thought not.

Did it matter if I passed or failed? What matters is to do my best...to give my all, to run the race to its end. To seek to love and to give love. To find joy in the seeking, hope in the darkness, and serenity in the quest for the good. To find beauty in the faces of children, to protect the innocent and vulnerable...to reach, and to strive. To give, and to never give up.

I grabbed my phone and coffee, waved goodbye to the mother and child, and strolled into the brilliant Arizona light. Pausing outside my Jeep Cherokee, I leaned against the door, savoring the sun's warm and soothing touch on my face and arms. A loud flutter above my head made me glance skyward. In the tree branches above, two hummingbirds flitted and danced.

I swung open the car door, stripped off my T-shirt and tossed it on the seat, snatched my red Hawaiian shirt and pulled it on. *Time to let go and celebrate life, come what may.*

My mobile buzzed and I ignored it. I was in no mood to talk. I sipped my coffee and the phone buzzed again. *Time to change that ring tone. Too many memories.* I looked to see who was calling.

It was Viva.

I hesitated. She might have left something in my car. Probably wanted me to mail it to her. I let it ring.

When it rang minutes later, I relented.

"What's up?"

"Hi, Jaden."

"What can I do for you?"

"Look...I'm really sorry."

"About what?"

"Everything. I don't know what got into me."

I was silent. There was nothing to say.

"Jaden..."

I said nothing, listening to my heartbeat.

"Jaden...I was thinking. I mean...I'm just so dumb some-times. Do you still need someone to navigate on your road trip?"

There was a brief stillness as my mind raced. *Why are you tormenting me like this? Probably gonna suggest Lyla.*

"Umm...maybe. If it's the right person. Qualifications are tough. I'm beginning to appreciate the solitary life."

"I can imagine. But...if it's not too late, I'd like to apply for the job."

My breath stopped, and my heart smiled without permission.

"You sure about that?"

"A hundred percent."

I paused, absorbing the impact of her words before I spoke.

"Well, you know…competition is stiff, and the tests are hard. Not easy to land the job. Great benefits, though."

"Yeah, like what?"

"Oh…you know… excitement, danger, deadly combat, run-ins with the law. Then comes the hard stuff." Viva giggled softly.

"Jaden."

"Yes, Viva."

"You know…what I said when I sang the song…the lyrics, I mean. The part about, 'If I stayed, I'd be in the way.' I realize now…I don't believe that's true. At least, I hope not. I miss the feeling of being together."

There was a long silence. My mind blanked. "I'm open to that," was all I managed to say.

"My bags are packed and ready. I…I love you, Jaden."

The silence felt like an eon.

"You still there?"

I breathed out slowly. "Let's just take it a day at a time and explore our world."

"Thanks for trusting me…I want to help you navigate the journey."

As I drove toward the Sedona hills, my heart sang a melody I'd never heard before.

My road trip was about to begin.

Child sex trafficking . . .

is one of the worst human rights abuses. Every country in the world is impacted by this appalling crime. Children between the age of 11 and 14 are the most commonly victimized. If you believe you may have information about a trafficking situation, call:

NATIONAL HUMAN TRAFFICKING HOTLINE
1-888-373-7888, or

SAVED IN AMERICA
(760) 348-8808

Author Bio

Emory J. Michael is the former owner of four bookstores and author of numerous popular books, including *Queen of the Sun*, which was translated into more than a dozen languages. He and his wife live in Sedona, where they enjoy the bountiful sunshine and red rock trails.

To receive his free monthly newsletter,
sign up at:

www.emoryjohnmichael.com